A TALE OF FABLES AND FORTUNES

GABRIEL'S CITY

LAYLAH HUNTER

RIPTIDE
PUBLISHING

Riptide Publishing
PO Box 1537
Burnsville, NC 28714
www.riptidepublishing.com

Gabriel's City: A Tale of Fables and Fortunes
Copyright © 2014 by Laylah Hunter

Cover art: Imaliea, imaliea.deviantart.com/gallery
Editor: Rachel Haimowitz
Layout: L.C. Chase, lcchase.com/design.htm

ISBN: 978-1-62649-164-9

First edition
November, 2014

Also available in ebook:
ISBN: 978-1-62649-163-2

A TALE OF FABLES AND FORTUNES

GABRIEL'S CITY

L A Y L A H   H U N T E R

RIPTIDE
PUBLISHING

For Kiwi, whose storytelling turned my life into an adventure.

CASMILE

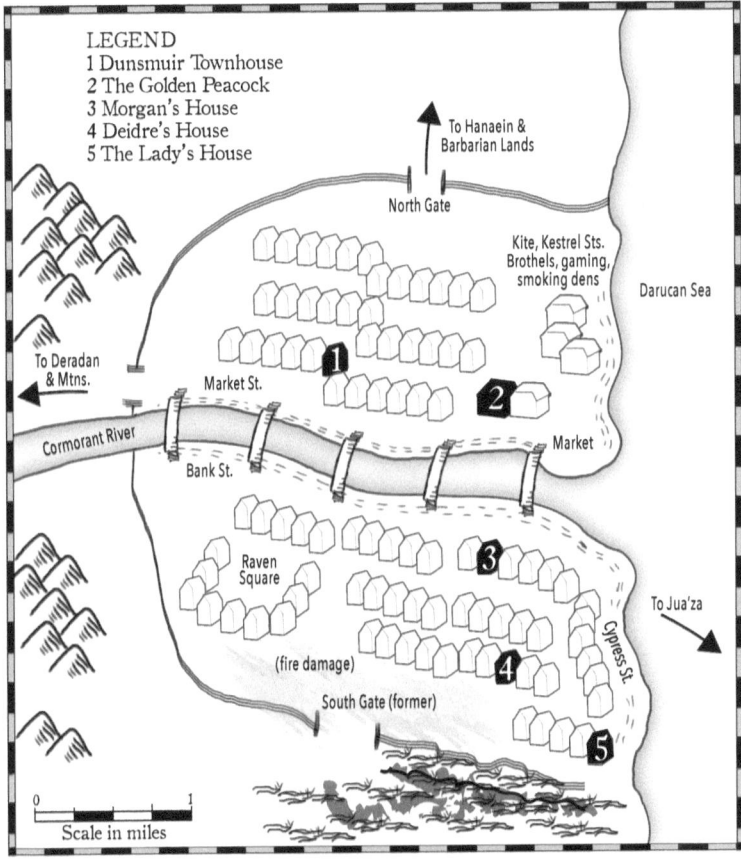

LEGEND
1 Dunsmuir Townhouse
2 The Golden Peacock
3 Morgan's House
4 Deidre's House
5 The Lady's House

To Hanaein &
Barbarian Lands

North Gate

Kite, Kestrel Sts.
Brothels, gaming,
smoking dens

Darucan Sea

To Deradan
& Mtns.

Market St.

Cormorant River

Bank St.

Market

Raven
Square

To Jua'za

Cypress St.

(fire damage)

South Gate (former)

0   1
Scale in miles

TABLE OF CONTENTS

Part III: Spring

PART I
AUTUMN

CHAPTER
ONE

C olin fidgets, wondering how much longer this dinner party can drag on. The rest of his table has just burst out in politely scandalized laughter at someone's prettied-up version of a bawdy gaming house joke. He's had enough lectures on how these people are his peers that he could recite them back to his father word for word, but compared to the company he'd rather be keeping, they remain excruciatingly *dull*.

At least he's had the fortune to be seated across the table from Captain Darius Westfall of the city guard, who's a falcon among finches if Colin ever saw such a thing. His blood's common, to judge by his tan skin and black hair, and his features are too sharp to be truly handsome. Likely he was never invited to this sort of party at all before he was appointed captain. Colin smiles at him.

"What about you, Captain?" he asks. "You've been so quiet. Surely you must have some entertainment to offer."

"I would hate to give offense," Captain Westfall replies. His voice is smooth, carefully free of any trace of a dockside accent. "I've no fit entertainment to offer such polite company." He reaches for his glass of wine, and there are raw scrapes on his knuckles.

"But you must have stories to share," Colin persists. "I expect your line of work gives you no end of exciting tales."

"Master Harwood," Madame Hewitt says, her lips pursed. "That's not decent conversation for young ladies, and you should be ashamed to encourage it."

The only young lady in their immediate circle—Julia Mear, one of the more tolerable girls of Colin's acquaintance—rolls her eyes. "Don't keep all the fun to yourself." She glances sidelong at

Captain Westfall. "I promise not to faint away in horror, no matter what you say."

Madame Hewitt *harrumph*s disapprovingly, but Colin grins. When his sister is old enough for society parties, he'll introduce her to Julia. They'll like each other.

"I cannot refuse, then, if the lady would make me such a promise." Captain Westfall smiles at Colin. "What sort of story strikes the gentleman's fancy?"

Colin says the first thing that comes to mind. "Tell me about Gabriel."

The captain laughs, low and rough, but Colin imagines there's a ferocity to it and shivers in anticipation of the tale. "No wonder your mother worries about you, if you're keeping company with the sort of rogue who tells stories about Gabriel."

"I heard of him from Sebastian Dunsmuir," Colin protests.

"I hope you don't think that'll make me retract the statement," Captain Westfall says. "He should still know better than to talk of such unsavory things with well-bred young gentlemen."

"But clearly he doesn't, and I do hope you don't, either." Colin leans forward, elbows on the table. "Sebastian made it sound like Gabriel doesn't really exist. Is that true?"

"There's *something* in Casmile that goes by that name," Captain Westfall says. "I've seen what's left of men who run afoul of Gabriel, and no matter how prettily you plead, Miss Mear—" here the captain looks over at her, and she blushes; really, he's quite the showman "—you won't get me to describe that horror in polite company."

"You make him sound like a monster." The servants are coming around to clear away the dishes from the meat course; Colin waits until the table's bare between them before he goes on. "It's hard to believe you're not simply toying with me."

Captain Westfall takes a sip of his wine, amusement clearly written across his face. "He may be a man. He may be an excuse, a bogeyman blamed for the crimes no reasonable man wants to confess." He leans back in his chair so the serving girl can set the last course in front of him, stewed late-season berries bleeding into thick cream. "I've heard grown men swear he enjoys the favor of the Green Lady—and not only in battle, if you take my meaning."

Madame Hewitt flinches. "Captain!"

"That's perverse," Colin adds before he can help himself. Arhon, the Green Lady of the Grave, is the eldest of the Fates; Colin's not entirely sure he believes in them, but if she does exist, then the idea of anyone seeking her rotting embrace is grotesque.

Captain Westfall doesn't look at all contrite. "My apologies," he says with a self-satisfied smirk, as though he's just won a hand on an outrageous bluff. "Madame Hewitt is right after all. I have no conversation fit for civilized company."

The rest of supper offers no scandal to match the captain's outrageous assertions, and Colin's attention wanders. When the party adjourns from the dining table to the ballroom that takes up the back half of the house, Colin hangs behind and slips off the other way when his father isn't looking.

The Ashfords' butler is sitting up in the front hall, still on duty because of the party. He starts out of his chair when Colin comes toward the door. "You are leaving, sir?"

Colin nods, reaching into his pocket. "Should my father—should Isaac Harwood come looking for me, tell him I'll make my own way home, and he needn't wait." He presses a half shilling into the man's hand—he can't use cut coin on the gaming tables anyway—and adds, "Don't hunt him down to tell him. Let it wait until he's searching for me."

"As you wish, sir," the butler says, and Colin is fairly sure he only imagines the reproach in the man's tone.

The evening air is crisp outside the house, and the sky not quite fully dark. Colin takes the first block at a jog, expecting someone to call after him at any minute, and doesn't slow until he's out of sight of the Ashfords' townhouse. Even after that, he tries not to pass too close to the streetlamps, and keeps an ear out for sounds of pursuit.

His father will be angry with him, of course, but right now Colin finds it hard to care. These society parties are barely tolerable when Danny's around to keep him company, but now, with

Madame Sheffield taking the waters in Nothwn for her health and insisting that the entire family go with her, there's nobody to keep Colin entertained. The other young men are too serious, and the young ladies are all worrying about whom to marry.

Fortunately there's always an interesting party going on somewhere in Casmile, if you know where to look and have a bit of coin to spare. Colin heads east, deeper into the city, and toys with the idea of going up to one of the Kite Street brothels and hiring himself some attractive company. But the houses on Kite are expensive, at least half a guinea for a tumble, and half a guinea's worth of silver will buy quite a few hands of cards even if his luck's awful—and tonight his luck must be good for him to slip out of the party as easily as he did.

He makes his way toward the gaming houses instead, the streets between Alder and Market blazing with lamps and alive with laughter. There's company to be bought here, too, if he wants it; he turns down a girl in red silk and a boy with his hair in tight Cabirile braids before he's passed the first block. The Golden Peacock's doors are open, despite the cool night air outside, and that's tempting, but Barron owns a stake in the Peacock, and Colin owes Barron rather more money than he cares to think about at the moment. Perhaps if he does well enough tonight, he'll take his winnings from one of the other houses and go pay down a bit of his debt before he heads home.

The Quartermaster is almost as good as the Peacock, and it's less likely he'll run into anyone there whom he owes more than a few shillings. Colin steps into the warmth of the light and the sweet haze of smoke. There are three tables open so far this evening, one for dice and two for cards, and Colin's spirits lift as he recognizes a familiar face at the far table. There's even an empty seat to his left.

"Sebastian," he says as he reaches the table. "Tell me this table's lucky tonight."

"Of course it is, darling." Sebastian smiles in that warm, conspiratorial way that makes him seem almost like a boy as young as Colin, instead of a man twice his age. "You know I only play at lucky tables."

"I'll take your word for it," Colin says as he settles in his seat. Sebastian seems to be doing well, as always; he is sitting at ease, and the rings on his fingers glitter elegantly as he arranges his cards. His coat looks new, a pearly velvet that calls attention to the pale gray of his eyes, and somehow he makes the tousled wildness of his hair—still black with not a thread of gray, despite years devoted to mastering Casmile's vices—look fashionable rather than sloppy. Not for the first time, Colin thinks it would be a blessing to have an older brother, like Sebastian does, who could inherit the family estate and all its responsibilities.

"And you, Colin?" Sebastian asks as Colin antes for the next round and the dealer shuffles the cards. "How do the Fates find you tonight?"

"Counting my blessings." A serving girl passes with a bottle of brandy, and Colin motions for her to bring him a glass. "I narrowly escaped dying of boredom just a short while ago."

"Congratulations are in order, then. That would have been such a disappointing way to go." Sebastian picks up his cards, rearranges them, hesitates over one and discards another. Colin looks down at his own and tries not to betray his surprise when he discovers two knights and a maiden among his cards. The first hand of the night is almost always a throwaway.

"Wouldn't it have been?" Colin says. The man on Sebastian's other side is glaring at them, but he pays it no mind. "Just a terrible waste." He gives up the pip cards that round out his hand. "Tell me you have some interesting news to share."

Sebastian pushes two shillings toward the center of the table. "Of course I do. Do you want to hear about Sophia Betteridge threatening divorce, or about the dismal state of the *Maiden's Mercy* when she limped back into harbor yesterday?"

It's no real secret that Henry Betteridge takes mistresses from the slave quarters; that's gossip Colin could have heard if he'd stayed at the Ashfords' party. Disasters at sea sound far more exciting. "Was it pirates?" he asks. His newly dealt cards net him the ace of blossoms, which matches up to the maiden and leaves him with the winning hand. A few more like that and he might be able to stop by the Peacock after all to show some goodwill by paying down his debt a bit.

Sebastian nods as he antes his shilling for the next hand. "Up from the islands, apparently." Colin nudges a coin from his winnings back into the center of the table. "Burnt black as pitch, from what I hear, and fierce as northmen. The *Maiden*'s captain will likely never walk again."

The man to Sebastian's right spares them another irritated glance and gets up from the table, either out of luck and coin or simply out of patience. Colin doesn't much care; someone else will be along to fill out the table soon enough.

Sebastian leans over and rests one hand on Colin's back. "There's a story I'd like to hear out of you too, you know," he murmurs. "What on earth have you done to get Barron's attention?"

"What?" Colin asks in alarm.

"If you're in trouble, you can tell me, darling, and I'll help." Sebastian looks so sincere, it's almost impossible to believe him. "A few of his boys were here looking for you earlier."

Colin winces. "It's nothing serious." If he tells Sebastian his troubles, the entire city will know by week's end. "I'm touched that you'd worry, but I'm fine. I promise." He really will have to start paying down that loan soon.

"If you're certain," Sebastian says.

"Completely." Colin reaches for his cards. "Don't give it another thought."

CHAPTER TWO

B y the time Colin leaves the Quartermaster, it's late enough that he has to pay his shilling up front before the hired carriage will take him out past the west gate. He doesn't mind so much; his luck held for most of the night, and he's going home almost two guineas richer than he left. It's not until they've passed the gate and driven all the way out past Mockingbird Lane that he remembers he meant to stop in at the Peacock and look for Barron before going home.

Well, there's always next time. Even if he winds up in terrible trouble for this evening's adventure, he can't imagine it'll be more than a week or so before he goes out again. He can always enlist Anna's help to get out of the house—she's only fifteen and a girl besides, so there's no way their parents would let *her* go out in search of adventures, and she depends on Colin to bring home stories. She'll love the tales Sebastian was telling tonight.

Colin gets the carriage driver to let him out at the top of the private lane to the main house. It's not terribly likely he'll manage to sneak up to bed without having a row with his father first, but he can always hope. He's beaten worse odds tonight already. His breath fogs in the moonlight, and his boots kick up drifts of fallen leaves. The Lady's feast night has already come and gone, so winter's almost here—the dry chill that leads up to the Longest Night, and then the miserable cold rain that lasts right into spring. Danny had best come back from Nothwn soon, because it'll be snowing in the mountains, and having him stuck so far away for the entire winter would be just awful.

The lamps are lit outside and in the front parlor. His parents must be waiting up for him. Colin slows, a bit of the swagger dropping out of his stride. There's no avoiding the lecture he's in for, he knows that, but it would be so much easier to take after he's had a few hours to sleep off the exhaustion and the brandy headache. Perhaps his mother will have gone up to bed already, and that'll keep his father from really getting blustery about it.

Only then he gets closer to the house, close enough to see the cracks in the doorframe, the raw splintered wood where the lock used to be. Colin takes a few more steps, catches himself looking to the shadows as if whoever did this might still be there, waiting for him. But that's ridiculous, isn't it?

The door swings open silently when Colin pushes, and he steps inside. He feels queasy, like he did the very first time he smoked a pipe. The hallway is dark, save for the moonlight filtering in through the glass of the back door. Why would burglars smash their way in the front door and leave the glass in the back alone?

He startles, nervous as a barn cat, when he hears a sound on the stairs. It's only Anna, coming down the steps in her nightgown, her hair tumbling loose over her shoulders and her eyes wide in the dark.

"Colin," she whispers. "Thank the Maiden. Are you all right?"

"Fine," Colin whispers back. "What—" He gets no further before Anna throws herself into his arms, holding on tight. "What happened?"

Anna takes a shaky breath, and it sounds like she might be crying, of all the awful things. "You've never seen anything so terrifying," she whispers. "Papa was already angry when they came home, because you'd gone, and then just after we put out the lights, the door burst open, and these men came storming in yelling for you, and—"

The parlor door slams open behind them, and Colin flinches. "Anna," their father growls, "go back to bed. The last thing he needs now is coddling."

Colin turns, squinting against the light spilling from the parlor. "What's that supposed to mean? I haven't—"

His father crosses the hallway and backhands him. "Don't dare to tell me what you have and haven't done. Bad enough that you abandon respectable company to waste your money in gambling dens, but this . . ." Colin's face stings, feels hot; his limbs tremble with the desire to strike back. "Borrowing money from thugs and ruffians to further compound your troubles!"

"Papa," Anna says, and Colin raises a hand to warn her to stay back.

"I never meant to— I mean, I was going to pay it back! It's not as though I thought—"

"I doubt you were thinking at all," his father says. In the parlor, Colin's mother is sobbing softly. "Fifty guineas, Colin! How did you even get *in* that much trouble?"

The figure stuns Colin nearly as much as being hit again. He knows he never borrowed so much from any one person; he was careful not to let any of his debts grow too unwieldy.

A chill creeps up Colin's spine. Barron must have bought up the rest of his loans. If he bought them all, and compounded the interest together… "We can still pay, though, can't we? You said the plantation yields almost a thousand a year. Fifty isn't so much of that—"

His father raises a hand as if to hit him again, and Colin flinches, but it's Anna's distressed noise that saves him. "No," his father says, "I won't be paying extortionate sums to a pack of arrogant criminals because of your thoughtlessness. Upstairs, both of you." He steps forward, shepherding Colin and Anna up the staircase. At the top, he lets Anna go and follows Colin down the hall.

"Look," Colin says as he gets to his room, hoping he can head off the additional lecture, "I know I've made a mistake, all right?"

"Do you?" his father asks, stepping into Colin's room and lowering his voice. "I'd like you to think about how lucky we've been tonight. You should thank the Fates that your mother and I had come home, and that one of the serving girls had the sense to run to the stable and rouse the boys before those thugs had a chance to do too much damage. I don't even dare to think what they'd have done if they'd caught your sister alone."

His father leaves before Colin can recover from the shock of that awful idea enough to protest—of course he'd never want such a thing, never meant to put Anna in danger—and punctuates the slamming of the door with the heavy *thunk* of the bolt sliding home.

"Wait!" Colin says, grabbing the doorknob, rattling it fruitlessly. "Come back!"

His father doesn't answer, footsteps fading down the hall. Colin pounds on the door, and then winces when all that does is sting. Well. Fine. He turns away from the door, crosses to the window, and pushes it open. He's not going to sit here like some child being punished for tantrums, waiting to be allowed out of his room.

It's the work of but a few minutes to change out of his fine dinner party clothes and into something more suitable for Casmile late at night: a plain shirt with no lace at the cuffs, dark cotton trousers instead of embroidered breeches, the high cavalier boots that he's always thought make him look like a highwayman. He even has a jacket that's wool instead of velvet, with deep pockets to keep his coin out of easy reach. He pushes his hair back off his face, catches it in a cord at the base of his neck.

He'll go back to town tonight, he thinks as he studies his reflection, and he'll talk to Barron. He'll put up what money he can, and he'll apologize for those jokes he made last month to the man's friends, which of course he didn't mean but perhaps were a bit over the line in any case. They'll get all this worked out before it gets any worse. Things will be fine.

The night's taken on a good deal more chill already when Colin boosts himself out the window. Perhaps it's only that he's more sober now. He lowers himself down as carefully as he can, hanging from the sill for a moment and taking a few deep breaths before he lets go and drops to the grass.

There are clouds drifting over the moon, dimming its light, but the route through the gardens and the orchard is one he could manage in his sleep, after all the times he's gone out with Danny before now. He finds his way with barely a false step, over the fence and back to the road, and is already thinking about how he's going to tell this story once Danny comes home from the mountains. It'll sound like a grand adventure by then, he's sure.

When he tells the story, Colin decides as he walks down the road, he's going to leave out the part about how cold it gets when one is tired and sober and walking back to town in the middle of the night. Or the way the distant baying of dogs makes him shiver and reminds him uncomfortably of children's tales of the Lady's hound. Or how dismal the western road seems when it's late enough that all the plantations have doused their lamps, and he has no company to help him pass the time. Most likely, he'll leave out the walk back to town entirely.

When he reaches the west gate, it's already shut for the night, and there's a guard on duty in the gatehouse, slouching out to meet him as Colin walks up. "Late for honest business, isn't it?" he asks, propping his duty pike beside him so he can lean on it.

"Never too late for Kite Street," Colin bluffs. Probably it isn't strictly true; the brothels must shut their doors eventually. But Colin's never been there late enough to see it happen.

The guard doesn't move to unlock the gate. "If you're headed up to Kite, your lordship, you must have coin to spare."

Colin stares. *That* certainly doesn't happen earlier in the evening, when there's more traffic coming through. "You can't be serious. My father knows your captain personally. I was at supper with him just this evening."

"That so?" The guard has a tooth missing in front, which only makes his smile uglier. "You going to run back home and complain that you couldn't go whoring in the middle of the night?"

Colin grits his teeth, clenches his fist until he's sure he has control of himself. He'd gain nothing by fighting here. He digs a shilling from his pocket and tosses it at the guard's feet. "Open the gate."

The guard waits another few moments, but Colin can read that for the bluff it is, and when he doesn't produce any more coin, the man does turn at last and dig out the heavy iron key to unlock the gate. "Enjoy your business in Casmile, your lordship," he says. Colin can't bring himself to say thanks.

He'll definitely leave out the parts about how he got back to town, when he's telling all this to Danny. None of it is worth repeating.

It's next to impossible to find a carriage for hire this late, of course, so he doesn't really have any option but to keep walking. Colin stuffs his hands in his pockets, hunching his shoulders against the chill, and starts down Market Street into the city. The later it gets, the less this seems like a good idea. He's cold, he's tired, and his head aches. His steps grow slower the closer he gets to Alder Street and the gaming district. Surely it's too late to find Barron at the Peacock by now. Only the most dedicated players would still be at the tables at this hour. Tomorrow would be soon enough, wouldn't it? When he has his wits about him and can explain himself properly.

Colin passes the turn he ought to take, and immediately feels better. Not entirely relieved, of course—Market Street is dreary at night, the shops all shuttered and the open stalls bare. Nothing moves save in the alleys, and there the rats are the most wholesome thing awake. He walks a little faster. It *is* late for honest business, and he might be the biggest troublemaker among his friends, but that's still a far cry from the worst the city has to offer.

He'll stay the night in a tavern, he decides, and straighten out this mess with Barron tomorrow. When he makes it all the way down to Front Street, there are plenty of places still open, light shining from their windows. Sailors, he remembers hearing once, keep time by the tide, not the sun. Of course, that presents its own problems—the door to the Mermaid opens as he passes, a few men staggering drunk out of a room alive with song and laughter.

There's no way he'll see a decent night's sleep with that sort of lullaby, so he walks onward, past the busiest part of the street near the main docks, and turns onto Ash Street a little further north. About halfway up the block, he finds a tavern whose sign is shaped like a dragon's head, with light in the windows but no sound spilling out into the street. It should be passable enough.

The light in the Dragon's Head comes mostly from the fireplace, with a few lamps behind the bar to help it along. The furniture is rough wood, unfinished, and plain where it hasn't been scored by guests leaving their mark. Apart from the innkeeper, who's a woman probably Colin's mother's age but considerably the worse for wear, there are only two other people in the room. One is an old sailor with a wooden leg who's nodding by the fire. The other is a skinny boy about Colin's own age who looks up with wary eyes, inspecting Colin suspiciously before he turns his attention back to the wooden cup in his hands. All three of them are ordinary Casmilan stock, with dark hair and eyes and skin similar shades of dusty tan, and Colin wishes he weren't quite so pale, nor his hair so tinged with red.

But for all that he feels awkward, nobody's actually challenging him. He crosses the room and steps up to the bar, trying to act as though he does this sort of thing all the time. "Have you a room free tonight?" he asks.

The innkeeper barely glances at him. "Three shillings for the room," she says, "or four with meals." She has a faint lisp when she speaks.

"Just the room is fine." If he does want breakfast in the morning, he's sure he can find better than the dull porridge they no doubt serve here. "I'll take a pint now, though," he adds. His nerves could use it, and it's probably polite.

"Three pennies a pint," the innkeeper tells him, and turns away to pull his pint while Colin fishes in his pocket for some copper. She puts his mug on the bar, he drops his coins into her hand, and after a moment of hesitation, he decides to take his drink to a table. No point in saddling either of them with the obligation to converse, is there?

Casmilan ale somehow manages both to be bitter and to taste of almost nothing. He lifts his mug to his lips and congratulates himself on managing to not make a face, though he's not sure how he'll get through the entire pint. The lager imported from the northlands is far better, but a place like this probably doesn't carry something that expensive, and he wouldn't want to give offense by suggesting he preferred the barbarians' craft, especially when he's so white-skinned himself. So he sips his bitter ale, and stares at the scars beaten into the tabletop, and wonders just how awful it will be to get Barron to agree to reasonable terms for repayment.

He's making himself miserable for no purpose, he thinks, and takes a long pull on the ale as though it's medicine enough to calm him. This mess won't get straightened out tonight, and it won't help matters any for him to worry.

The boy in the corner is watching him again, eyes too intent and focused for any sort of polite or well-intentioned interest. Colin glares, daring the boy to come give him trouble. He could take down a skinny little rat like that, and it might even make him feel better, with the way this night's turned. The boy just smiles, though, or possibly bares his teeth—he looks amused enough, but not at all friendly. Brat. What makes him think he's so tough?

Colin's about to get up and go over there, ready to ask what the boy thinks is so rotting fascinating about him. Then the door opens, and the boy looks away immediately.

"Good tip," says the man in the doorway. "He's in here."

Colin's heart stutters in his chest, panic locking his limbs as the man steps inside and brings three of his friends with him. They're big, broad-shouldered as dockworkers, one of them dark like an islander, and all four of them are carrying cudgels. But they don't even glance at Colin, instead heading straight toward the boy in the corner.

The boy gets to his feet, uncoiling into a ready, tense stance, and bares his teeth at them, too. "The dogs come snapping at my heels, do they?" he asks. His voice is smoother than Colin would have expected, a light tenor that sounds almost friendly.

"Morgan's not happy with you," the leader of the thugs says as his companions spread out between the boy and the door. "He wanted his girl back in one piece." Colin glances over to see if the innkeeper is going to try to intervene, at least to tell them to take the trouble outside, but she's disappeared.

"Well." The boy shrugs, shifts his weight, and somehow there are knives in his hands, glinting in the firelight. "You're good dogs who do as you're told. Maybe he should have sent you after her instead of me."

"You think you're clever?" the leader asks. His men close ranks, weapons ready.

The boy hisses, low and threatening, like a barn cat cornered by the hunting hounds. Colin almost can't stand to look. This is going to be awful.

They all move at once, sudden as a flock of crows startled off a corpse. One moment they're glaring at each other, and the next they lunge. The boy is fast, ducking low and catching the leader's arm with one knife as he twists out of the way of a swing. A fine spray of red arcs across the floor, but it's not enough to slow the man down. The thugs swear and yell as they fight, but the boy stays quiet, hissing sharp little breaths between his teeth as he dodges their blows and shoves furniture between him and them. A chair splinters under a cudgel blow, and Colin winces. Out of the corner of his eye, he sees the old sailor hobbling for the door. If he had any sense, he'd follow, but he can't bring himself to move. He's never seen anything like this; even the best theater can't capture this feeling.

The boy snarls—the first real sound he's made since the fight started—as he loses one of his knives, caught between the ribs of the most aggressive thug. It unbalances him, and the islander's next swipe sends him sprawling to the floor. He rolls away, dives toward the fireplace and comes up with the poker, iron scraping stone as he pulls it free. He jabs it into the islander's stomach as he regains his feet, and the man goes down howling, clutching at the burn. The air reeks of seared flesh.

But the poker's too heavy for the boy to use one-handed, and the leader knocks it from his hand. The boy springs back, dodging and swiping at his attackers when he has the chance. He looks like he's trying to get past them, but they're driving him into the corner. Once he has no place left to run, this won't last long.

He should be *doing* something, Colin realizes abruptly.

He gets up, crosses the room to take the cudgel of the man who's been stabbed. It's heavier than he expects, unbalanced, weighted at the end. The last two thugs have the boy cornered, so there's no time left to hesitate. Colin steps up, swings the cudgel, and there's an awful, wet crunch when it connects with the back of the first thug's head. The impact jars up Colin's arm, solid and final, and the man drops gracelessly to the floor.

The last one, the leader, turns toward him, and the boy lunges immediately, grabbing the man's hair with one hand and drawing a knife across his throat with the other. Blood sprays; the man makes terrible gurgling noises as he collapses.

Then, thank the Fates, it's over.

The fire pops and settles, loud in the sudden stillness. Colin stares at the boy, his blood pounding in his veins. The boy grins back, fierce and proud. "Ah," Colin starts, not even sure what he's going to say, "I—"

The boy shoves past him, knocking Colin out of the way with a snarl, and buries his knife in the eye of the man he'd burned before. Colin catches himself against the edge of a table, swallows hard against the feeling that his throat is closing up. He starts to shake, his nerves overtaxed, as he takes in the long, thin blade in the dead man's hand. He could've— If this boy hadn't been so fast, he'd—

Lady's luck, this night is going all wrong.

CHAPTER THREE

"That went pretty well, didn't it," the boy says, more a statement than a question. He pulls his knife free—Colin winces at the rush of fluids—and wipes it on the dead man's shirt before he tucks it away in his clothes somewhere. Then he shrugs, rolling his head from side to side, and his neck cracks audibly. "Help me with the bodies."

"Help you?" Colin sways on his feet. He could have died just now. He fears his legs won't hold him if he tries to move.

The boy nods. "This is a nice place. It's polite to clean up your messes." He pries the knife out of the dead man's hand and tucks it into his belt, then takes the body by both wrists. "A big strong monster like you ought to be able to help me carry them, right? I'll share with you."

There are so many things wrong with that explanation that Colin doesn't know what to object to first—from the description of this dingy tavern as "nice" to the lecture on manners from a savage little street killer. His wit fails him, and he says nothing at all, only takes the dead man's feet and helps the boy carry him out the door. They leave the body in the alley behind the Dragon's Head, where he'd almost look like he was just dead drunk instead of dead, except for the blood and fluids on his face.

Colin feels numb and feverish at the same time. He finds himself nursing a vain hope that he's dreaming as he follows the boy inside to retrieve the second body. This is the one with his throat slit, so there's much more blood, and the man's head lolls back too far when they pick him up to carry him out. It's too vivid. This isn't a dream.

"All . . . all four of them are dead, aren't they?" Colin asks as they drop the second body beside the first. "I mean, even the one I . . . the next one." He hadn't *meant* to kill anyone, never wanted to—he hadn't realized how much harder the cudgel would strike than the light fencing rapiers he's used before.

The boy gives him a pitying look. "Don't know your own strength, do you? You were very good, Drake."

Colin tries to restrain his dismay, because he can't imagine it would go well for him if he insulted this boy. "Thank you," he says as they head back inside.

The boy holds the door for him, incongruously polite again. "You're good luck, aren't you?"

"For you, maybe." Colin can feel panicked laughter trapped in his chest, threatening to bubble up and spill from his mouth. He takes deep breaths, trying to calm himself down.

"For me," the boy agrees. "Very good luck." They pick up the third body, and Colin tries to stop thinking about the fact that *he* killed this one. He remembers the wet crunching sound it made, the way he felt the shock all the way up his arm. Blood drips on the boy's boots.

"Why were they after you?" Colin asks to distract himself. Maybe this will feel less like a nightmare and more like an adventure if there's some kind of grand story behind it all.

The boy shrugs awkwardly as they carry the body out the door. "Their master hired me to retrieve something he'd lost. It . . . ." He pauses as though he's thinking about the answer. "It got broken in the scuffle." He shakes his head. "The whole thing would have gone so much better if she hadn't started screaming."

On the other hand, perhaps Colin would be better off not knowing. He could do without more adventures like this. He doesn't ask any more questions as they dump the third body with the others and go back for the last. At least it's almost over.

The boy kneels beside the last body and reaches for the knife stuck between the dead man's ribs. He tugs at it, rocking it back and forth to make it come free, and more blood wells up, thick and dark, around the blade. Colin has to turn away.

"Notched it." The boy sounds petulant. "Well. Maybe they'll have enough coin to pay the blacksmith, mm?"

Daring as it sounds in ballads about highwaymen, Colin finds he doesn't have any desire to go loot bodies. Everyone says disrespect to the dead causes the green rot. Just this much—he picks up the last man's feet—brings him closer to death than he'd have liked.

"We're going now," the boy calls as he backs out the door, the last body swaying between them. "Sorry for the trouble."

There's no answer from the innkeeper. Colin isn't surprised.

"Right," Colin says when they get outside, "I— Thank you for saving me back there. I'm very grateful. So, ah. Have a good night, and Fates keep you." He'll have to find someplace else to go. There must still be other taverns with rooms free.

The boy looks surprised. "You can't go yet. Don't you want to see what we got?"

For an instant Colin pictures himself paying Barron off in coin looted from corpses, but the idea makes his stomach lurch. "You— you can have it," he says as the boy kneels to paw through the dead men's clothes. It's too dark to see anything in detail, but he seems to be working mostly by feel, anyway. "I'm fine."

"Very noble of you." The boy shakes his head. "But silly." He stuffs something in his pocket and moves on to the next body. "I'm taking the first share, because three of them were mine. But you helped. Here." He stands up, reaching out to offer something to Colin. "You can have this. It'd suit you. Then," he adds, in a patient tone that suggests he's trying to explain something important and Colin is slow to understand, "the dogs get the next pick, and in the morning the captain gets whatever's left."

"The— You mean the captain of the guard?" Colin tries to imagine telling Captain Westfall, possibly over the fowl course, that in the natural order of things, he gets fourth pick of a murder's spoils, after the killer, his accomplice, and the city's stray dogs. The idea is so appalling that Colin would laugh if he dared.

"Nastiest dog in the city," the boy says. "He runs all the others off." There's just enough light in the alley to make his grin look utterly ghoulish. "Now go on, take this. You're going to need it."

That doesn't sound good at all, but still Colin reaches out to accept whatever he's . . . earned here. His share is heavy and cold, and it takes him a moment to figure out what it is: a single piece of metal, four rings forged together in a row and a bar laid over one side. Brass knuckles, he realizes, when he discovers how easily the rings fit his fingers. The damage it would do, to punch someone with these . . . He shudders. "I'm going to need this?"

"Yes." The boy finishes with the last body and dusts off his hands. "We're going to see Morgan, and ask him why he thought this—" he kicks the dead man in the ribs "—was a good way to tell me he had a problem."

"What?" Colin steps back nervously. He's already gotten in enough trouble tonight; he has no desire to go haring off after someone who hires thugs and murderers to take care of his business. "No. Not me. Maybe you're going to see Morgan, but I don't want anything to do with him."

The boy stares at him as if he's touched. "One of his men tried to kill you. You can't just let him get away with that."

"I—I trust you to take care of it," Colin improvises. "In fact I'd like to hire you to take care of it for me. I'm sure you're capable."

"You flatter me, but I don't want your silver. You're my luck tonight. You have to come with me."

It must be true, Colin thinks, that the Fates laugh hardest when men's own vices trip them. How many times has he used that very excuse to drag Danny all over town? "My luck's gone from bad to worse tonight. It won't do you any good to have me along."

"I want you to come with me, Drake," the boy says, and the petulance in his tone would be laughable if they weren't having this argument over the bodies of men he's killed. "Don't make me ask again."

That last sounds like a threat, and while the boy glares like a child being refused extra dessert, he's also running his fingers over the hilt of his knife. Colin takes a deep breath and lets it out shakily. "I'm not going to kill anyone." He never wanted to in the first place and certainly not more than once. "And stop calling me Drake. I have a name."

The boy smiles, like they're sharing a secret. "Of course you do. Even I have a name, and you're a much finer creature than I am. This way."

They head further into the city instead of back toward the harbor, taking cramped little streets and turning at almost every corner until they come out on Market near the second bridge. The boy starts across the bridge without a second of hesitation, and Colin's stomach lurches in a way that shouldn't be so much like the thrill of rolling high-stakes dice. Right by the river, the south bank is still respectable enough, but beyond that, it grows wild quickly. In the maze of streets there, the houses are still scarred by the last big fire in the city, though that's ten years past.

"Don't hang back," the boy says in a low murmur that Colin would swear sounds excited. "Plenty of nasty things prowl around the city this late."

"You'd know all about that, wouldn't you?" No more than one in every four street lamps is lit, wherever they are now. This clearly used to be a nice part of town, years ago—the houses are big enough, some of them even fenced in front, but they aren't all whole anymore.

"Of course. All the hunters know each other's names."

That's not reassuring in the least, and Colin nearly says so. He can see his breath, thin plumes like smoke, when they pass under the lit lamps, or when the moon peers out from behind the clouds.

"Not that Morgan's a hunter himself," the boy adds. "Not anymore. He's found all the treasure he knows what to do with, like—mm, do you know the story of the king of the wolves?"

"No," Colin says slowly. "I don't think I do."

"Deirdre told it to me when I was small," the boy says, as though that explains everything. "The king of the wolves is huge and shaggy, tall as a house and nearly as broad. He takes human girls as brides, sends his pack out hunting for them at midwinter, and that's why they don't let northlands girls go anywhere alone in the coldest part of the year. Because the dire wolves will come and carry them off to the cavern where their king is waiting." He brightens, entirely too enthusiastic about this whole business. "Anyway, he's wronged us now, so we're going to make him pay."

Colin thinks only exhaustion is saving him from real terror. His head aches and his limbs feel heavy, and they're stopping now in front of one of the houses, one whose fence is in good condition and whose grounds look well kept.

"Look," he tries one more time, "I'm not going to be any help to you in there. I'm only going to slow you down."

The boy pats his arm reassuringly. "You won't slow me down. I'll do all the hard parts."

He turns and takes hold of the front gate, boosting himself up with a hiss of effort, his boots wedged in the narrow spaces between the iron bars. If Colin wanted to run, now would be the time, wouldn't it? But he thinks of how fast the boy lunged after the thugs in that fight, thinks of how many knives the boy has, and doesn't want to risk it.

The gate is cold under his hands, and wet with dew. Colin climbs over it carefully, trying not to let his coat snag. He wonders if the reason the boy wears only a heavy vest, instead of a proper coat, is to avoid that problem.

On the far side of the gate is a path up to the door, the slate flagstones cracked, weeds sprouting between them. The house is dark inside—it's late for anyone to keep the lamps lit, by now—but it looks decent, for something this far south. The paint is fresh, not yet peeling in Casmile's humid air, and the balcony supports are sturdy, unbowed.

"Up here," the boy says, standing on the porch railing and reaching up for the balcony over his head.

This is ridiculous, Colin thinks. He takes his coat off and drapes it over the railing—the sleeves were pulling under his arms when he scaled the fence, and tearing out the seams wouldn't do anything to make this excursion better. The night's chill prickles down his back as he reaches up.

And it may be ridiculous, but it's also *real*. The muscles in his arms and chest ache with the effort of climbing over the second-story railing. His heart thuds hard in his chest. The boy is waiting for him, watching.

"Why come this way?" Colin asks softly. "You can kill a man in a heartbeat, but you can't break in the front door?"

The boy grins. "We're sure to run into the dogs if we go that way." Colin can't tell if he means real dogs or more hired thugs. Do criminal overlords hire house guards the way respectable families do? The boy turns away, knife in hand as he kneels to attend to the latch on the balcony doors.

Colin licks his lips. "Are we— Are you going to kill him?"

"No," the boy says, and Colin relaxes, a breath too soon. "Not unless he's difficult. I'd rather just hurt him. Then he can tell people it was me." He gets the door unlatched before Colin can protest, and then he's slipping into the dark inside.

This is a terrible idea. If Colin had any sense, he'd run. He'd leave this mad boy killer here and flee, walk all the way home if he had to, and deal with his troubles like a civilized person tomorrow. He'd forget all about this night, what he's seen, what he's already done. And nothing like this would ever happen to him again.

He follows the boy inside.

The hallway's even darker than the street, cramped and narrow. Colin can just make out the boy at the end of it, where dim light comes in the window to silhouette him. The doors along either side of the hall are open, like they've already been tried and abandoned, and now the boy is standing at the last one, head cocked as he waits for Colin.

It's too late to back down, isn't it? Colin walks down the hallway as quietly as he can, and the boy eases the door open. There's light inside, a faint red glow from the fireplace, where the coals have been carefully banked against the draft. Morgan seems to be still asleep in the big bed in the middle of the room, so Colin takes a moment to glance around. It looks more comfortable than he would have expected from the ringleader of a criminal gang—not as nice as his own room, of course, but nicer than most of the inns he's seen. The furnishings are solid, and the curtains heavy enough to block the cold air from outside. Morgan himself is perhaps Colin's father's age, his temples gray and his cheeks just starting to soften to heavy jowls. The bed's big enough for two easily, and there are a few pieces of women's jewelry on the nightstand, but no sign that Morgan's had company tonight.

The boy shoves a chair under the doorknob, and the loud scrape wakes Morgan. He sits up abruptly, shoving back the blankets. "You," he says. "You should be—"

"Dead?" the boy interrupts in a chilly, too-bright tone. "Don't be silly." He has knives in his hands before Morgan can make it more than a step. "You've forgotten who she really favors, haven't you? You can't kill me."

"Bullshit." Morgan looks about half-ready to fight the boy, knives or no, so Colin takes a step closer. The brass knuckles are heavy and cold against his hand. He might be in over his head, but he's not about to fold now—they've made this gamble together. "Those superstitions might frighten children, but don't try that line with me," Morgan says. "Everyone dies."

The boy laughs. "Like your boys did earlier?" He brings up one of his knives to point at Morgan's face. "Sit down. Let's talk about that."

"You son of a whore. I have nothing to say to you." But the boy doesn't back down, and Morgan clearly knows he wouldn't hesitate to use the knives. Morgan takes a step, and then another, and he winds up backed into the chair beside his desk.

"Good," the boy says. "Now tie him down, Drake."

This time Colin doesn't mind the name so much—it's better if someone like Morgan doesn't know who he is, right? "Tie him down with what?"

"Tch, you were clever enough in the fight," the boy says without taking his eyes off Morgan. "Don't tell me you only know one trick."

Colin bristles. He saved this boy's life earlier tonight, and he's let himself be dragged along for luck; already he's done more than he needed to. He rummages in Morgan's chest of drawers, finds a stash of bright silken cravats that look near as eye-catching as some of Sebastian's. Out of the corner of his eye, he sees the boy smiling as he uses them to bind Morgan's arms to the chair.

"You'll regret this, the both of you," Morgan growls. "I'll make you curse the day the whores who whelped you ever spread—"

Colin hits him in the mouth, and his head snaps back. An instant later Colin freezes, alarmed by his own thoughtless daring.

"Now, Drake," the boy says mildly. He sounds like a tutor scolding a child too restless for lessons. "You're getting impatient. Talking first. *Then* we hurt him."

"He should leave my mother out of it," Colin mutters. Morgan smirks, and Colin steps back before he'll be tempted to throw another punch. This isn't his fight.

The boy perches on Morgan's desk, his muddy boots crumpling the blank paper laid out there, and the smile slides off his face. "Why'd you send your dogs for me, Morgan?" It might be the first time Colin's heard him sound completely serious. "Why would you do that? I got your job done for you."

"You didn't." There's blood at the corner of Morgan's mouth. "She's dead because of you."

"She's dead because of the man who slit her throat, and that wasn't me. Or maybe she's dead because her man decided to play tough and hire *me* to go looking for her, instead of taking the safe route and paying her ransom. Don't see how that's my fault." The boy hops down off the desk, goes over to crouch by the fire and poke at the coals with his knife. The flames flicker back to life, giving enough light for Colin to see Morgan break out in a sweat.

"You said you could do the job," Morgan rasps. "And you let her die."

The boy looks up, though he doesn't take the blade out of the fire. "What was it you said? Everyone dies. Some of them even do it without my help." It's like going to the penny theaters, Colin thinks. Except the knives are sharp and the blood is real. "You shouldn't have asked me to do it if you wanted her back more than you wanted them dead."

"I wanted both." Morgan's voice is still steady—he bluffs well—but a trickle of sweat runs down his temple all the same.

"Greedy." The boy shakes his head. "And then you sent your dogs after me. I probably can't go back to that tavern now, and I liked that one."

Morgan snorts. "Your tavern can rot, you mad bastard. You've cost me something much harder to replace than a pint of beer."

"Wormwood," the boy corrects him. He turns his knife, examining the blackening blade. Colin imagines that hot steel touching flesh and feels queasy. At home they don't even brand the slaves; his father has always said it's unnecessary and barbaric.

"The big problem here," the boy goes on, the firelight playing across his face, "is that you still think you're in control, don't you? You've had too many lap dogs for too many years. The ones from earlier, that girl, the other girls you used to have. None of them so much as bare their teeth, do they? So you've gone soft."

"You think so?" Morgan turns his head and spits. "I'll kill you myself."

The boy smiles into the fire. "Promise?"

"On the Lady's bones."

Colin flinches away as soon as the boy moves, turning so he won't see what comes next, and that almost makes it worse when the screaming starts. He's not going to look, doesn't want to know, just wants to get *out*. He crosses to the door, shoves the chair out from under the knob. Before he can open it, though, a dog starts to bark from the other side, loud and deep, and then the door shudders with an impact. Colin jumps and steps back. The room smells like burning meat, blood, and the sour tang of piss.

The window, then, if he can't use the door. Colin turns, and can't help looking, just for a second. The boy is stepping back now, blood dripping from his knife to the carpet. Morgan's face is a wreck, blood and thick clear fluids running down from the raw, red hollows where his eyes should be. His screams have faded to wet gurgling whimpers.

Colin has almost nothing to bring up, but his stomach heaves all the same. He yanks back the curtains, claws at the latch so he can shove the window open. The air outside is cold, sharp in his lungs, stinging at the corners of his eyes. But it helps, keeps him from losing what's left of his composure. He half expects the boy to attack him, or at least laugh at his weakness, but it doesn't happen.

After a minute or so, the gurgling stops. Colin doesn't dare look again. Then the boy touches his shoulder, and he jumps. "We're done, Drake. Let's go."

Colin looks up at the boy, whose expression is solicitous now, almost kind—despite the knife still in his hand, the stink of blood on the air. "How could you," Colin says before he can think better of it. "I mean—what kind of person *are* you?"

The boy lets go of him. "Don't you know?" He steps back so he can offer Colin a flourishy actor's bow. "I'm Gabriel."

CHAPTER FOUR

"That's not possible." Colin gapes at the boy. "Gabriel's just a legend! He doesn't really exist."

"Well," the boy says, "that gives us something in common, doesn't it?" He smiles brightly, as if that solved a problem instead of being utter nonsense, then winces when the dog starts barking again. "We should go. If there are any guardsmen around, that might get their attention."

Colin nods. Lady's cowl, he wouldn't want the guard to find him here, not after . . . what they've done. "That sounds like a mastiff. If we're going back through that door, you're going first."

The boy who claims to be Gabriel laughs. "You've already found us an escape." He pushes the window the rest of the way open. "Ready, Drake? Out of the tower we go." He climbs through the window, holding on to the sill and lowering himself down to hang before he drops. His knuckles are scarred, and Colin thinks of Captain Westfall again.

It's not so much like theater now as like a bad dream, things half familiar and half horribly strange. How many times has he climbed out his own window like this?

He can't help looking back into the room once more as he gets a leg over the sill. Morgan isn't moving anymore, his head fallen forward, his nightshirt soaked dark with blood. Black Mother Ket, it's a lot of blood. Either he's fainted from the shock and the pain, or else . . . Gabriel . . . really did kill him after all. Colin's not sure which is worse.

"Come on," the boy—Gabriel—calls from the ground. "It's clear."

Colin shakes himself, tears his eyes away from the wreck that was Morgan, and makes the drop. He lands hard, and for an awful moment, he fears he might have turned his ankle, but it still takes his weight, so at least his luck hasn't *entirely* deserted him yet.

The houses on either side are still dark, despite the screams and the dog's barking. Gabriel—Colin realizes he can believe this boy is the sort to frighten even other criminals—is walking toward the front gate. He has Colin's jacket in his hands and he's going through the pockets.

"Stop that," Colin says, jogging to catch up with him and snatching it back. A moment too late he realizes how reckless that is.

Gabriel just grins at him, though, like he's pleased that Colin would try to make demands of him. "We should hurry. The night guard would rather be in taverns than on the streets, but that makes them mean if they do catch up to you." He hauls himself over the fence, and Colin thinks that when he manages to get out of this mess, he'll have to remember to tell Danny how much of being a street tough is actually a matter of good climbing skills.

He follows Gabriel over the fence and shrugs back into his coat. The night air feels even colder after the warmth of Morgan's room, but at least it helps to clear his head.

"This way, Drake," Gabriel says. "It's late. We should go home." Colin almost asks how long Gabriel intends to keep him around, save that he's too likely to get an answer he doesn't want to hear. Once the sun's up and the city's awake, he can try to talk Gabriel into taking him to Market—there'll be crowds there to get lost in, and he can get a carriage home and be done with this whole terrible mess.

"It's not far, is it?" he asks. The cobblestones are slick with dew, and his footing is uncertain as anything else tonight.

"Not too far. Had enough adventures for one night?" Gabriel sounds sympathetic. "Don't worry. We can rest soon."

Not soon enough—every turn they take leads further away from anything Colin recognizes or wants to. The houses grow smaller and more decrepit, the streets more narrow and filth ridden, like they're heading straight south. Some of the huddled shapes in the alleys are *people*, Colin realizes when one of them stirs. He knew Casmile grew wild south of the river, and of course every city has beggars, doesn't it? But being close enough to smell the stench of human waste, to see the rats scurrying in the streets, is nothing he ever thought he'd do.

"You could take me back to the port, if you'd like," he ventures. "I could take a room there and not put you to any more trouble."

"It should be fancier, shouldn't it?" Gabriel says sadly. He makes one last turn and stops in front of a door, jiggling the knob until it turns. "You'll want silks and jewels to make you happy."

"I don't mind," Colin lies. Is it really that obvious where he comes from? He hopes Gabriel won't follow that line of thought any further.

They climb a creaking, narrow set of stairs and walk down a dark, foul-smelling hallway, and Gabriel pushes open the door at the end. One night of this, Colin tells himself. He can stand this for one night, and then he'll go home and bathe in pennyroyal until he doesn't have any fleas left to remember it by.

The room is nearly bare, and as cold as the night outside—the one window is broken, two of its six panes gaping empty instead of filled with cloudy glass. There's a small stove on one side of the room, and a crooked little table with nothing on it on the other side. The squat shape on the floor beside the table is probably a chamber pot. The dark lump to the left of the door, Colin realizes as Gabriel kicks off his boots and sits down on it, is supposed to be a mattress.

"I've left you room," Gabriel says, stretching out beside the wall. "Time to sleep now, Drake," he adds when Colin hesitates, as if his offer simply wasn't clear.

Colin's fairly sure Gabriel still has all his knives. "I can take the floor. It's fine."

"You'd be cold," Gabriel says as Colin sits down on the floor and tries to pretend he's content. "There's only the one blanket."

"I don't mind," Colin insists, even though he's already chilled through. "Thank you, though. You're very kind."

"And you're stubborn." Gabriel crawls off the mattress, grabs Colin by the shoulder, and pushes him toward it. "You take it, then."

"But—" Colin starts, and isn't sure how to go on.

"Hesitate and I'll change my mind."

That sounds like a threat of some sort, so Colin stretches out on the mattress. There isn't a pillow. "Thank you," he says.

Gabriel nods, and curls up on the floor with his head resting on his arm. "Good night, Drake."

He drops off to sleep almost instantly, his breathing changing and his limbs deadweight limp. Colin lies awake in the dark and listens to Gabriel breathing, to the distant scratching that he fears is from rats in the walls. The mattress isn't comfortable at all, a bit of straw poking at the bare skin of his neck. He reaches for the blanket crumpled beside the wall, a ragged old thing that's stiff in a few spots and threadbare in others. How does Gabriel—*why* would Gabriel live like this? When he's so dangerous he's practically a myth, why would he be stuck in some filthy little hovel like this?

Colin rolls over to peer at Gabriel again, as if there's a visible answer to that question. He must be freezing. And that doesn't make sense either: why would a remorseless killer insist on giving Colin his bed and blanket when he clearly needs them himself?

When Colin sits up, Gabriel doesn't move. Maybe if he were to leave very quietly . . . But then he'd be lost in the dark in the far south end of the city, and that might be worse than Gabriel's company. So Colin reaches out to spread the blanket over Gabriel's thin shoulders, and lies back down on the mattress himself. He tucks his hands in his armpits to keep them warm and closes his eyes. It should be hard to sleep like this, but the weight of the whole long impossible night bears down on him, and despite the cold, despite the fear, he sinks under it.

CHAPTER
FIVE

C olin wakes pinned beneath something heavy and warm, and for a moment he's completely disoriented. "Maddie?" he mumbles, reaching up to push his way free before he remembers that it's been years since he had a dog. Then he takes a deeper breath that smells of muddy straw, damp wood, and sweat, and more recent memories come back to him in a nasty, sobering rush like cold water down his back. His eyes snap open. "What are you doing?"

Gabriel has draped himself over Colin with the blanket covering them both. "You're so warm," he says, thin fingers curling tight around Colin's arms. "I knew you would be."

"That's . . . natural, isn't it?" Colin holds very still, trying to figure out how he can decline if this really is what it seems like, whether Gabriel will even *let* him refuse.

"It's a very good disguise," Gabriel goes on. He levers himself up on one elbow and looks Colin in the eyes. "Most people probably never even suspect, do they?"

"I don't know what you mean," Colin says. Gabriel's eyes are so dark, he can't tell where the color fades into the black. He looks away nervously. "What disguise?"

Gabriel shifts to move back into his line of sight. "It's very clever. But you don't have to worry. I won't tell anyone."

Colin hears his own heartbeat in his ears, and wonders if Gabriel can smell fear, like a dog. "Won't tell anyone what?" He looks away again.

"What you are," Gabriel says. He takes hold of Colin's jaw, turns his face so they're eye to eye again. His eyes widen like he's surprised. "You're so soft." He runs gentle fingers over Colin's face, and Colin closes his eyes, trying desperately not to think about what Gabriel did to Morgan last night. But Gabriel's touch remains gentle, and Colin is starting to believe that this might be an appallingly clumsy romantic overture after all, when Gabriel says, "Such a clever dragon."

Colin opens his eyes again, unsure if that was just fancy, or if Gabriel really is mad enough to mean it literally. "What?"

"Don't worry," Gabriel tells him again, petting his hair. "I'll keep your secret. I'm good at that."

"Gabriel," Colin says slowly, "there's no such thing as dragons."

Gabriel nods solemnly. "I know. I told you last night, I'm like that too. Except there are more sightings of me." Colin glances toward the door, and Gabriel hisses like an alley cat. "Don't do that. I'm your friend, Drake. I won't hurt you. Where did you come from? Why did you come to Casmile?"

"I've lived—" he almost says *here*, but that's not right, not even close "—in Casmile all my life. I'm a boy just like you."

"Nobody's just like me," Gabriel says. "Look at me, Drake. It's better when I can see your eyes." Colin flinches; it feels like a challenge, like he's exposing himself. But making Gabriel angry would be worse. He looks up reluctantly, and Gabriel relaxes a fraction. "There. Much better. If you can't tell the story to a stranger, that's all right. I'll wait."

"I don't have any stories to tell," Colin says helplessly. He tries to picture himself relating society rumors to Gabriel: Lady Montrose's scandalous festival dress, or the gossip about whose engagements were likely to falter for want of income. "Not good ones, I mean." The longer he keeps looking at Gabriel, the harder it gets. He closes his eyes. "I'm just a boy who—"

"You're lying again!" Gabriel slams his hand down on the mattress beside Colin's head. A little puff of straw dust rises from the fabric, and Colin coughs. "Don't look away, Drake."

He needs to get out of here, and the sooner the better. He makes himself meet Gabriel's stare, and tries to stay calm. It's like bluffing high, isn't it? Too high, but he won't think about that. "I'm nobody special," he says, and he can see skepticism on Gabriel's face. "But I *am* hungry. I'm not sure I'd even remember a story before I've had some breakfast."

Gabriel laughs, and sits back so the blanket slides off his shoulders. "Then I'll have to feed you. What do dragons eat for breakfast?"

Maidens with jam, Colin almost says, save that it would be a nightmare if Gabriel believed him. He can bluff his way through this. He knows his nursery rhymes well enough. "I can't speak for the race of dragons, but I'd like some sweet rolls." No, he should be more specific, demand more luxury. "Cakes with cinnamon and honey."

"You see? You give yourself away, Drake. Normal boys don't have such fancy tastes." Gabriel shifts his weight to let Colin up at last, and reaches for his boots. "But we'll go find you some cakes anyway."

"Thank you," Colin says, sitting up gingerly.

Gabriel's room doesn't look much more appealing by daylight than it did the night before. The walls might have been white when the plaster was first applied, but now they're more of a dingy yellow. The ceiling has water stains in several places, and sags in a way that speaks ill of its future. Near the window, the floor has a few sagging spots too, where the boards look to be rotting away.

And Gabriel is watching him. "You came from someplace glorious, didn't you," Gabriel says. "Some glittering cavern full of treasure."

Colin thinks of his parents' house, of the ballroom with all its fixtures polished and the lanterns blazing for the first party of the winter season. "Something like that," he says. He tugs on his boots and stands up. "Shall we go?"

He follows Gabriel out of the room and down the stairs. The building feels cramped in the daytime, less the looming threat it seemed last night and more simply pathetic. There's no lock for the front door, just like there was no lock for Gabriel's room.

"Don't you worry about people taking your things?" Colin asks. Granted, he didn't see much in Gabriel's room to begin with, but it still seems strange.

"No." Gabriel grins in a horrible, predatory way. "It's only happened once."

Outside, the street is dreary, the colors drab and waterlogged even in the bright morning sun. The best of the houses might be salvageable with some fresh paint and the attention of a skilled carpenter; the worst of them seem to be collapsing slowly inward, into dark caves with mouths of jagged, rotting beams. There are a few men loitering on corners and in doorways, not doing anything in particular, just watching as Colin and Gabriel pass. Colin hopes he's imagining the challenge in their dark eyes. "Where are we? I mean, what street?"

"Cypress," Gabriel says, stepping over a hole in the street where the cobblestones are entirely gone. "Near the south end. Not far from the Lady's house."

"The what?" Colin tries to think if he's ever even heard of a Cypress Street, and whether it will take them back to the river.

Gabriel reaches into his shirt and pulls out a bone pendant on a string. "The Green Lady's house. I go to visit with her sometimes. She gave me this." The pendant is of northlands make, carved in the shape of a little howling wolf.

"She gave you . . . You robbed someone's grave," Colin translates. The Green Lady's house can only be the graveyard, where she grinds men's bones to powder and presses their flesh for blood to water her wild gardens. Colin thinks of the rumors Captain Westfall repeated last night. They sound less far-fetched now.

"She *gave* it to me," Gabriel insists. "I saw her take a man right into the black earth, swallow him up whole, and she gave me a present for not being afraid." He glares, like he's waiting for Colin to call him a liar.

Colin doesn't dare. He holds his tongue as they walk up Cypress Street, coming north, slowly making their way out of the pits of filth and misery and back toward the Casmile that Colin knows. They pass a few shops with tradesmen's signs hung outside, candlemakers and glassblowers. Soon, now, they must reach safety.

Cypress empties into a larger street, where they cross one of the smaller bridges, and then finally they reach Market Square, with the auction house broad and sturdy along its south side and the specialty traders opening their doors for the morning crowds. There's a band of travelers telling fortunes and selling love charms, and a group of musicians have claimed one corner to play for coin. Colin takes a deep breath—salt air from the harbor, baking bread, the morning's fish catch—and lets it out in relief.

When he glances sideways, Gabriel is smiling at him. "You like it here," Gabriel says. He sounds pleased, and sweet, not at all like a killer or a madman.

"Don't you?" Colin asks. "There's so much going on." He hadn't realized it would already be so busy this early in the day. Most times it's past midday when he comes into the city for fun.

Gabriel nods. "That makes things much easier, doesn't it? Come on. There's a bakery up the street a bit that puts their wares out front."

They make it most of the way across the square, and then Gabriel stops again, pulling Colin with him as he shrinks back against the wall. "Actually, you should wait here." He reaches up to pet Colin's hair fondly. "Someone might notice you."

He doesn't wait for an answer, just slips into the growing crowd, the urchins and house servants and townswomen come to buy the fresh food their households will need. It's the chance Colin's been waiting for. He doesn't see any carriages for hire in the square itself—a few private ones, but those won't do him much good.

But there's no help in cursing the cards once they're dealt, and besides, it shouldn't take that much searching to find one. Colin keeps his head down and weaves his way through the crowd, out of the square and onto Market Street itself. From somewhere up ahead comes the snort of a horse and the jingle of harness, so maybe when he reaches the next turn—

"Very clever," Gabriel says, falling into step beside him. "Now walk quickly, but not too quickly. And take this." He presses something sticky into Colin's hands. "We'll turn as soon as we reach the bridge."

Colin blinks and looks down. Gabriel has brought him the honey cake he asked for, slightly flattened in the center by a thumbprint but warm and so sweet-smelling that it almost makes up for the fact that he's stuck with Gabriel again. "Did you steal this?" he asks, and then feels silly. Of course Gabriel must have, or they wouldn't be fleeing, would they?

"Mnh," Gabriel says around an outrageously large mouthful, then swallows. "Morgan never gave me the second half of my money, and his boys didn't have much. Not a good time to go wasting pennies."

"I would have thought," Colin starts, and then doesn't finish the sentence. He would have thought someone like Gabriel wouldn't need to worry about money, but if that were true, then Gabriel wouldn't live in a single blighted room at the bottom of Cypress Street. And he'd have a coat for nights like last night. Colin considers his stolen breakfast and takes a guilty bite.

It's possibly the best cake he's ever tasted, drenched in honey and rich with butter. The first taste makes him realize how hungry he is, and then he's stuffing the rest in his mouth with no better manners than Gabriel. He devours the entire thing before they've gone a full block.

Gabriel laughs when Colin's reduced to licking the honey off his fingers. "Hungry dragon. Should I get you more?"

"You don't have to do that," Colin says, though his stomach still feels empty. "You shouldn't go back there right now anyway, should you?"

"I'd manage," Gabriel says loftily. "I'm tricky. And I wouldn't want it said that I didn't give proper hospitality to a dragon."

"I'm sure nobody would say such a thing." If this *were* a children's story, now is about the point when one of them would turn out to be a prince in disguise, and the other would be rewarded according to his courtesy. And Gabriel's been by far the more generous of them, hasn't he? Colin's coin purse feels heavy in his pocket. "No. You've—you've been very kind already. Why don't you let me, ah, buy you some sausages or something? To thank you for your hospitality last night."

The hunger on Gabriel's face is almost hard to look at. But it only lasts for an instant, and he sounds almost formal when he says, "I'd be honored, Drake."

"It's nothing." Colin takes his bearings quickly. "Up this way, a bit past the bridge. Have you—" and then he realizes how unlikely it is that Gabriel frequents the Bloodied Boar, so he doesn't ask, just explains. "There's a place up Bank Street that I've always liked."

If Gabriel finds it odd that a dragon would have a favorite place to go for sausages, he doesn't say so. He walks along beside Colin, sucking the last traces of honey from his fingertips, his stride easy and confident. He acts like a prince of the city, for all that he looks dirty and underfed.

They cross the bridge over the river, the water churning dark and slow on its course. The old stone of the supports is mossy, stained black up to the high-water line, where the winter's rains will make it swell. They pass vegetable carts headed to market, children playing a counting game, shopkeepers propping open their doors. *I killed a man last night*, Colin almost wants to tell them. *I saw men die, handled their bodies, and now I'm walking down the street with the boy who killed them. He thinks I'm a dragon.* It sounds ridiculous, impossible in the bright light of morning. The sky is too blue, the air too crisp. Those dark, slippery streets feel far away.

"What are you smiling about?" Gabriel asks.

Colin looks up sharply. He hadn't realized he *was* smiling. "How—how strange all this is, I suppose. It's as though we're in a different city today than we were last night."

Gabriel nods. "I think sometimes it does change. There are so many things you just can't find if you go looking in the daytime."

"Like dragons?" Colin asks, before he can help himself.

"And the Lady," Gabriel agrees. "All the most interesting things come out at night."

Colin can imagine himself having said something like that to Anna before last night, and likely with that very same expression. What did he know, anyway?

There's a pack of bravos coming up the street from the other direction, the sort of flashy toughs that Colin sees around the gaming houses often enough. As they get closer, he thinks he may even recognize one of them by the neat row of Jua'zan tribal scars along his cheek—and as they pass each other, one of them grabs Colin by the shoulder and shoves him toward the wall.

"Colin Harwood, is it?" the tough says. Colin pushes his hand away. "We've been looking for you."

"Rot and die," Colin says. He hopes Gabriel didn't hear his name. The brass knuckles are a heavy weight in his coat pocket.

The tough who has him against the wall is grinning. He has a broken front tooth. His friends close in, putting themselves between Colin and any hope of escape. The last thing Colin sees of Gabriel, he's wearing a detached, curious expression, as if he wants to see whether Colin can handle himself.

"You talk big, boy," the tough says. "Where were you last night when we came to call?"

"That's no business of yours," Colin snaps. His voice shakes.

"Isn't it, when you owe our boss so much?" The tough's ugly grin gets wider. His breath smells foul. "Last thing he said to us was that we ought to see about selling you for it, since you're so slow with coin."

"You can't do that," Colin says, even though he's less sure of that than he wants to be; it turns out all sorts of terrible things are possible. And there's a little part of him that's furious, hot and red beneath the fear: he *knows* what a slave is worth, and it's far more than all his debts put together. "I need a little more time to get the money together, that's all." Why isn't Gabriel stepping in? What's he waiting for? "I'll give you what I have now, and I'll come up with the rest. Soon." He reaches into his coat.

The tough pretends to think it over. "I'm not so sure. Do we wait, and hope you're as good as your word, or just take your pretty ass down to the docks for a southbound ship now? Barron's already been plenty patient, what with you thinking you could talk such rot about a man who gave you so much."

They're bluffing. They must be. If they really wanted to carry him off, they'd have just done it, instead of stopping to threaten him first. "I'll get him the money, and a public apology, I promise."

Gabriel is still there, beyond the pack of thugs. He must be waiting for Colin to prove himself, mustn't he? Colin has to believe it. "All I have for you right now," he says, and slides his fingers into the brass rings, "is—"

Then one of the thugs makes a wet choking sound. Colin doesn't look, doesn't waste the moment Gabriel's bought him; when the man in front of him glances over to see what happened, Colin throws a punch.

The soft give of flesh and the awful crunch of bone underneath almost make him sick. But he doesn't have time for that now, not when the others are pulling weapons too. He flinches back, trying to get out of the way of a knife, wishing he had more room to move—he can't get past them like this, and even with two of them down, the odds aren't good.

Colin deflects a strike with his forearm, realizes that he's taking comfort from Gabriel's little hisses and snarls. He has an ally here, someone to help him fight his way free. Fates, what he'd give for some *distance*. His sleeve tears as he tries to block one of them, and then he's left himself open, too exposed, and a blade bites along his side, a sharp, hot pain. He yelps, lashes out at the man who cut him, and this time the impact doesn't bother him at all when he feels ribs crack against his hand. He sucks in a quick breath, and his wound stings—and down the street there's the shrill blast of a whistle.

He spares a glance—Barron's thugs are tripping over their fallen comrades as they scramble for the alleys—and realizes it's not just any of the guard; he'd recognize his rescuer by that dappled stallion alone. Colin sags against the wall in relief.

"Drake," Gabriel calls, his voice tight with panic, "*run!*"

Colin bolts before sense catches up with him. What must it take to make Gabriel sound that frightened?

"That way," Captain Westfall barks as another guardsman rides up. "Don't lose them!" That sounds like— Does the captain think they're to blame for this? Colin doesn't stop to argue, just follows Gabriel, tearing down a narrow side street after him. His boots skid on the cobbles and he slides, nearly falls, catches himself on his hands just in time to see Gabriel turning a corner into a tiny alley. His side aches and his shirt clings to his skin, wet through.

When he turns the corner, he doesn't even see Gabriel. "Here," Gabriel calls, and Colin looks up. Gabriel's on the roof of a building halfway down the block, where a bare-branched skinny tree must have given him a way up.

"Why are we running?" Colin pants as he reaches for the first branch of the tree. "We didn't start it." His hands slip, stinging against the bark, and he grits his teeth as he tries again. "I know Captain Westfall. If we just told him—"

"We were winning," Gabriel says, reaching down and grabbing him by the wrist to haul him the rest of the way onto the roof. "That makes us guilty too."

"That's—" *stupid*, Colin's about to say, or *not how it works*, and then a crossbow bolt cracks against the shingles beside him. "Arhon's bones," he says, looking back down.

Captain Westfall is already snapping another bolt into place. "Bad company you're keeping, Harwood. Bring him down, and it'll go easy for you."

Colin hesitates. "What'll happen to—" he almost says *Gabriel*, and then catches himself in time "—to him?" He presses a hand to his side, where it hurts, and his stomach lurches at the wetness soaking through his coat.

"I'm not going," Gabriel mutters, like he wants Colin to have warning.

"He'll get no worse than he deserves," the captain says coolly. As if *that* makes it any better. Captain Westfall might not believe in Gabriel's legend, but he's still a killer. In the eyes of the law, what he deserves is to hang. "Come down, Harwood. You don't belong here."

Colin swears he can feel it the instant before Gabriel moves, a tension gathering in the air and then snapping as Gabriel scrambles over the peak of the roof. Captain Westfall fires again, and Colin doesn't see the bolt strike home but he hears Gabriel hiss.

He moves without meaning to, without thinking, his bloody hand slipping as he grabs for purchase. He should be doing as he's told, giving in, but instead he's heading after Gabriel, his heart pounding in his chest. Behind him the captain is cursing him and all his line, but in front of him Gabriel's beckoning him to hurry, and he does.

"Get your boots off," Gabriel says as Colin slides down the roof beside him. His trousers are wet with blood down the left side. "They'll slip."

"Are you mad?" Colin asks, tugging his boots off anyway as Gabriel does likewise.

Gabriel smiles, quick and wry. "People seem to think so." He picks up his boots and takes off running again, sprinting along the roof to gain speed and then leaping the alley to land with a thud on the other side.

He must indeed be mad, and Colin must be mad to follow, but all the colors are brighter, the sounds crisper than they should be, and Colin's blood sings in his veins with the thrill of being alive. His bare feet don't slide on the shingles as he runs, gathers himself, and jumps. There's a second of pure terror, so strong he can taste it sharp and stinging in his mouth—and then he's landing, awkward and off-balance, scrabbling for purchase and trying not to drop his boots at the same time.

When he recovers, Gabriel is waiting. He nods once and takes off again, up the roof's slope. The idea that Gabriel is taking care of him seems so bizarre that Colin would laugh if he had the breath to spare.

Taking the roofs was a good idea, he realizes quickly. As they head south from the river, the houses grow closer together, and they're more or less of a height, so there's no point that'll force them to come down. They can change direction almost anywhere, crossing from one house to the next, and the cramped streets will make it hard for the guards to follow them on horseback. Colin makes another leap—he's lost track of how many that makes, or where they've turned, only that the gray-blue of the sea is nearly always on his left. He stumbles on a landing and has to stop as spots swim in front of his eyes.

"You're all right?" Gabriel says, almost a statement but not quite.

Colin shakes his head. "I got cut." He presses his hand to his side again and holds it up to show Gabriel the blood. How much can a man bleed before it becomes truly dangerous? He has no idea.

Gabriel hisses through bared teeth, his brow furrowing. "Come on, then. We should get down before that gets any worse."

He peers down at the street, checking for pursuit, and nods decisively. Then he turns right, leading Colin away from the harbor, and stops at the edge of the next block, where an old oak grows by the edge of the road, its leaves turned brown and paper-dry for the winter. Gabriel climbs from the roof into the branches, and Colin clumsily follows him. The pain in his side is getting worse without the thrill of the fight to buoy him up anymore. He drops his boots as Gabriel shimmies down the trunk, because there's no way he can manage this climb without both hands free.

By the time he reaches the ground, cursing the roughness of the bark and the dizzy swimming of his head, Gabriel is already stamping his feet into his boots again.

"There you go, Drake." He pats Colin's arm. "That was the hardest part."

Colin picks his own boots up off the street. "You're hurt too, aren't you?" Gabriel is leaning on the wall, not putting any weight on his left leg, and Colin would swear the bloodstain on his trousers is worse than it was only a few minutes ago.

"It's not so bad. I'm more used to it." He meets Colin's gaze very seriously as Colin straightens up. "You'll get used to it too, if you stay in Casmile. It's nasty here, not like in your fancy castles."

"Caverns," Colin says, and then regrets it when Gabriel smiles; the last thing he needs is to encourage all that dragon nonsense. "You said caverns last time." He looks away. "Used to it or not, we're both *bleeding*, Gabriel. We need to—"

"We need to hurry." Gabriel's tone is sharp, and Colin falls silent. "We're on our way to get help."

"Oh." Colin feels stupid. Gabriel might seem a little touched, but he's had enough sense to stay alive so far, hasn't he? "Do you know a doctor, then?"

"Something like that." Gabriel turns to start down the street. He's limping, but he still moves fast. "Mama Deirdre is at least as good as a doctor."

"Deirdre?" Colin echoes. He presses his hand to his ribs, trying to think of anything but the pain as he walks at Gabriel's side. "That's an uncommon name, isn't it? Is she a . . ." But he doesn't know if he'd give offense, calling her a barbarian, and who knows if Gabriel even notices the difference between the men of Casmile and the north?

"Yes," Gabriel says, as if Colin had finished the question. "She is."

CHAPTER SIX

G abriel's path through the streets feels random, as if he's still trying to shake pursuers, or expects to be followed at all times. But he must know where he's going, because they never turn down a blind alley, even when they cross into the fire-damaged southern quarter and the houses are falling to ruins. Their pace slows, though, as Gabriel's limp gets worse.

"Are you sure you're all right?" Colin asks.

"You're too kindhearted, Drake. Where did you learn a thing like that?" He stops at a house with a patched roof and crooked shutters, blue paint peeling off the front door. He raps on the nearest window, and the glass rattles.

For a moment there's no response, and Colin's heart sinks. As far from ideal as it is to rely on Gabriel's acquaintances for help, it would be worse to have none at all.

But then there's sound from inside the house, the hollow tread of footsteps, and the curtain in the front window twitches. If he were on the other side of that door, Colin thinks, he wouldn't open it to let them in. Deirdre must be more forgiving than he is, though, because she throws the bolt with a thunk and opens the door.

"Deirdre," Gabriel says, hunching his shoulders and scuffing his boot against the paving like a boy ten years younger. "We're in trouble."

She *is* a northlander, with ashen blonde hair drawn back off her pale face and slate gray eyes. There are worry lines at the corners of her mouth that grow more obvious when she speaks. "You always are, these days." Her accent clips the words in strange ways, and Colin has to listen hard to be sure he understands her. "I remember when you used to come see me without the Lady on your shoulder."

"Sorry." Gabriel shifts his weight—and then has to clutch at the doorjamb for balance. Colin reaches out instinctively to steady him, and catches a faint softening of Deirdre's expression.

"I'll have time enough to scold you later, won't I? Come in before you let out all the heat." She steps back, opening the door further. "I've not seen you around here before," she says to Colin. "Who are you, then?"

Colin barely hesitates. "Drake," he says. "I'm . . . I met Gabriel last night."

Deirdre nods, but Colin can't read her expression. He follows Gabriel into the house, through the dark front room and back to the kitchen, where south-facing windows let in enough light to keep it from seeming completely dismal. There's a fire in the stove, and a table in the middle of the room with benches on either side. A plate on the table still has a bit of brown bread and hard cheese on it.

"Well?" Deirdre puts a pot of water on the stove and tosses in a handful of herbs. "Let's see what trouble you've brought round this time."

Gabriel kicks off his boots and unties the laces of his trousers, letting them fall without any care for decency. The blood comes from a raw, ugly wound in the back of his thigh—the bolt must not have really sunk home, but it's nasty enough. He's even thinner than Colin thought, skin stretched taut over sinew and bone, and he's marked with other faded, white scars.

"You've no sense at all," Deirdre says, crouching beside him and inspecting the wound. "Walked on this all the way here to make it worse, didn't you?"

"Ran, most of the way," Gabriel says. "And jumped."

Deirdre shakes her head, and opens a cabinet to pull down a brown glass bottle. "There you go. Have a drink, if you're going to want it."

Gabriel doesn't take the bottle. "Let's just do it. Drake's hurt too, and he doesn't do this all the time." The particularities of Colin being a dragon seem to slip Gabriel's mind rather conveniently when things get serious.

"All right," Deirdre sighs. "Down you go. Let's get this over with." She fetches some cloth and a needle and thread from another cabinet as Gabriel stretches out on his stomach across the nearest bench. She dips the cloth in the pot on the stove and wipes the blood from his skin, then picks up the needle. "Now. I'll do my best to be quick, and you do your best to be still." It almost sounds as though it's meant to be a joke, as though neither of them needs to be told how this routine goes.

"Come talk to me, Drake," Gabriel says. "I hate this part."

Colin kneels on the floor beside him—and almost reaches out to touch his shoulder, but loses his nerve at the last moment. "I'm sorry I got you into that," he says, wincing in sympathy when Gabriel grimaces at the first bite of the needle. "I hope those guys don't give you any more trouble."

"If we're lucky, your friend the, ah, captain rounded them up." Gabriel's voice is tight, but doesn't shake. "Then they won't be, *ow*, trouble for either of us anymore."

"He's that bad, is he?" Colin says. The thought isn't terribly reassuring.

"Told you, didn't I? Nastiest dog in the city." Gabriel squeezes his eyes shut and grunts, his hands clenching white-knuckled around the edge of the bench, and then he takes a deep breath and continues. "Nobody ever comes back once the captain's got them."

"What happens to them?" Colin asks against his better judgment. Captain Westfall seemed so reasonable, so polite, at the party yesterday evening—a bit rakish, maybe, but civilized. He was nearly a different person this morning.

Gabriel stares at Colin curiously. "They hang. Eventually." He swallows another little injured sound. "Do they not have hangings where you come from?"

Colin glances up and catches Deirdre watching him; Gabriel might have a head full of fancy, but she probably has little doubt where he comes from. "I've never seen one," he says. He supposes that the way Gabriel means it, he does come from a place where they don't happen.

"Maybe we'll go see the next one," Gabriel says. Colin hopes the Maiden will have more mercy on him than that—he'd rather just go home, if he can manage it. "We can see if the hounds really did catch up with the men who were after you."

Deirdre finishes with her needle, sparing Colin the awkwardness of responding. "There," she says to Gabriel as she leans back. "You know how to take care of that, with as many times as it's been. And don't strain it while it mends, for light and mercy."

Gabriel looks at least a bit chastised. "I'll be careful. I wouldn't want to waste your hard work."

"Or your health, you silly boy," Deirdre says as Gabriel gets up gingerly off the bench. She turns to Colin. "All right, Drake. What do you have for me?"

"If you don't mind," Colin says as he peels off his coat, "I think I'd like that drink first."

"Help yourself," Deirdre says, though she doesn't offer a glass.

It feels a bit like admitting he's not so tough as Gabriel, to take the drink, but that's true, isn't it? And he's never been hurt so badly that he needed stitches before. He uncorks the bottle and lifts it, breathing in the sharp scent of whiskey as he raises it to his lips.

It's not bracing, like he hoped it would be. Instead he just feels dizzy as the heat of the whiskey slides down his throat to burst in his stomach. He clutches the edge of the table and wishes he were home. "There isn't any way you could do this without stitches, is there?"

"Won't know until I see it," Deirdre says. "Take your shirt off, please."

Colin unlaces his cuffs and collar and pulls his shirt off slowly. The cotton peels away from his skin reluctantly, stinging where it's stuck to the edges of his wound. He straddles the bench and raises his arm so Deirdre can take a look.

"Sharing Gabriel's luck, are you?" She wipes his skin with a warm, wet cloth. It would be soothing if he didn't hurt so rotting much. "A little lower and this could have gone deep. All he had to do was miss your ribs."

"I don't f-feel especially lucky right now, but I'll take your word for it." Colin's teeth are chattering, though it's not really that cold in here, with the fire.

"Gabriel's luck, I said. Remarkable, but not easy." She touches Colin's side carefully, her fingertips brushing the skin on either side of the wound. "I'm still going to have to stitch this up if you want it to heal clean instead of taking rot."

Colin grimaces. "Do what you have to, then." He tries to think about his breathing, about staying calm.

"Here," Gabriel says, sitting down in front of him. "Look at me, Drake. First time, isn't it?"

Colin nods. Of course it's obvious.

Gabriel's gaze wanders over Colin's bare chest and stomach, and Colin fights the urge to cover himself. He has nothing to be ashamed of, but Gabriel looks at him much too intently. "You have no scars at all. What kind of life is that?"

"A comfortable one," Colin says, "where nobody tries to kill you just for—" Deirdre's needle bites into his skin, and he chokes on the words. It's worse—much worse—than being cut in the first place, the needle pushing into flesh that already aches. "Mother's blood," Colin swears, squeezing his eyes shut. He feels like he might be sick.

"It'll make you better, Drake," Gabriel says softly, fiercely. "Hold on, and look at me."

Deirdre takes another stitch, and Colin whimpers as she pulls the thread taut. When he manages to open his eyes again, Gabriel looks so nervous that Colin would probably try to say something reassuring if he dared to open his mouth. He can stand this, can't he? He can—

Darkness rises up around him the next time the needle pushes in, and there's a roaring in his ears that covers up the words someone is trying to say, and his eyes flutter shut again as he slides down into the dark.

When Colin wakes, he doesn't know where he is. His right side aches, and he feels stiff, like he's been sleeping in an awkward position for a while. He sits up, and a blanket slides off his shoulders, leaving him bare-chested in the cool air. He reaches down, prods gingerly at his side, and finds the row of tight, coarse stitches just above his bottom-most rib. They hurt worse when he touches them, and he swallows hard.

Deirdre. Gabriel. Captain Westfall treating him like he was no better than the toughs who'd attacked him.

There must be a way out of this.

Colin stands up carefully, trying not to pull his stitches. It appears they left him in the kitchen, rather than try to move him. Neither his coat nor his shirt are at hand, but he can hear voices from the other room. He pauses in the doorway, just out of sight, and listens.

". . . would have thought he'd run right then," Deirdre says.

"Run?" Gabriel echoes. "Never. Drake helped."

"Now you're telling tales. One of his kind?"

Gabriel makes a soft sound that Colin thinks is laughter. "I didn't know what to expect. I've never known one of his kind."

Deirdre sighs. "Haven't you?"

"No." There's a pause, and Colin realizes that he's waiting to hear if Gabriel will say anything more in his defense. Which is ridiculous.

He steps through the doorway. Deirdre and Gabriel are sitting by the fireplace in the front room, which provides nearly as much light as the north window. Colin wonders how long he slept.

Gabriel straightens when he walks in. "Drake. You're feeling better."

That's sort of an appalling overstatement, Colin thinks. He's lost, hungry, injured, and cold, and he needs to stop this now before the trouble gets any worse. "I want to go home."

The way Gabriel's face falls almost makes him sorry. "You can't," Gabriel protests. "You can't go now, Drake. We've only just begun."

"I have to." Colin tries to choose his words carefully, so they'll fit into Gabriel's mad fancies. "I don't belong here, Gabriel. You saw that right away, didn't you? Already I'm being hunted. I should go back to . . . my own kind."

"We'll hide you," Gabriel offers. "I know all the best hiding places in the city. The hunters will never catch you if you stay with me."

Colin glances to Deirdre for help. She must know better than to encourage this. "You can't go anywhere as you are now," she says. "At the very least, you should come eat something while your clothes finish drying. It'll help you get your strength back."

The thought of food makes Colin's stomach growl, and he crosses his arms over his stomach sheepishly. This morning's honey cake wasn't much to break his fast, and last night's supper might as well have happened in another lifetime. "I'd be grateful."

Deirdre nods. "Come on, then. We'll get you fed and then we'll talk about what you've planned for after."

"There's nothing to plan," Colin mutters, but he goes. Gabriel gets up from the fire and follows, still favoring his left leg. Colin tries not to meet his eyes when they sit down on opposite sides of Deirdre's table, because the hurt in them doesn't seem fair.

"You can start with this," Deirdre says, setting a little round loaf of bread and a thin wedge of cheese between them. "But midday's come and gone, so I'm guessing you'll want a bigger meal than that."

"Yes," Colin says, reaching for the knife, and then remembers his manners enough to add, "if it's not too much trouble."

"You can bring payment next time you're here," she says, but there's a twist to her expression, behind Gabriel's back, that makes it clear she doesn't expect to see him again.

"I'll be sure to do that." He cuts some bread and cheese for himself, and then some for Gabriel, too. Gabriel takes it without a word. The silence between them is uncomfortable as they eat. Deirdre puts something on the stove. The bread is dry, and the cheese earthier than Colin prefers, but his mouth waters all the same. It seems being hungry enough can make even plain fare appetizing.

As he's finishing the bread and cheese, Deirdre sets down a bowl in front of him, full of steaming porridge with scraps of dried apple scattered over the top. "Maybe it's no lord's dinner," she says, "but it'll keep you, won't it?"

Colin feels like the prince in a nursery tale again, his cheeks hot. "Of course. Thank you for all your care."

Deirdre nods, as though he's just passed a test, as though she really is a witch with the power to turn an ungrateful boy's bones to powder.

"How do you know so much about Drake's kind?" Gabriel asks. Deirdre sets a bowl down in front of him, too. "Thank you."

"I worked for some of them when I was first brought to the south." Her tone is clipped and final, her gray eyes cold and flat when Colin dares to meet them. He can guess what she's not saying outright. Almost all of the servants of Casmile's landed gentry are property. So she either won her freedom somehow, or escaped her master, or . . . The challenge in her stare makes him blush and drop his eyes.

"You know all the important things," Gabriel says, stirring his porridge, burying the apple pieces. "You should explain to Drake why he can't go away."

Deirdre hums thoughtfully, sitting down with her own bowl. "He might still be able to," she says. Gabriel makes an outraged little noise, but she doesn't pay it any attention. "Though I'd be surprised. You've killed a man, haven't you, Drake?"

Colin puts down his spoon. "Maybe two." It's almost worse that he can't say for sure.

"One that his lordship the captain is certain of, though?" she asks. When Colin glances up, she's smiling wryly. "You're only guilty of the ones the law knows about."

"Probably one, then." He doesn't feel so hungry anymore, thinking of it.

"He's so fierce in a fight," Gabriel adds. "He tries to hold back, but once you make him angry enough—"

"I'm nothing like that," Colin protests. He's not the killer Gabriel wants him to be, not really. He's a boy who walked into the wrong tavern last night and wishes on the Maiden's eyes that he could take it back now.

"Whether you are or not," Deirdre says, holding up a hand to stop Gabriel from arguing, "you've killed a man that Westfall knows of. And Gabriel says he called you by name."

Arhon's rotting shroud, how much worse can his luck get? "He did," Colin admits.

"Then you'd best be careful." Deirdre has a stare like a hawk's, sharp featured and merciless. Looking at her, Colin can believe that women of the northlands go to battle with their men. "He'll know where to find you. He'll know who would shelter you. And you can bet he'd love a chance to make it clear that even the highborn are still subject to the law."

Colin laughs weakly, but it feels like a bad bluff and sounds worse. "He wouldn't. He's a— We *know* each other. I was at supper with him just last night. I've danced with his wife. It's not . . ." He trails off, not sure whom he's trying to convince. Certainly this morning it didn't seem like any of that mattered.

"You could be right," Deirdre says, shrugging. She doesn't look as though she cares much, one way or the other. "But watch your back. And if he comes looking for you, don't expect any mercy."

"Thank you," Colin makes himself say. He pushes away his half-eaten bowl of porridge. "For the advice and—for everything. But I should be going. Before it gets any later."

"No," Gabriel says, getting up. "Haven't you been listening? It's not safe to leave, Drake."

"Hush," Deirdre says. "He'll come back. He just has to go away first to know why." Her tone sounds like a threat, but Colin's grateful all the same. Gabriel believes in her, so let her tell what lies she will, if it means he can walk out of here.

Gabriel glares at him. "I'm not going to show you the way back."

Colin rolls his eyes. "Then I'll find the way myself." If he just walks north, he'll find the river, won't he? "Thanks for the help. This morning."

"See you soon," Gabriel answers, or maybe demands.

"Farewell," Colin says. It seems polite.

CHAPTER
SEVEN

Neither of them follows him when he goes into the front room to recover his clothes. His shirt is dry, and the blood mostly washed out of the cotton; only a faint dark stain around the gash torn by the knife remains. Pulling it on is tricky work, with his stitches tight and aching, but he manages, and the fire-warmed cloth feels good against his skin. His coat's still damp, but he doesn't plan to stay here until dark, waiting for it to dry. One of the pockets is ruined, but if he goes home needing only a new coat and some time to heal, then his luck isn't entirely gone after all.

There's a heavy weight in the right pocket when he pulls his coat back on. He reaches in, and draws out the brass knuckles that Gabriel gave him the night before. They've been carefully cleaned so there's not a trace of blood on them, and the metal shines softly in the firelight. Colin stares at them for a long moment, picturing Gabriel sitting here by the fire with a polishing cloth. He shakes his head to clear it, and sets the brass knuckles on the mantel. He'll have enough reminders of this adventure without them.

He has nothing left to say to either Deirdre or Gabriel, so he doesn't try, only lets himself out onto the street. The chill that came in last night still hangs over the city, and the light feels weak and wintry. Colin shivers. He'll have to hurry to get back to the right side of the river before sundown.

He finds his way north by trial and error, keeping the sun mostly to his left. He doesn't have Gabriel's luck or knowledge of these streets, and turns down blind alleys more than once. But in time he reaches a street wide and well-maintained enough that it seems likely not to give out on him. A bit further north he'll reach Bank Street, and even if he doesn't find a carriage there, he can cross any of the bridges to try his luck on Market.

And perhaps his luck is turning, because the first carriage he finds on Market stops for him. "Can you take me out the Deradan road?" Colin asks.

The driver examines him, then squints at the angle of the sun. "How far you looking to go?"

"Not far. Just past Mockingbird Lane." It's never seemed like such a distance as it does today.

"Climb on, sir," the driver says with a grin. "Had a bit of a rough night, have you? Seen a few too many of the city's sights?"

Colin laughs ruefully, relief easing the tightness from his chest. "Quite a few," he says, climbing up into the back of the carriage. It's a light model, meant to carry no more than two or three passengers, and pulled by a single unremarkable bay. Despite the ache in his side as they rattle over the street, Colin's never been so glad to take a carriage anywhere.

The driver steers them past slower carts and foot traffic, his eyes on the road. He leans back, though, so his voice will carry well enough as he ventures, "Bad night in the city, from what I've heard."

Perhaps it was too soon to relax entirely. "Is that so? What happened?"

"Bloody murder." The driver glances back for a moment to grin ghoulishly. "The guard found four bodies by the docks this morning, laid out end-to-end like they was a present for someone. Or a message."

"A message," Colin repeats weakly.

"Smugglers, maybe," the driver suggests. "Someone trying to move in on routes they shouldn't. Or payback for that bad business with the girls being taken out of the Scarlet Rose last month. Can't say who done it without knowing who's been done, though."

Already it's less like his memory and more like a tale, the very next day. "Gabriel," Colin says, without really thinking about it. Surely he'll be fine. He had that fight under—well, almost under control before Colin stepped in.

"Not likely." The driver is practically *leering*. "You know how you can tell?"

"No."

"The bodies still had all their parts," the driver says triumphantly. "If it was Gabriel, he'd have taken some pieces with him."

Right. Gabriel can take care of himself.

They leave the city by the western gate, and the driver flicks the reins to urge his horse into a quick trot. Colin winces, holding on to his wounded side, but he can't very well ask the driver to go easy for the sake of the stitches he's just had from an escaped barbarian slave after he got knifed in a street brawl and fled the city guard. He'll live with the discomfort, as long as it gets him home.

"Nearly there?" the driver asks, after they pass the turn where Mockingbird Lane curves away into the indigo fields.

"Almost." The road curves, coming up alongside the orchards, the peach trees half-bare for the winter already. Beyond that they'll reach the main house, where—where a too-familiar dapple stallion is tied outside, decked in the guards' burgundy.

"Keep driving," Colin says hoarsely, "until we're out of sight of that house." He feels chilled, like he has a fever coming on, and he's not sure if it's better or worse to know he's likely only sick with fear. The captain has come for him after all.

The driver doesn't argue, moving on past the Harwood estate and over the next hill before he reins in his horse in the fading light. "Bit of an odd request, your lordship. You care to explain yourself?"

He can't go back to the house now. Not with the captain there. His father would be angry, yes, but his parents would at least listen to him. They'd find him someone to stay with in Nothwn or Port Clair until this all blows over. But if Captain Westfall is already there, waiting to arrest him for this morning—which wasn't even his fault! He hadn't been the one looking for that fight—then he can't very well come driving up to the house as though everything is fine. The captain shot at him this morning, knowing who he was.

"I've changed my mind," Colin says. His voice shakes, and he feels pathetic. Where's the dragon Gabriel was so impressed with? "I want to go back to town."

The driver turns to look at him, eyes narrowed with suspicion. "I think you might have to pay me now for the return trip. And I think you might have to pay me double."

Gabriel would have a knife at the man's throat for that, if Gabriel would ever get into a mess like this in the first place. But Colin doesn't have any weapons, and he doesn't think he has Gabriel's nerve, either. "You'd have driven back to town either way, and now you want me to pay you twice?"

"It's that or I take my time to let your friend in the guard catch up to us."

You'd best hope I never see you again, Colin wants to say. But he holds his tongue, because it'll only make things worse to make threats he can't back up.

He fishes in his pockets and comes up with three loose shillings. "That's all I have," he lies, dropping them in the driver's grubby, outstretched hand. "It'll do, won't it?"

The driver shakes the coins in his hand as if he could hear the difference between false silver and true. "It'll do. I don't suppose there's much of a reward for you, anyway."

"Your luck," Colin says, and realizes with a cold shock that he might be capable of turning two murders into three, if he has to. "If there were, I'd likely be dangerous and desperate, willing to kill a man who tried to collect it."

The driver laughs shortly, and wheels the carriage around toward the city. Colin sinks down in the seat, holding his breath when they pass his house as though that'll keep him from catching the Lady's attention. He doesn't relax until they reach the city gate without having heard any hoofbeats pursuing.

"Where should I leave you, your lordship?" the driver asks when they've come back inside the city walls.

Colin grits his teeth at the mocking tone. "Front Street," he says. If he were Gabriel, he'd—

He's thinking too much on what Gabriel would do.

When they reach the docks and the driver says, "A good evening to you, sir," Colin doesn't bother to answer him, just jumps down from the bench to the cobbles. Pain washes outward from his stitches in a queasy wave, and he tries not to let it show. The driver's laughing as he turns his carriage and heads north toward Kite.

"I'll kill you next time," Colin mutters, too low to carry, and tries to get his bearings. He's not so far from where he started hunting for a tavern last night. This time he knows better than to go looking down the side streets; he'll stay someplace along Front, noise or no, and perhaps tomorrow he'll be able to see some way of fixing this awful mess he's been dragged into.

The Mermaid is even rowdier than last night—it sounds like there may be an actual brawl happening inside—but the Flying Fish isn't so bad, and nobody gives Colin any trouble as he shoulders his way through the crowd to the bar. "I'll take a room for the night, if you have one free," he says, raising his voice to be heard over the noise. Somebody's playing a fiddle in the corner by the fire, and a few of the sailors know the words that go with the tune.

"Two shillings a night for the room," the innkeeper says, "or you can have it for the week for nine, if you're ashore for a while."

Nine for the week is plenty reasonable, and he'd have somewhere to stay while he gets his feet back under him. But he finds himself saying, "Just tonight, thanks. And some hot food, whatever's on the stove, and lager if you have it."

"If we have it," he says. "There's not a drink you could want that the Fish can't provide." The man turns away, rolling up his sleeves and producing a heavy mug. Colin's tempted to ask for a glass of Dormier's ten-year brandy just to be difficult, but that'd run him another shilling by itself, and he has a limited supply of those at the moment. "Your dinner will be right up," the innkeeper says as he sets Colin's pint on the scarred bar. "That's another ten pence together for the food and drink."

Colin comes up with three shillings out of his ever-lightening purse, and drops them into the innkeeper's hand. "There, dinner and the room. I'm a bit short on copper."

"Can't have come up from the south, then, can you?" the innkeeper asks, grinning. He pockets Colin's silver and comes up with two copper pennies, so old and worn it's hard to make out what city's crest they bear. "Not that I'd have guessed south, to look at you."

Colin takes a sip of his beer to cover his uncertainty about what to say. He'd rather not look memorable at all, even if the man's taking him for a northern half-blood instead of a highborn Casmilan. Should anyone come looking for him, asking after a young man of his height and coloring—

His worry is interrupted by the kitchen boy bringing him a steaming bowl of stew with a thick slice of bread. The sauce is a warm gold, and it smells rich with cumin and allspice. Colin's mouth waters. For once, it seems he's gotten something better than he was expecting.

The stew is spicier than he's used to, flavored with little pieces of red and orange peppers, but they're a good balance for the flaking white fish, and he has the smooth northlands lager to sooth the burn on his tongue. He cleans his bowl, wiping up the sauce with the heel of the bread, and drains his mug to the last stray foam. He's starting to feel properly human again with some decent food in him. It's tempting to stay for another pint, but he'll want to be clearheaded in the morning, and likely he'll find a better use for the coin, so he beckons for the key to his room instead of for a second drink.

"Up the stairs, third door on your left," the innkeeper tells him. "Maiden keep you."

"Thank you." Colin rises carefully from his barstool. The lager has softened the edges of his aches and pains somewhat, and he's grateful for it; perhaps he'll manage to sleep decently despite them. He threads his way through the crowd to the stairs, holding on to the rail and climbing by feel. There aren't any gas lamps in the upstairs hallway, only a few hooded candles along the wall, and Colin pauses for a moment to let his eyes adjust to the dim light before he counts off three doors and fits his key into the lock.

The room's plain, but clean enough, and a low-banked fire in the fireplace has kept it warm. After a day like this, Colin thinks he can't ask for much more luxury. He takes off his coat, kicks off his boots, and crawls under the blankets. They're soft Deradan wool, far warmer than the threadbare one Gabriel had, and the mattress is much better stuffed. Colin stretches out gingerly, trying to keep from pulling his stitches, and closes his eyes.

And yet, despite the warmth and the comfortable bed, he sleeps badly. Once he wakes to the sound of shouting in the street below, men arguing in loud, slurred voices while others encourage them to fight. He listens, only half making sense of the dispute, until someone comes to drive the fighters away. Later, he wakes again to silence, his heart racing in his chest and his dreams dissolving reluctantly from his mind—wolves in ball gowns trading gossip behind their fans, the shingles of roofs turning to ravens under his feet and flying away.

When dawn comes, the sky turning from black to gray outside his window, Colin finds he's ready to leave. He isn't rested, but lying awake in the half dark isn't helping. He pushes back the blankets and sits up to reach for his boots.

The Flying Fish is quiet at this hour, nobody moving in the upstairs rooms at all. Colin finds his way down to the public room, where a girl around his age is coaxing life back into the fire.

"Something you needed, sir?" she asks when she sees him, rising and brushing ash from her apron.

Colin shakes his head, holding out his room key. "I'm on my way. It seemed best to make an early start of it."

The girl drifts close enough to take the key from his hand and offers him an awkward, unpracticed curtsey. "Anything else we can do for you before you go?" Her eyes are nervous, her mouth drawn just slightly too tight at the corners. Colin wonders for a moment what villainy she expects of him, and stops when he realizes he can think of too many possibilities.

"Nothing, thank you." He nearly asks her not to tell anyone looking for him that he was here, but decides he'd only make himself more memorable if he did. He nods to the girl and lets himself out the front door onto the street.

Gulls wheel over the harbor, screeching, and among the moored ships a few merchant sailors and fishermen are bringing their vessels in to port. The eastern horizon is red with the rising sun, but clouds hang heavy over the shore, blanketing Casmile in an ashen gray. The water is as sluggish as Colin feels, and steel gray in answer to the clouds. He turns, following Bank Street into the city, watching the curl and drift of fallen leaves in the slow currents of the river. He stuffs his hands in his pockets to chase the aching chill from his knuckles. There are fewer signs of life here: smoke curling from chimneys, and the sweet, warm smell of baking bread.

At the second bridge, he crosses to the north bank and Market Street. He's awake enough now to be hungry, and there should be bakeries nearby. The pennies he has left from the night before buy him two sweet rolls filled with peach jam, and a mug of warmed cider with cloves that he drinks too fast, scalding the roof of his mouth.

He'll have to figure out what to do now, he thinks as he leaves the bakery behind. If the captain's as clever as everyone says, he'll be watching the Harwood estate, so it won't be safe to go back there for a while. But staying in taverns isn't a good solution, either—he'll run out of money, and quickly, with as poor as his luck's been lately.

His wandering takes him south again. He doesn't remember crossing another bridge, wasn't thinking about his path at all, but it seems unpleasantly appropriate. He turns down another crooked street and realizes he can see old scorch marks in the brick on some of the houses. He wonders what Gabriel thinks of Deirdre, if he believes she's some kind of witch. An oracle, perhaps.

Time to see if her divination's as good today as it was yesterday.

CHAPTER EIGHT

H e makes slower progress once he knows where he wants to go. Half this route he's only done in one direction, when the sun was going down and he was thinking more about avoiding people than remembering landmarks. He takes as many wrong turns as right ones, startles more mangy cats in alleys than he cares to count, but eventually Colin manages to find the house with the crooked shutters and the peeling blue door. The latest of the street cats—this one a dull orange—bolts from the stoop as he walks up to knock at the front window like Gabriel did.

"Still hungry, my lord?" Deirdre asks when she opens the door. "Shall I put the kettle on?"

Colin shakes his head. "I wouldn't presume." She's sharper, talking to just him, than she was with Gabriel around. "I already owe you without imposing any further."

Deirdre laughs, short and harsh. "I was just about to make some tea for myself, so I suppose you can have a cup, if you care to come in."

"That's very kind of you." Colin follows her into the house. It's almost comforting to be here, he realizes as they cross the front room toward the kitchen, where the stove keeps the room warm and the air smells of crushed herbs. Gabriel isn't the only one who thinks she'll have answers.

"How are your stitches?" Deirdre asks as she sets the kettle on the stove and feeds the fire a bit to wake it up.

Colin has to stop and take stock; he's been trying to pay them as little attention as possible. "Tender," he says, tracing the line carefully through his clothes. "Tight, I suppose. Like the skin doesn't fit so well."

Deirdre nods. "That'll happen. He's complained about it a time or two. Not much to be done but bear it, I'm afraid."

"I figured as much." Colin watches Deirdre measure out tea for the pot—white glazed earthenware, plain but probably decent enough before the end of the spout got chipped like that. He waits a bit, but she doesn't ask his business, doesn't prompt him to explain himself, and eventually he has to just come out with it. "You were right about Captain Westfall."

"I was," Deirdre says, as unsurprised as if he's just told her the sun rose this morning. "You're here, though, instead of in prison waiting for the gallows, so you must have come to your senses at some point."

"I must have." Colin waits while Deirdre pours hot water into the teapot. "But I don't know what to do now."

"Hmm." She cradles the pot in a towel and sets it down on the table between them. The steam rising from it is fragrant and soothing; Colin thinks there might be some blossoms mixed into the tea. "And you haven't the money to get yourself safely out of town?"

Colin shakes his head. "Probably not." He's not sure what the coach fee is to Deradan, but he's fairly certain it's counted in guineas, not shillings. "Everything seems to cost more than it should, once it's something you really need."

Deirdre sets a pair of teacups on the table. The handle of hers is broken off. "That's an important lesson to learn." She sits down across the table from him to pour.

"Somehow my tutors must have skipped that one," Colin says, and doesn't sound nearly as casual as he'd like to.

"You were never meant to need it." She wraps her hands around her teacup. They're bony, the knuckles swollen; her hands look older than her face. "So you'll be staying in Casmile, then, unless you want to go get hired on a ship." She looks at him, eyes narrow and lips pursed, passing judgment that's clearly not favorable. "And if I were you, I wouldn't."

"No," Colin agrees. "I'd be a miserable sailor." He's only traveled by ship once, a trip to the islands of Jua'za when he was ten or eleven years old, and he still remembers how sick he was for all four days out and three days back.

"There's that, too," Deirdre says. "I meant you're too pretty, and too soft, for that kind of use." She doesn't give him time to decide which part of that is most insulting, only goes on, "But you're not skilled in any trades, are you?"

"Of course not." Where would he have picked up a trade? He's only barely started to learn to manage the family estate.

Deirdre goes quiet, watching him again, and Colin takes a sip of tea to soothe his nerves. There's definitely something floral in it, and he tries to distract himself with guessing what the additive is. It doesn't really work.

"What do you think I should do?" he asks at last.

"I think," Deirdre says, setting down her teacup and watching him as if she's pronouncing a sentence, "you should go see Gabriel."

Tension unknots in Colin's stomach, and then a moment later he's angry with himself for being relieved. "What, so I can kill more people with him? He's the reason I'm in this mess." But that isn't true, not entirely, and he doesn't need Deirdre's raised eyebrow to let him know he's being an ass. "He's mad," he says next. He's more certain of that. "He thinks I'm a dragon."

Deirdre nods. "He's had a bit too much of the moon," she agrees. "It comes and goes, and on his bad days, he's barely seeing the same world as the rest of us. But he'll watch your back if you've caught his fancy that much, and it's true he knows better than just about anyone how to stay clear of Westfall's boys."

"There must be some other choice. Someplace else I could stay until things settle. I—I could stay here, even. Not for free, I mean. I could pay you for—"

"No. You couldn't." Her eyes narrow, and the room feels suddenly darker. "How many of my kinsmen work your father's fields, boy?" Colin hesitates, and she spits. "You don't even know."

"I never," Colin says helplessly. "I don't—"

"Any kindness you get in this house is for his sake, not yours," Deirdre says. "Were it up to me alone, I'd have no trouble leaving you to rot. But Gabriel's taken a liking to you, and there's little enough as makes him happy. I'll keep you in one piece as a kindness to him, but I won't help you to turn him away."

He should flee, make his excuses and leave and never think on this again. But then he'd be back where he started, a wanted man with no place to go. Perhaps just for a little while, until the guards find someone else to pursue and he can get a letter home to ask his parents for help . . . "I'm not sure I could find him," Colin says. "I don't know if I can find my way back to his . . . house . . . from here without a guide."

"You'll likely not find him at home right now anyway." Deirdre's face smooths into calm again, and the feeling of a brewing storm eases. "He went off in a sulk of his own after you left yesterday."

The idea's ridiculous—both that Gabriel sulks like a child, and that he'd do it over Colin. "Where should I look for him, then?"

"The first place he goes when he's upset," Deirdre says. "The Lady's house."

"The cemetery," Colin translates. He's had enough of people talking in tales and riddles.

"The old one at the end of Cypress." Deirdre nods. "She does look after him, unbelievable as it is to tell."

"I thought you, ah, your people believed in different gods," Colin says, curiosity getting the better of him. None of his family's house staff came from the north, so he's never really spoken to any of them.

Deirdre shakes her head. "My gods are far from here, and nobody has luck like Gabriel's without some kind of help."

Colin frowns and sips his tea. "They say the Fates don't play favorites." It's a proverb that's always annoyed him, mostly because people repeat it when he wants to stay at the tables for just a few more hands, but it seems true enough.

Deirdre snorts, a sort of small, private laugh. "Of course they do. No man wants to think a lady's playing favorites when her favorite's not him."

That surprises a little smile out of Colin in return. "No, I suppose not." It *would* be grand for the Three to be real, to be at his side when he wanted them. He sets down his teacup. "How do I get to the Lady's house from here?"

"You head east," Deirdre says. "Take Sparrow, that's the next real street south of here, and follow that almost to the water. That'll put you on Cypress—it's the broadest street there is, this far down. You'll not miss it. Then turn south, and just follow Cypress straight to the end. You'll be there by midday, if you've no trouble."

"That almost sounds too easy," Colin says as he rises from the table.

Amusement flickers in Deirdre's eyes, gone as fast as it comes. "You might not be completely hopeless after all. That's with no trouble, and you, my lord, look like an invitation to all kinds of that." She leans forward to tug at the stray lock of hair that's come loose from Colin's ponytail, too long and too light to be ordinary. "Trouble's going to be quite interested in you."

Colin huffs in frustration, pulling away from her. "Can't say that's a surprise, after the last two days." Maiden's mercy, is that all it's been?

"Wait here." Deirdre leaves him in her kitchen. He can hear her footsteps on the house's creaking stairs, and he fidgets, looking around for something to hold his interest while she's gone. The jars on her shelves have labels he can't read, the letters all angles and straight lines without near enough difference for him to make out what they are. He wonders if it's a personal cipher, or if the northlanders have writing of their own after all.

When she comes back, she's carrying a battered cloth cap, dull coal gray, like the one the Harwood stable boy wears when the weather's cool. "You can give it back to him when you catch up to him," she says as she holds it out to Colin. "And in the meantime, it'll make you a little less of a beacon."

"Thank you." He takes the hat, trying not to think too hard about the vermin that must be living in it. Between this and his torn, stained coat, he doesn't think he looks much like heir to an estate anymore. He puts Gabriel's hat on and tries to tuck his hair up under it.

"You should cut it," Deirdre says, which seems a bit much to Colin, really—he hasn't had his hair short since he was out of nursery. "But that'll do, most likely. Have you weapons?"

Colin thinks of Gabriel's ever-present knives. "No. I'd never needed them until the night I met him."

"Take what you left here, then." Deirdre shepherds him into the front room. The brass knuckles are still sitting on the mantle. The metal is cold in his hand. "And take one last piece of advice, if you'll have it."

"Of course," Colin says. He's not bound to follow it, is he? And she's helped him so far.

Deirdre looks him straight on, her eyes cold and gray as the sky outside. "Be the dragon," she says. Colin opens his mouth to protest, and she raises a hand to still him. "It's madness, true. But it'll help you all the same. Gabriel didn't take in some wayward lordling in a fancy pirate costume. You've more to you than that. Remember it."

The comment about his clothes makes Colin bristle, even though he thinks she meant for there to be a compliment in there, too. He makes himself take a deep breath and answer politely enough for a tale. "Thank you again for the tea, and for all your help." He gives her a little bow, and she nods.

"You're welcome to both of them, Drake. Now go find Gabriel."

No wonder Gabriel thinks she's a witch, Colin thinks as he sets out from her house. She's not above twisting things to make her prophecies come true.

To be fair, he could be fighting it more vehemently; he's found what he thinks is Sparrow Street now, and is following its gentle incline toward the harbor. The day has stayed cold, the sun too stubborn to part the clouds, and the air feels thick like winter's rain might arrive early tonight. Colin stuffs his hands in his pockets and walks faster.

He finds Cypress with no difficulty, and parts of it are even familiar, the sunken cobblestones and ragged holes in the street, the houses he'd swear have seen battles, not just storms, to wear them down.

At one of the cross streets, he pauses, not sure if he's found Gabriel's tenement house after all. A boy about his own age slinks out of the destroyed houses off to his left and looks him up and down with slow, calculating familiarity. It's a stare that asks what he's worth, what he could be taken for.

Colin thinks of dragons, of bright blood pooling on dusty floorboards, and meets the boy's stare without flinching. His lip curls back in a snarl, and he fits his hand into the shape of his weapon. He's killed two men in as many days, hasn't he? And they were more fearsome than this.

The boy only smirks, and steps back casually, leaning against the wall to let Colin walk past. There's more noise after that, as Colin keeps going south—shifting and settling sounds among the wreckage, as if more people are coming out of the shadows to watch him pass. The hairs stand up on the back of his neck as he tries not to turn around, tries to pretend he has no reason to worry. There are higher stakes to this bluff than he likes; he's more than half sure the only thing saving him right now is the fact that each of his watchers wants someone else to try him first.

He can see the gates of the cemetery up ahead now, half-open and rusted, black iron hidden by dead vines and drooping cypress branches. Colin clenches his fists and reminds himself not to hurry. He'll get there just fine.

Right before he reaches the gate, there's a scrape of masonry and a clatter of stone, like someone moving in a hurry on unstable footing. He looks back when he's halfway through the gates, and sees the street people slinking away, fading into the broken buildings instead of following him any further.

Somehow, he doesn't find that reassuring.

Even without that ill omen, he's not sure he'd be terribly at ease inside the gates. The ground is uneven, sunken in some spots, tombs leaning drunkenly as though the earth is trying to escape from under their weight. The granite is mostly covered by moss, and the memorial sculptures are weathered, limbs broken off and faces worn down to blank, empty stares. Nothing comes here to graze, so the grass is knee-high where it's not crowded out by brambles or overshadowed by the spreading cypress trees. The remnants of a path, broken flagstones giving way to weeds, lead back past the first graves, toward the more elaborate mausoleums in the heart of the cemetery.

It's hardly the Lady's *house*, unless there's some particular monument in the back somewhere that's grand enough to suit her. More like the Lady's garden, all these wild things growing without restraint, feeding on the deaths of men. Colin edges down the path, looking for signs of life.

"Gabriel?" he calls when he's come around a bend in the path and can't see the gate anymore. "Gabriel, it's Drake. Are you here?" There's no answer, and he's starting to feel like this was a mistake. He should be too old for ghost stories, but the blank, water-stained faces of carved stone children unnerve him, and the street toughs' refusal to follow him inside makes it worse.

If he were more clever, he thinks, he'd be able to track Gabriel; he'd know how to catch the signs of a human passing, and follow them—and then what? He'd have Gabriel at bay when he didn't want to be found, and that wouldn't be any good either.

A rustle of brush off to one side makes Colin start. Despite his better judgment, he looks for the greenish white of a trailing shroud as much as for the drab browns of Gabriel's clothes. There's nothing, only the slight movement of the brambles where a squirrel or a rat must have dived for cover a moment before. Gabriel's stories are only that, Colin reminds himself. Nobody *sees* the Lady.

All the same, he tenses at a new sound, this time a scrape of stone that no small animal would make. "Gabriel?" he calls again. "Deirdre sent me to find you."

Bits of gravel fall from one of the larger mausoleums, rustling into the grass, and Gabriel peers over the edge of its roof. "Drake?" he asks doubtfully.

"Come down," Colin says, looking up at him. "I've come back after all."

"Have you?" Gabriel sounds wary, like he doesn't trust his own eyes and suspects a trap. He perches on the edge of the mausoleum, his knees drawn up in a crouch and his hands resting on them. "Are you sure?"

Colin hesitates. Deirdre's advice didn't include the answer to questions like that. "Yes," he says after a moment. "I'm sure." He makes himself meet Gabriel's eyes, since that seemed to reassure him before. "Come down from there, Gabriel. I can't see you so well."

Gabriel makes a thoughtful noise, cocking his head to one side like a crow. "You really did come back, didn't you? I thought maybe I was just having another bad time, but you talk like the real Drake."

"I am the real Drake." A prickle of foreboding raises the hair on the back of Colin's neck. That's three times he's called himself Drake, once to Deirdre and twice in the cemetery. If you tell the same lie three times, people say, then all of the Fates have heard it. "I couldn't go back to my own kind," he says carefully. "Because of the city's guard.

So I—I can stay with you for a while." A little shiver wracks him, and he tells himself it's just the chill air. "Until my people come for me."

"Ah," Gabriel says. "Do you think that'll take long?"

Colin swallows uncomfortably. "It might. I don't really know. This has never happened to me before."

Gabriel nods, silent for a moment, then pushes himself off the mausoleum's roof to land on the grass in front of Colin. "Well," he says as he recovers his balance, "I suppose you'll need looking after, if you're going to learn to live in the city." He brushes his hands together, dusting off dirt that Colin can't see.

"Gabriel . . ." Colin hesitates. He doesn't particularly want to ask, but he needs the answer: "You do *know* that I'm not really a dragon, don't you? You know it's fancy?"

Gabriel glances at him for barely an instant and then drops his gaze. "I know sometimes I see things that aren't what people think I'm supposed to see. And sometimes they get upset if I say so." His voice is tight and unhappy. "You're a rich man's son, filthy and lost, somewhere you don't belong. Is that what you want to hear?"

"It's what I needed to know." Colin bites down on the urge to apologize. It was a reasonable question.

"Right, then." Gabriel nods decisively and straightens up like he's feeling better, even if he still isn't looking Colin in the eye. "You promised me sausages yesterday."

"I did." Relief washes through Colin at the reprieve. "Come on, we've probably got a walk ahead of us before we get to anyplace we can buy sausages."

At the cemetery gates, Gabriel pauses and finally meets Colin's gaze. "Still," he says, smug and airy, "I like the dragon you better."

CHAPTER NINE

The next few days are blissfully less eventful than the first two. In the mornings, they go up to Market Street, and Colin does his best to look inconspicuous while Gabriel steals food—bread, apples, and once a soft, flaky pastry full of ground, sweetened nuts. By the third morning, Colin stops feeling guilty about not paying; his silver is disappearing much more quickly than he'd like as he pays for their other meals, which are more difficult to steal. Gabriel remarks on the voracious appetites of dragons when Colin keeps asking about the meat in the taverns where they find their supper; Colin realizes only then that it might be a luxury he'll have to go some days without. They aren't in the taverns only for food, either; sitting by the fire is free of charge, if they've bought food or drink, and the company's less of a gamble than it is around the stray fire pits of Casmile's south end.

When Colin complains of the cold, after a night when he could see his breath on their way home, Gabriel takes that as a challenge. He leads the way on an expedition through the southern half of the city until they find an ill-guarded washing line, where he helps himself to another blanket. They boost their way up onto the roofs for a giddy, rushed escape that leaves them both laughing breathlessly when they collapse in a heap on a rooftop some dozen streets away, the damp blanket draped over them both like an odd-smelling woolen trophy. Colin's stitches ache and itch, but it's bearable. The air is crisp and sweet up here, and the sky overhead is a vibrant, glorious blue.

The weather turns that night; Colin wakes at one point in the dark and listens to the drum of rain on the roof, the soft huff of Gabriel's breathing, the slow drip of water into the weak floorboards beside the window. He misses the warmth of his own room, the ease of having meals ready when he wants them, the way he can make Anna laugh. But he's been having quite the adventure, hasn't he? And Gabriel never leaves him time to be bored. There's always some new kind of trouble they can get into. The thought is a strange sort of comfort as he drifts back to sleep.

By morning, the rain has stopped. When he opens his eyes, Gabriel is already awake, already sliding out from under the covers to find his boots.

"In a hurry?" Colin asks sleepily.

Gabriel nods. "We've a ways to go if we want to get there before it starts."

Colin scrubs the sleep out of his eyes and sits up. "Before what starts?" Sometimes he wonders if Gabriel imagines conversations they haven't actually had, and picks up in the middle of them thinking he's making sense.

"The hanging," Gabriel says. "It's week's end today."

"You're keeping better track than I am." That means it's been six days since they met, since the night that Colin chose the wrong tavern in which to find a room and fell into Gabriel's blurry reflection of Casmile like a boy in a nursery tale.

Gabriel shrugs, as if that's nothing to remark on, as if he hasn't seemed more than half moon-touched for most of the week. "You've never had reason to keep count of the days, have you?"

"And you have?" Colin reaches for his boots. "I haven't seen you working an honest trade yet."

"We have so much in common," Gabriel says, with a smile that looks so ordinary it's disconcerting. "But the hanging's as good a reason as any to keep track, isn't it? My coin's run out completely, and your purse is looking thin lately, too."

Colin shoves his feet into his boots. "You're going to get money at a hanging. You pick pockets?"

"And cut purses. It's also a good chance to see who's run afoul of the guard lately, and that's an important thing to know." Gabriel stands up and stretches. "Come on, Drake. It's a long way off."

The clouds haven't completely cleared from the night's rain, but there are a few patches of blue in the quilt of gray. The holes in the street have become puddles, mirror-still until Gabriel kicks pebbles into them, and the air smells cleaner than usual. They cut north and west toward Raven Square, a place Colin's heard plenty about but never actually gone to see. People are already gathering in the street leading up to it, lining both sides of the way between the prison and the square. It feels like the start to a festival, people waiting for something exciting. This parade won't be anything like the midsummer celebration of the Mother's bounty, though—it'll end in Raven Square, up ahead of them, where a triple gallows waits.

Gabriel ducks out of the press of the crowd, stopping at one of the dozen or so handcarts around the edges of the square. He buys half a dozen jam tarts, and Colin stares.

"How?" he asks, as Gabriel offers him a stack. "I thought you had no coin."

"I didn't," Gabriel agrees, the words muffled by his first bite of breakfast—fully half a tart at once. "It's a good thing we came here, isn't it?"

Colin retraces their path in his memory, trying to pick out a moment when Gabriel could have found the chance to lighten someone's purse. He can't figure it out.

"Aren't you hungry?" Gabriel asks. "Because I'll eat yours for you if you're not."

"No!" Colin protests, pulling his tarts out of reach. "I mean, I am." He takes a bite of the first tart, blackberry jam oozing out onto his fingers as the pastry crumbles. He still feels a little self-conscious, bolting his food on the street like he doesn't know any better, but it bothers him less than it could, and anyway, nobody here is gentry enough to care. "Thank you," he says between one tart and the next. "These are good."

Gabriel beams. "We'll eat like lords tonight," he promises. "Meat and spices, something really fit to grace your table." He polishes off the last of his breakfast and licks his fingers. "Now you stay here, and be careful of your purse once the show starts. I'll be back when it's done."

Colin still has a mouthful of tart, so he can't even manage a coherent protest before Gabriel is off, slipping into the thick of the crowd. It makes sense—of course he'd have an easier time cutting purses without Colin shadowing him—but that doesn't make it any more comfortable. The whole crowd has a bloodthirsty feel to it;

everyone is waiting for the spectacle to start, and Colin thinks he'd feel better with Gabriel's knives to depend on.

He loses track of Gabriel in the crowd within moments—just one more thin, dark-haired urchin, when the place swarms with them—and tries to distract himself studying the other people who've come to see the hanging. He doesn't spot any of the gentry, but just about all of Casmile's other types are there, beggars and sailors and merchants, dun-colored Casmilans and darker-skinned islanders and even a few blond northmen scattered through the crowd.

The midmorning bells ring, the sound carrying from the river, and when their peals die away, noise erupts from the street where people are waiting. The crowd surges back, trying to clear the way as the guardsmen's procession advances toward the square. Captain Westfall rides first, dappled stallion tossing its head, his eyes sweeping the crowd. Colin's stomach tightens in a moment of pure awful terror, and he tugs his borrowed hat down to better hide his face. The captain's gaze doesn't linger, thank the Fates. He's safe for now. This macabre show has nothing to do with him.

Behind the captain comes the cart with the condemned, drawn by two huge black draft horses. The prisoners are chained to a frame in the cart, standing, on display. The crowd gets louder as they pass by, and a few people throw things at them. One of the men spits back.

When the cart passes by him, Colin sucks in a sharp breath. They're the same men who attacked him a few days before, the ones he and Gabriel fled from when the guard arrived. The men Barron sent after him. They weren't nearly that battered when he saw them last, though—now they're bruised and bloodied, filthier than he remembers, their clothes torn. One of them keeps nodding, as though he can barely keep awake. Colin tries to tell himself it wouldn't have gone so roughly for him if the captain had taken him in, but he's not sure he believes it.

Gabriel would have faced exactly this.

He shouldn't care so much, shouldn't worry when Gabriel is plainly able to handle himself just fine, but the thought makes him queasy all the same. Fates, he nearly feels sorry for Barron's men as they're dragged up onto the scaffold to have nooses fitted to their necks. They attacked him. They broke into his parents' house. They could have hurt his sister. That last makes him want them to get what they deserve, at least, even if he's still not sure he wants to watch.

He expects a speech of some kind when Captain Westfall climbs onto the scaffold himself. The condemned men fidget as the ropes are drawn up and secured, and the crowd slowly goes quiet, waiting. Anticipation knots Colin's stomach, heavy and cold.

"For murder," the Captain says, his voice pitched to carry as if he's on a stage of a battlefield, "and for brawling in the streets, the law demands that you hang." Whose murder? Were they already wanted for something else? Did they kill someone on their way to being captured? He and Gabriel were the only ones who did any killing in that fight.

The captain steps closer to the first prisoner, the one who was nodding off, and Colin waits for him to deliver the rest of the lines— asking for the condemned man's last words, or at least commending him into the arms of the Three—but all he does is smile and pull the lever for the trapdoor. The rope snaps taut and the prisoner dangles, barely kicking before he goes limp and just sways there. The crowd cheers, and Captain Westfall bows to them. Colin's heart pounds. The man makes it look easy. How does it become such a simple thing to take a man's life?

The second man bares his teeth when the captain turns to him. His lips move as he says something, likely a curse, but the crowd's making too much noise for Colin to catch it. The captain's answer is likewise lost, but he smiles the same way he did when he was telling that awful rumor about Gabriel and the Lady. He gestures as though he's explaining something entertaining, and the prisoner lunges for him like a dog on a too-short leash. The captain steps back, just out of reach, and eases the second trapdoor lever down almost gently.

It's no kindness at all. The prisoner jerks and struggles like a fish on a line, twisting, gasping horribly for air. The crowd jeers and howls, and Colin feels sick, but he's not looking away any more than they are. The man's face swells as he hangs from the noose, darkens past red to an awful, blotchy purple, and a spreading wet spot darkens the front of his trousers.

After too many minutes, when the body has gone still and the noise of the crowd begins to die down, someone off to Colin's left says admiringly, "I've got five shillings says he'll do the last one like that." Colin pushes his way through the crowd, away from the gambler, before he can hear whether anyone takes the man's bet. He sure wouldn't.

The crowd nearly quiets as Captain Westfall steps up to the last man. The prisoner doesn't disappoint them, either—he raises his head and spits, "The Lady take your eyes, you rotten bastard."

That provokes more shouting and even a few cheers from the crowd. The captain waits, like an actor who knows better than to deliver his lines when the applause will drown him out. When the crowd hushes, no doubt curious, he says with obvious relish, "She'll have yours first." He drops the lever to the sound of cheering.

Colin's had about all of this he can stomach. He turns away from the spectacle as the final prisoner starts the last fight of his life. If this is what Casmile is really like, then maybe Gabriel's right after all. Gabriel's Casmile and Colin's Casmile *aren't* the same place, and there's only one of them whose rules he knows. He searches through the crowd, trying to catch sight of a familiar, sharp-angled face, but his luck isn't with him. Gabriel's too good at disappearing.

Something brushes against his thigh, too intimate a touch for a crowd full of strangers. Colin reaches down instinctively to deflect it, and catches the bone-thin wrist of a boy who's trying to pick his pocket.

For a panicked moment they just stare at each other. The boy is tiny, skull plain under taut skin, his black eyes huge in his face. There's a bright, angry sore on his lip. "I'm sorry," he says. His voice hasn't changed yet. He tries to pull free, and Colin lets him. Enough people have been killed this morning. Colin's in no hurry to hand over someone else—or get caught himself.

They've attracted attention, though, their stillness making the nearest spectators turn toward them. "Here," a woman says loudly as the boy takes a step back, "he's picking pockets!"

"Run," Colin breathes. The boy doesn't wait to be told twice, turning to shove his way through the crowd. The charge gets repeated, other people taking up the cry, the way the entire pack will start to bay after the first hound catches the scent. Some of the guards look their way from the gallows, and Colin's heart hammers in his chest. If he's recognized here and caught—

He pushes through the nearest knot of people. "After him!" he calls. "Don't let the brat get away!" Some of the more bloodthirsty members of the crowd move with him, and Colin fights his way through the throng, keeping his head down. Two of the guard are coming down off the gallows to investigate. Colin falls back, letting some of the other pursuers take the lead so he can ease sideways out of the hunting crowd.

"What's happened?" a man asks him as he pauses to get his bearings.

Colin shakes his head. "Someone says there was a pickpocket loose." He prays it's the Maiden watching him now, and not Gabriel's Lady.

"Good luck finding him in this mess," the man says, and Colin spares him a quick smile.

"Don't have to tell me, but my friend's run off after him. Excuse me." The lies come easily enough, and he'd rather flee trouble than stand around waiting to see if anyone else is set to die. He slips through the press of the crowd toward one of the alleys that lead off the square. Behind him there's a roar of voices—sounds like they've found someone to be their thief—and he thinks it must be true that the Maiden can't care for all men at once.

He slides into the alley, takes a few steps into the shadow, and leans against the wall. Gabriel's back there somewhere, but Colin isn't sure he dares to go search for him, not with the captain on the prowl and already in a killing mood. He'd have terrible odds of finding Gabriel in that mob anyway, wouldn't he? He could probably make it back to Cypress Street on his own by now, for all the good it'll do him if Gabriel isn't headed there too.

He's still trying to choose his next move when Gabriel slips out of the crowd and into the alley. He looks so focused, so worried, that Colin nearly panics all over again. "Did someone spot you?"

Gabriel stops dead, staring at Colin. He squeezes his eyes shut, opens them again, and his shoulders sag in relief. "Drake," he says. "You didn't go away."

This could have been his chance, Colin realizes. He could have found himself a carriage while both Gabriel and the captain were occupied. It didn't even occur to him to try.

"I was waiting for you," he admits. "I only came this way once the guard started hunting the thief."

Gabriel nods. "Clever. I saw you go, and I thought you were leaving again. But you shouldn't. Not when I finally have the money to give you things as fine as you deserve."

Even if Gabriel has cut a dozen purses in the last half hour, Colin doubts it could amount to enough coin to provide him the luxuries he was used to at home. "Thank you," he says anyway. He wonders what sort of finery Gabriel imagines he deserves.

"You're welcome," Gabriel says seriously. He starts down the alley away from the square. He doesn't look back even when he reaches the corner, like he's just expecting Colin to follow him.

After a moment's hesitation, Colin does.

CHAPTER TEN

He starts to suspect after a few minutes that Gabriel isn't going anywhere in particular; Gabriel's routes through the city are always capricious, but this is even more random than usual.

"This way," Colin suggests when they pass a corner he recognizes, mostly to see if Gabriel will let him make the decisions.

Gabriel turns. "Where are we going?"

"I don't know." The clarity that Gabriel woke up with this morning is lasting longer than usual, as if even someone as dangerous as he is needs to keep his wits about him when the city itself is mad for blood. "Down by the riverside, I suppose."

"Mmm." Gabriel nods. "Keep to the left, then. There's a good spot up by the Wren Street Bridge."

It's near enough to having some control, Colin decides. And Gabriel does know the city better, so it's not that hard to follow him.

They come north and west to the river and skirt down along Bank Street, mostly silent. This morning's fresh horror is starting to settle in Colin's mind; not only the way that people treat the hangings like free theater, but the way that Captain Westfall encourages them to do so. It's almost hard to believe—the sort of thing that should happen in the northlands, or on the far side of the mountains, somewhere distant and barbaric. Not two miles from where Colin grew up. No wonder Casmile needs villains like Gabriel, if its protectors are so vicious themselves.

The sky is dark and threatening again by the time they reach the bridge, and Gabriel steps off the street to climb down a rough, muddy path toward the water. Colin almost asks what's down there, but decides it isn't worth the bother. It won't matter what the answer is; he'll follow anyway.

Gabriel's path leads under the bridge, where the stone supports form a shelf just wide enough to sit on comfortably. The pillars have crude drawings and badly spelled insults scratched into them. The water churns by, smoke-dark, only an arm's length below.

"What," Colin teases, "we're under the bridge, and there's no troll?"

Gabriel laughs, as though that was far more clever than it was. "There used to be," he says. "Black Tom, his name was. But he didn't like me coming down here, and we had a fight."

He should have known better than to ask, Colin thinks. Now he'll likely lose Gabriel to fancy again. And yet, he thinks he can make out enough of the truth through Gabriel's telling of it. Perhaps Black Tom was another street tough, or a madman taking shelter here from the weather. It doesn't really matter; it rarely does, when people start fights with Gabriel. "So you vanquished the troll?"

"Well, you don't see him here now," Gabriel says. He sounds proud of himself. "In early summer, in the dry season when the river runs low, sometimes you can see the stone he turned into, out there." He points into the middle of the river, and Colin squints at the dark water even though he knows better. "Not right now, though. Not with all the rain we've had."

"Looks like it's picking up again," Colin says, peering out from under the shadow of the bridge. The rain's just started, a slow patter that's gaining speed, making the surface of the water shiver to dull stone gray. "Hope it doesn't last too long." Before now, he's always had warm places to go when he wound up outside in Casmile's winter rain. He wonders if the little potbelly stove in Gabriel's room is safe to use, and how much it would cost to buy some coal for it.

"Does it rain much, where you come from?" Gabriel asks, sitting down with his legs folded under him. He pulls his spoils from his pockets, loose coins and little cloth purses, piling them on the stone in front of him. Right now it seems more like *he's* the dragon, hoarding his pittance of treasure.

"I've told you, I'm from—" Colin stops when Gabriel raises an eyebrow. "It's a lot like here," he says instead. In the right light, it's true. He speaks the same language and knows the same seasons, but he can't honestly say he's ever lived in Gabriel's Casmile. He sits down, trying to ignore the chill of the stone through his clothes.

Gabriel makes a thoughtful noise, emptying the purses to count their coins. "That's sort of a shame, isn't it." He looks up. "I sometimes think I'd like to see snow, instead of just having Deirdre's stories. Listening to her, sometimes it almost sounds like it can't be real."

Colin reaches for a half shilling in the pile, the sharp edge cut through the mountain crest of Deradan. "You can believe in trolls and dragons, but not in snow?"

"I've seen those," Gabriel says. "I'd believe in snow if I could see it, too."

"It's pretty enough. You'd want a good fire to sit beside, though. Maybe someday—" Abruptly Colin realizes he's about to make an absolutely ridiculous offer. "You'll get a chance to see it," he says instead.

"Maybe so," Gabriel says. His smile is calm, satisfied, like he could hear what Colin almost said. He's quiet for a minute, sorting through the last of his coins, and then he says, "We should celebrate."

Colin laughs weakly. "What do we have to celebrate? Escaping with our lives from that awful display?" He thinks of it again, the desperate kicking of the dying men, the cheers of the crowd, the vicious delight on Captain Westfall's face.

"Even if you didn't have fun watching, you should at least be grateful," Gabriel says in his advice-giving tone, which Colin suddenly realizes he must have learned from Deirdre; the inflection's almost identical. "One of our enemies just slew three others, and that means the city's less a danger to us now than it was at dawn."

"They weren't the real problem, though," Colin points out, leaving aside the way that Gabriel has taken on Colin's enemies as his own. "Barron can always hire more, can't he?"

Gabriel nods. "He probably will. But they won't know where to find you." He meets Colin's eyes, as clear and steady as he's ever been. "They'll be looking for a fancy boy in a fancy house, won't they."

Colin's stomach rolls over slowly, and the cold grows far sharper. "Yes," he says. His voice cracks. He wants to go back to being a dragon.

"So you'll have them fooled. Well done." Gabriel scrapes his plunder into a single pile of copper, and starts to put all the coins into one purse. "And that means we should celebrate."

"Do you know what happened to him?" Colin asks, though it's probably a bad idea. "The boy, I mean."

Gabriel studies him for a minute, head cocked like a raven's. "He got away."

Colin lets out a sigh of relief. "Really?"

"Don't know," Gabriel says. "But you want him to have, so you might as well believe it." He puts the last of his coins away with a clink of metal and tugs the purse's strings shut. "When this lets up enough to walk in, we should go get some food. We could both have meat today."

The rain has settled in for a long stay, though, and doesn't lighten in any sort of hurry; the toll of distant bells means that midday's come and gone. They sit under the bridge like a pair of trolls themselves, and Colin tries to keep himself occupied thinking about things like whether trolls come in pairs, instead of things like whether the pickpocket escaped, or how Gabriel has managed not to fall prey to the fever when he doesn't even have a proper coat.

"Tell me a story," Gabriel says at last. "To make the time pass."

Colin shifts, looking over at him. The interruption's more welcome than he'd like to admit. "What kind of story?"

"The story of the dragon who came to Casmile," Gabriel suggests. Colin opens his mouth to protest, but Gabriel goes on, "Or if you still won't tell me that one, then pick something else." His voice sounds petulant and young, as though the clarity he had this morning is reaching its end, guttering out like a candle burned down to the nub.

Colin takes a deep breath, trying to think back on the stories he used to beg for when he was little. He tells the story of how fox singed his tail white, which he heard from his nurse, who was imported from the islands. When he closes his eyes to remember it better, he catches himself repeating the words in her rhythms, her accent. He tells the story of the boy who played dice with the Fates, which he heard for the first time only a few years ago, and which he sometimes thinks Danny was making up to flatter him. Gabriel, in turn, tells the story of the Battle of Troll Bridge—in rather more detail than Colin might actually like—and then the story of the boy who wooed the moon, which Colin has never heard before. It sounds like a northlands tale, mixing everyday things with utter fantasy; Colin wonders if Deirdre told it to Gabriel, or if there are more barbarians in the south than he'd always believed.

After that, it's his turn again, but the surface of the river is still, the rain stopped. "We could go now," Colin says. "Couldn't we?"

Gabriel boosts himself up immediately, like he's just been waiting for the word. "We could. Let's."

CHAPTER ELEVEN

They'd need a change of clothes and a bath before they could get themselves served at any of the truly fancy places along the river, but they do find a tavern where they can order steaming, hearty portions of a chicken pie that leaves Colin feeling pleasantly sated. From the look on his face, Gabriel is just as content, though Colin's not sure if that's due to the food or to Colin's enjoyment of it. He watches carefully, trying to figure out if the odd mood that took Gabriel under the bridge has passed yet; Gabriel's madness feels like the rain, coming sometimes in sudden thunder and other times in slow, creeping mist.

"Where shall we go next?" Gabriel asks, pushing the last bit of piecrust around his plate to sop up the gravy. "We have coin to spare. We could go see a show, if you'd like."

Likely that's a sign of reason returning, an offer designed to appeal to the young lord Gabriel sometimes knows him for. Colin thinks of the theater on Kestrel Street where he and Danny went last spring, how outrageous it seemed at the time. No doubt Gabriel could suggest less wholesome places, where the Mother only knows what sort of barbarity happens both onstage and off. He'd rather not try his luck with something like that tonight, not when this morning's show was so far from entertaining. Although if Gabriel is looking for some way to treat him, perhaps he does have an idea.

"I'll pass on the show for today, but if you know someplace where I could throw some dice, that wouldn't go amiss."

"My dragon throws dice with the Fates?" Gabriel asks. He doesn't wait for the answer that Colin is hesitant to give, just shrugs. "I can find some places, but I don't know if they're fancy enough for you."

Colin shakes his head. "I met Barron in a gaming house. Somewhere that isn't expensive enough to catch his attention would actually be better." Assuming they even have enough silver to *play* at the Peacock's tables, which he doubts.

Gabriel smiles broadly. "In that case, we should go down to the docks."

It's harder than it should be to stay calm as they leave the tavern and head toward the harbor. Colin can feel the excitement humming just under his skin, the certainty of luck tingling in his fingertips. He's had so many more pressing worries to deal with in the past week, there hasn't been time to miss gaming.

It's gray dusk when they make it down to the harbor, a fitting end for a gray day, but the taverns spill golden light onto the streets, and the tide must be at an advantageous turn because there are ships moving out in the gloom. The two of them pass a few open doors before Gabriel finds their destination: a smoky little half-underground room full of rowdy people and the smell of burning herbs. There are three tables going, with a handful of players at each one, and spectators crowded behind them. One or two of them might be betting on the players at the far table, from the way coins are changing hands. Some of the watchers are clearly whores, too cheap for the licensed houses of Kite Street, here to make money off the luckier gamblers. Most of the whores are girls, but there are a few pretty boys who might be selling, too.

Colin picks his way through the crowd, Gabriel following close at his heels, until he has a good vantage point to watch one of the tables and see how the action is moving.

It's a three-penny table, considerably lower stakes than the shilling tables Colin's used to at the Quartermaster or the Peacock, but that suits his reduced funds just fine. The players mostly look like sailors, weathered and windburned, their hair cut short or tarred back where it'll be out of the way. One of them is dark-skinned enough for Cabiral; another tips his dice-cup with a hand that's missing its last finger; another is a woman with a sharp, barking laugh and a crooked smile. Colin watches them play for a few rounds, studying the players' styles.

A girl comes around in the employ of the house, offering pipe tobacco blends, lumps of opium resin, and small bottles of liquor. Colin doesn't have his pipe with him, and he doesn't like the way Gabriel's lip curls at the resin, so he buys them a bottle to share instead. It turns out to be rum, cheap and harsh, burning as it slides down his throat. He swallows with a grimace and passes the bottle to Gabriel.

"You like it here?" Gabriel asks when he's had a long pull of the rum himself.

Colin nods. He has to lean close to make himself heard over the noise of boasting and laughter from the tables. "It looks like a good time." Gabriel's fingers brush his when handing back the bottle, and a little shiver thrills up his arm. Gaming always makes him restless, makes him daring, so he hears himself say, "You'll be my luck, won't you?" before he's realized just what a horrible idea that is.

Gabriel laughs. "I'd be honored, Drake." He reaches into his pockets and comes up with a few rounds' worth of copper that he presses into Colin's hand. "Play well."

"Thank you." Colin takes another drink of the rum for the sake of his nerves. He'll have to play well, if he's doing it with Gabriel's money.

But he thinks he can read this table decently from watching the last few rounds. The Cabirile man plays cautiously and challenges early; the woman is reckless, raising the bid even when chance is set against her; the man with the missing finger plays viciously, goading his fellows on and challenging as soon as someone's overbalanced and ready to fall. The last two players are floundering, their patterns not nearly so clear, and Colin's glad when it's one of them who concedes defeat and gets up from the table.

"I'll take that seat," Colin offers, passing Gabriel the rum so he'll have his hands free. Across the table, another sailor who looked interested shrugs and gestures for him to go ahead. Colin slides into the chair and sweeps the dice in front of him into the cup, tossing his pennies into the ante in the middle of the table.

"Go on, handsome," the woman tells him as the others take up their cups to roll their dice. "Take the first bid."

Colin turns his cup onto the table. "Gladly." He tips it back so he can see his hand. Three, three, four, two, six. "Seven threes," he says.

"Six fours," the woman raises immediately, and the game is on. Play happens fast, almost pure chaos, with no fixed order to the bets, and the rattling dice and jingling coins have Colin giddy in no time. The rum's nothing to this rush. He takes two rounds in the first dozen, one on a challenge and one on a very lucky bet for a dozen fours, and by then he thinks he's starting to really know how to play this table.

He takes the next round, even, calling ten fives when he has a pair and an ace himself. And then, somehow, it all starts to go wrong. He loses the next ten rounds in a row, even when it seems like his challenge is completely reasonable. Gabriel's hand comes to rest on his back, either a reassurance or a warning, as the players turn their cups for the next round. Colin's lost all he's made now, and he's running out of the money that Gabriel gave him. His stomach tightens with nerves.

Five threes, the bidding goes. Seven threes, seven fours. Six fives. "Eight fives," Colin says. It's still a fairly safe bid, with five players at the table.

The man with the missing finger immediately tips his cup. "Call."

Gabriel's hand tightens in Colin's shirt. "You're cheating," he says loudly, as the other players start to reveal their hands.

Quiet ripples out from their table, and the pop and hiss of the fire is suddenly audible. Gabriel isn't deterred at all. "You turned two of your dice just now."

"That's an ugly lie," the man says. He pushes his chair back from the table, stares at Colin in challenge. "You here to game, or to fight?"

"The boy who played dice with the Fates, Drake," Gabriel says. He takes his hand off Colin's back, which means he's readying himself to fight. "Did he win?"

Colin reaches into his pocket and finds the heavy, solid weight of brass. He knows how this ought to go in a tale. "Yes, Gabriel." He can see a few people tense at the name, and the thrill that runs down his spine is every bit as good as throwing a winning hand. "He did." He has just enough time to draw another breath, and it feels like the whole room does it with him, before they all explode into movement.

The cheater tries to come over the table at him, so Colin braces his hands under the table and shoves it upwards as he stands. Dice and coins scatter, and space clears around them. Someone swings a wide punch at him, and Colin raises an arm to deflect it, stepping in closer and driving straight, knocking the wind from the man so he can shove him back into his friend. All those hours sparring in the practice salon keep paying off, despite how he resented them at the time. Behind him, Gabriel laughs as glass shatters. They can take this room, he thinks, grinning, staggering when someone careens into him.

It isn't them against the room, though, not really. People turn on each other like they've just been waiting for an excuse, like this is the game they were here for, and it's a blind free-for-all within moments. Even some of the whores get involved—Colin sees a girl break a bottle over the head of her would-be customer. People are grabbing whatever loose coin they can and running with it. Somebody elbows Colin in the ribs, and he lashes out without seeing what he hits. Gabriel appears on the other side of the room for a moment, driving his heel into the kneecap of someone who's trying to grab him, and then the chaos swallows him up again. A moment later, someone hits Colin in the face as he's punching someone else, and splotches of bright gold cloud his vision. His head spins. Then there's a thick, muscular arm around his throat and a deep, growling voice yelling at him to get out. He's dragged backward up the stairs and shoved out the door into the chill of the evening.

He's just been thrown out of a gaming house for starting a brawl. Colin bursts out laughing, and hasn't yet stopped when Gabriel stumbles after him.

"Have fun?" Gabriel asks, slurring a little from the bloody split in his lip.

Colin grins. His left eye is already swelling, tender, and his hair is falling in his face; he must have lost Gabriel's hat in the fight. "Yeah," he says, a bit to his own surprise. "I did."

The door opens again as the house's muscle throws out the woman from Colin's table, who's cursing in a language Colin doesn't know, and then the cheater, who's bleeding from a gash in his forehead. The cheater glares at the two of them like he's thinking of trying his luck out here. Colin, still drunk on the fight, bares his teeth and growls. The cheater spits, and turns away from them to limp off up the street.

Gabriel laughs, and that makes Colin feel warmer than the rum *or* the fight. A minute later he sobers, though, remembering the circumstances they're left in as a chill wind sweeps up the street from the harbor. "I'm sorry. For losing your money."

"Don't worry about the money, Drake." Gabriel lays a hand on Colin's shoulder carefully, as though he's not sure how it's done. "Money's not so special. We can get more."

Not easily, Colin almost says. *Not without risking our lives*. But Gabriel's luck is a strange thing that knows no proper laws, so perhaps that's enough. He leans into Gabriel's hand and smiles. "Yeah," he says again. "I guess we can."

CHAPTER
TWELVE

The next day, they return to the room after supper—Colin almost, when he's not careful, thinks of it as their room, like he almost thinks of himself as Drake—and find it already occupied.

"What do you want, Jack?" Gabriel asks flatly, staring at the man in the middle instead of the obvious hired muscle on either side of him. Jack is better dressed than Gabriel, but his face still has the pinched look that Colin is coming to associate with Casmile's lowest classes, the look like he's always at least a little bit hungry.

"You're three weeks late with the rent," Jack says. He looks up from studying the dirt under his nails. "Again."

"It's been a bad month." Gabriel shrugs. "I'll get you your money. I always do." His stance is still casual, but his voice has taken on the too-smooth tone it had the night they went to see Morgan.

Jack shakes his head. "I've been very patient with you." He smirks at Colin. "Maybe you should put your boy on the corner, if you're having that much trouble coming up with coin."

Colin tenses, but Gabriel's low growl makes him pause. They haven't killed anyone in days, and he sort of likes it that way. He particularly likes the idea that they haven't killed anyone where they sleep. If Gabriel starts moving, somebody is going to die here. It might not even be Jack's thugs, who look like serious, well-armed trouble.

"Gabriel, not here," Colin says gently. Gabriel makes another half-restrained snarling noise, like a hound on a leash, and Colin glares at Jack. "What do we owe on the room?"

The way Jack's lip curls makes Colin want to hit him, too—it's far too knowing, too lewd, the assumptions he's made about them plain on his face. "Eight. For the last month."

Colin's down to twelve shillings and change, after all the meals he's bought for the two of them. "I can give you four," he offers. He's seen how these bargaining games go. "But that's all I have. You'll need to give us a little time to come up with more."

"I'll need to, will I?" Jack raises an eyebrow, addressing Gabriel instead of Colin. "Your boy's got quite a mouth on him. Could get him in trouble one day."

Colin bristles, seething at the way Jack treats him like he can't vouch for himself.

"Not everyone prefers the company of whipped dogs," Gabriel says mildly. "You'll need to give us more time."

Jack's thugs tense, like they can feel the charge in the air and the way Gabriel is readying himself to spring. Jack laughs harshly, forcing the sound, his teeth bared in a poor imitation of a smile. "You'll need to hand over that four now, then. And I'll be back at the end of the week for the rest."

Gabriel nods graciously, another one of those exaggerated gestures he probably picked up in a cheap theater. "Give the dog his bone, Drake." He's toying with them now, Colin thinks as he reaches for his money. "Red Emma seeing visitors this week?"

"Could be. I make my living like an honest man, wouldn't know about her trade." Jack holds out a grubby hand for Colin's coins.

"Have to go see her tomorrow," Gabriel says thoughtfully. "We'll get your money for you."

"Vulture," Jack says, but he pockets the money and steps past them, toward the door. For a moment, Colin expects Gabriel to lash out and sink a knife into Jack's unprotected back, but it doesn't happen, and the tension ebbs as Jack and his thugs leave.

Gabriel drops easily onto his bed, rolls over, and arches his back, stretching like a cat. His shirt rides up just far enough to expose a narrow stripe of skin above the waistband of his trousers, and Colin looks away. He's been doing pretty well since that first morning at ignoring Gabriel's physical presence, but now he's thinking again about what this looks like—what it likely would *be* with someone less touched than Gabriel. They share the one mattress, lying back-to-back under the blankets, and though Colin hasn't woken with Gabriel pinning him since that first time, he's suddenly aware of how easily it could happen again. He can't decide whether there's enough of a thrill to the idea to offset how terrifying it would be. Especially since he can't picture Gabriel spreading his legs for anyone, and he'd never planned on doing it himself.

"Something the matter, Drake?" Gabriel asks, looking up at him.

"No." Colin's face heats. With any luck, Gabriel won't notice it in the last of the fading light.

"Come to bed, then," Gabriel says, squirming under the blankets. "We'll want rest, if we're going to do actual work tomorrow."

Colin exhales heavily. "Right." He takes off his boots, and strips off his coat so he can ball it up to use as a pillow. With two blankets and Gabriel's body heat, he doesn't need it for warmth.

"Good night, Drake," Gabriel says when Colin lies down. He sounds oddly content, like having Colin here makes him happy, which is something Colin doesn't want to think about too hard.

Gabriel's back is solid and warm against his own, almost comforting. "Good night."

CHAPTER THIRTEEN

Red Emma is a Jua'zan islander with a nasty smile and a pirate's brand. She holds court in a dockside tavern, brokering deals between men who need ugly jobs done and men who don't mind getting their hands dirty. She greets Gabriel like an old friend, and only looks askance at Colin for a moment. The first day they go to see her, she has nothing for them, but she promises to keep an ear out for things that would suit them. Two days later, she has something to offer.

The job she gives them isn't complicated, just nasty. They track down the first mate of a known smuggling ship, follow him until they catch him alone, and then Colin stands watch while Gabriel makes a grotesque, messy example of him in a rented tavern room. Colin doesn't let himself look too closely. It isn't as quick as the scrapes they've gotten into together or even that first night with Morgan. Someone who runs in the kind of circles that get Gabriel loosed on him can't be much of an upstanding citizen in the first place, but that doesn't make it easy to watch. He'll sleep better if he doesn't know the details.

The important part is they get paid a dozen newly minted shillings—not even a guinea's worth, but enough to keep trouble off the doorstep.

The day after that first job, feeling oddly pragmatic, Colin insists they spend a fairly large fraction of their earnings on practical things. They give Jack enough money to earn a week's grace on the rent, and buy a bucketful of coals for Gabriel's little stove. In the afternoon, they poke around the market, and when Colin finds a coat that fits decently across Gabriel's shoulders and isn't too moth-eaten, Gabriel manages to talk the seller down to eight pence less than she'd first asked for it. Overall, Colin feels good about the entire day. He catches Gabriel once or twice holding his hands out in front of him and admiring the tarnished braid that still hangs limply from the coat's cuffs.

And then Gabriel turns in to a chemist's, instead of heading south toward home.

"What are we here for?" Colin asks, squinting in the gloom of the shop, wrinkling his nose at the smell of dry, pungent herbs and bitter powders.

"Bottle of genepy," Gabriel says, as much to the old man behind the counter as to Colin. He looks over at Colin as the old man gets down from his stool to fetch the bottle. "You don't want laudanum, do you?" he asks suspiciously.

"No? I mean, why would I?"

"For the pain."

Colin tries not to look as alarmed as he feels. His eye's still nicely bruised, sure, ugly and purple in the reflections of shop windows, but he didn't need laudanum for that when it was fresh, much less now. "The pain?" he repeats. "Are we planning to get ourselves hurt?"

Gabriel pats Colin's shoulder. "Deirdre's needlework has to come out sometime. Mine's about done, so yours should be, too."

"And that hurts, does it?" He should have suspected it, Colin supposes. The stitches have never gotten comfortable, even when the swelling went down; now, with new skin forming pink and shiny under them, they've begun to itch whenever he pays attention to them.

"Be brave," Gabriel says. "I won't hurt you more than I have to." He smiles at the chemist. "That'll be all, thank you. We don't need any laudanum."

The genepy, milky green in the bottle, costs Gabriel a shilling by itself. Colin is shocked at the expense for a moment, and then feels ridiculous. A guinea's a lot of money; a shilling is the bet he used to place on a decent hand of cards. How many days has it been, that he's starting to get used to this?

"Gabriel," Colin says slowly as they head south along Cypress again, "how long have I been—" he almost says *with you*, but catches himself in time "—here?"

"Starting to worry?" Gabriel parries. "Are your people coming for you?"

They should be, Colin realizes. By now surely his father is more worried than angry. Even if Captain Westfall told his parents . . . awful things. They'd want him back, wouldn't they?

"I don't know," Colin says. "They—they might be. I thought they would. But I suppose they're not doing a very good job of looking, are they?"

"Well, you don't look much like you did that first night. And you had the sense to come and hide with me."

"That's not . . ." Colin frowns. He doesn't want to be *stuck* with Gabriel, certainly, and he still thinks he wants to go home eventually. But perhaps it can wait just a bit longer. They pass the house with the tower room whose roof has fallen in, and that means they're almost back to their own. "Thank you. For taking me in."

"My pleasure," Gabriel says. "How many men ever get this close to a dragon?" His tone is teasing, enough that Colin feels a jolt of surprise. From someone else that would sound like flirting. Even from Gabriel, it sounds awfully close to an admission of just how much he's invented between them.

Colin hasn't figured out how to ask about that before they reach the house. It's getting easier to be here, to step over the filth in the first-floor hallway and climb the rickety stairs by only putting weight on the relatively solid parts. Their door is closed and everything inside is still right where they left it, even the coals, which Colin had been a bit worried about. They seem like the sort of commodity that would be in high demand.

"The tinderbox is tucked under the stove," Gabriel says. "Light us a fire, Drake?"

Colin hesitates; he's never built a fire himself before. There were always servants to do that at home. But he's watched, at least, so he knows more or less how it's done.

"What are you doing?" he asks as he feeds some coals into the belly of the little iron stove. When he glances over, Gabriel is sitting cross-legged on the bed, studying something in his lap.

"Tricky work, drawing stitches." Gabriel holds up his smallest knife and tests the edge against his thumb. "It helps to have your knife freshly sharp."

That's not reassuring at all. One day, Colin thinks, he'll have the sense to stop asking Gabriel questions. He takes the battered tinderbox from between the legs of the stove and flips open the lid. The straw inside is so dry, it almost crumbles at his touch, but that should make it catch fire easily. Colin carefully lays the straw on top of the coals as Gabriel starts drawing his knife across a whetstone with a thin, high scraping sound.

Really, Colin decides, it's more shameful than anything else, the fact that he's sitting here hoping he's *guessed* right about making a fire. It's pathetic that he knows so little about taking care of himself. He holds the flint and steel above the tinder, striking them together with maybe a little more force than necessary. Sparks fly, but they die before they reach the straw. Colin holds the flint a little closer and tries again.

This time the spark catches, and a little flame blooms in the straw, wavering and then growing bolder. Colin draws a breath to point out to Gabriel that he's done it, and then feels silly. It's not that much of an accomplishment, is it? A child half his age could probably light a fire as easily, if he hasn't been coddled all his life.

"Good," Gabriel says. "It's a little easier to do this when you're warm." He kicks off his boots, then tugs at the laces of his trousers and lets them fall. Colin averts his eyes, but can't help glancing back as Gabriel sits down gracelessly on the mattress, twisting like he's trying to examine the stitches on the back of his thigh. "Hmm. I might need you to get these for me, Drake. It's a tricky spot to reach myself."

"Me?" Colin echoes. "I wouldn't have the first clue how to take stitches out. Wouldn't you rather go see Deirdre for that?"

Gabriel shakes his head. "You can do it. You're clever. Come here, and I'll show you."

"I wouldn't want to hurt you," Colin protests. "You trust me more than you should, Gabriel."

The look in Gabriel's eyes is piercing, too perceptive, too aware. "Do I?"

Colin swallows hard, not sure how to respond, and Gabriel smiles slowly.

"Sit down and take your shirt off, and I'll show you how to do it."

Whenever it really counts for anything, Colin seems to find himself doing what Gabriel wants. He tugs off his coat and shirt, and he's glad for the stove, even if the heat from it isn't much yet; he has goose bumps rising on his arms, and he wants to curl up under the blankets. "All right. I'll—I'll do my best." His heartbeat is loud in his ears. "Go ahead."

"You want a drink first?" Gabriel asks, offering him the genepy bottle.

Colin shakes his head. Considering how fast the whiskey overtook him when he first got the stitches, something as strong as genepy would wreck him. "You want my hands to be steady when I do yours, don't you? I'm afraid I'd best not drink until after."

"Brave dragon," Gabriel says approvingly. He leans forward, examining Colin's side, pushing Colin's arm back and out of the way. "You start at one end, and you have to cut each one by itself. Like this." Colin should be terrified, watching Gabriel's knife come closer. He's holding still for Gabriel to use a knife on him. Perhaps he *is* terrified, a little, but it's really more that he's afraid of something going wrong by accident; he honestly believes Gabriel wouldn't hurt him.

The very point of the knife slides under the first stitch, then sideways. Colin grits his teeth at the tension on the thread, the way it pulls—and then the thread gives, all at once, and Gabriel lifts the knife away.

"Brace yourself," Gabriel says, carefully catching the knot between his fingernails. "Sometimes this part is bad." He pulls, and Colin hisses at the pain, hot and ragged, like ripping off a scab too soon, except much worse.

"Ah, Black Mother," Colin curses as Gabriel tugs the stitch free and drops the scrap of thread. "Do they really have to come out?"

Gabriel shrugs. "Deirdre says if you leave them too long, they rot in your skin, and then sometimes it swells and festers and she has to cut you open to get the bile out." He raises his shirt and shows Colin a little knot of scar tissue low on his ribcage, thick and raised and still an angry pink in spots. "Then it heals like this."

"Right," Colin says as Gabriel pulls his shirt down again. "They have to come out."

"So sensible," Gabriel says, using that almost-teasing tone again, and leans down to cut the second stitch.

It's awful, Colin decides as Gabriel pulls the second stitch free, but less so than having his side fester and fill up with bile. He grits his teeth and tries not to make any more noise than he has to, even when it feels like Gabriel is tearing his skin to get the thread to come loose. Looking down is discouraging, because it means then he can see how little progress they've made, and also alarming, because there are little beads of blood rising to the surface in a few of the spots where the stitches are gone. He can get through this. Men live through worse. He's fairly certain that Gabriel has lived through far worse.

"There," Gabriel says at last, sitting back on his heels. "All done, my dragon."

"Thank you." Colin reaches for his shirt and pulls it back on. His side aches, and it feels hot, but at least it's over. Soon he'll be able to have a drink, and that'll do a lot to make it better.

First, though, he's going to have to take care of Gabriel. "All right," he says, picking up the knife. "Are you ready?"

Gabriel gives him a little wry smile, completely ordinary, completely reasonable. "Close enough." He stretches out on the mattress, facedown, head pillowed on his hands. He looks relaxed, like he doesn't even realize what a vulnerable position he's in, lying on his belly in his ragged small clothes.

For Gabriel, it probably *isn't* a vulnerable position. Colin tries to imagine himself—anyone—attempting to take advantage of Gabriel. It could only end in blood and pain.

He kneels between Gabriel's legs carefully, leaning down to examine the stitches. There aren't all that many, which is a bit of a relief. The skin right around them is bright pink, freshly healed, and fades at its edges into dusty olive. Gabriel doesn't have an ounce of fat on him, just lean muscle over bone, and the skin at the back of his thigh is pinched tight around the new scar. Older scars make finer lines, some raised and white, others flat and brown.

Colin almost reaches out to touch one, to see what it feels like, before he thinks better of it. "I'm, ah, going to start now."

"Go ahead," Gabriel says.

Gabriel's skin is warm and smooth under his fingers, and Colin tries to stop thinking about that as he eases the knife under the first stitch. It won't do him any good to notice. Wouldn't do him any good to try anything. If he's really that hard up, he can hire someone the next time they wind up in a gaming house—Gabriel is much too dangerous, and much too hard to predict.

The thread is tougher than it looks, even with the sharpness of Gabriel's knife. It pulls taut, then snaps, and the knife slides almost too fast for a moment before Colin manages to get it under control again. "Sorry," he says.

"You're doing fine." Gabriel's voice sounds smooth and distant. "Now pull that stitch." He's still completely relaxed, completely calm.

"Right." Colin catches the knot with his nails. The fine detail work is difficult, with the poor light and the way his hands shake. Drinking the genepy before this would have been a terrible idea. But the thread comes loose without too much trouble, once he can actually get a grip on it, and Gabriel makes a soft humming sound that he doesn't want to think about too hard. "Like that?"

Gabriel nods. "Just like that. You should have a little more faith in yourself."

"I'll do my best." Colin can feel a sort of helpless smile tugging at the corners of his mouth. He's done nothing, really, to earn the trust Gabriel has in him. But he has it and he's going to do his best to keep it.

It helps that Gabriel seems to be more healed than Colin was. He doesn't bleed when Colin pulls the stitches free, and most of the thread comes loose without too much effort. The fresh scar is thin and bright pink, smooth and shiny against the ordinary skin around it. Colin counts as he goes—eight of them, which feels like far fewer than he had. It seems unfair that Gabriel should be the tougher of the two of them and also get hurt less.

"All done," Colin says at last, sitting back and setting Gabriel's knife aside.

"Mmm, good." Gabriel sits up, curling his legs under him and reaching for the bottle. "Let's not do that again for a while."

"Gladly," Colin says; he'd be happy not to do it again at all.

Gabriel uncorks the bottle and takes a long pull from it, then hands it over. The genepy smells tangy, herbal, strange, overlaid with the sharp bite of alcohol. "Have some," Gabriel encourages. "You'll hurt less, and it's good for you."

"Thank you." Colin lifts the bottle to his mouth and takes a careful drink. It's stronger than the rum from the gaming house, stronger than the brandy he was used to before, turning to dizzying vapor in his mouth and making heat burst in the pit of his stomach. "Oh," he says, and takes another drink. "Oh."

Gabriel laughs. "Yes. Exactly."

PART II
WINTER

CHAPTER
FOURTEEN

I t's coming close to the Longest Night. Houses in the nicer parts of town are decked with evergreen branches, and when they leave the relative comfort of home, their breaths steam in the cold air. Drake's been here for more than a month: long enough to get used to Cypress Street and the tidal rhythms of Gabriel's madness, long enough to start answering to a new name, long enough to act more the part of Drake than that of Colin Harwood. Sometimes he still thinks of home, but less than he'd have expected, especially in the winter. With Gabriel, even the most mundane routines have a chance of turning into fantastic adventures, and the excitement has yet to fade. They walk the streets of Casmile, and hear stories in pubs, and play cards in dockside houses, and sometimes they take money from well-fed old men with hard eyes, and then go start fights that other people don't walk away from. Drake hears his new name come up in stories about Gabriel occasionally, and he tries not to let it go to his head, but it isn't easy when he sounds so much larger than life in the rumors.

Gabriel, for his part, only rarely asks to hear stories about dragons, and doesn't complain much when Drake still denies being one. He thanks Drake for doing practical things like bringing up a pitcher of water from the rain barrel outside so they have fresh water in the mornings, or setting aside some of their coin every week so the rent gets paid with no trouble. The one time Drake gets needy enough to hire a girl at a gaming house, Gabriel stands watch in the alley while Drake pins her to the wall and takes what he paid for. Afterward the girl asks if Gabriel would like to buy a turn, too, but he shrugs her off without bothering to hide his distaste.

After that, Drake doesn't want to waste their money again, when Gabriel so clearly thinks poorly of the whole prospect. The tension between them comes and goes, like everything with Gabriel; sometimes he seems to be flirting with Drake, but it never leads anywhere and often it passes so fast that Drake wonders if he's imagined it.

The shorter days make Gabriel more impatient to leave the house in the morning, even when it's cold, as if he wants to make the most of the daylight when it lasts for so little time. So they find themselves in Market Square one morning, when carts and carriages start to pull up to the auction house.

"Have you ever been to an auction, Drake?" Gabriel asks, perched on a low wall as he eats one of the apples they've gotten for their breakfast.

Drake watches the chattel being unloaded from a cart, the one man who's struggling with his chains and the dull, resigned expressions of the others. "Where would I have done that?" His father always managed the estate, and he'd generally done his best to duck the excruciatingly dull lessons on the plantation's business.

"I didn't think so." Gabriel tosses the apple core behind him. "Come on, then."

"What?" Drake asks, as Gabriel jumps down from the wall. They haven't anywhere near the money it costs to buy a slave, and Drake's not sure he wants to think about what Gabriel would do with one if they did. Which means— "You're looking for purses to cut again, aren't you?"

"And it'll make the morning more interesting. And warm." Gabriel starts across the square, toward the front door of the auction house, and after a moment, of course, Drake follows.

There's quite a line forming outside, but it moves fairly quickly. Most of the men in line—almost everyone in the crowd, it seems, is male—don't look like they have the money for a chattel auction, either, but almost none of them get turned away. When they get near the front of the line, Drake sees why: there are two tiers inside. It's the opposite of the theater, where the cheapest view is down front; in the auction house, there are proper seats near the platform, and then an open space for standing audience members behind that. Drake doesn't look too closely at the men in the seats down front. It's not likely that his father would be here, but it seems as though he'd be uncommonly lucky not to run into *anyone* who knows—who knew him.

When they get to the front of the line, the auction house guard doesn't even look twice. "Five pence each for standing room," he says. He sounds bored.

Colin would have been outraged at not even getting the choice to buy the expensive seats, but Drake doesn't care so much. He reaches for his coin purse and pays for them both, since Gabriel has the distracted expression that means either he has a fit coming on or he doesn't have any coin in his pockets.

"Enjoy the show," the guard says when Drake hands over the coin.

"How much does it cost down front?" Drake asks as they make their way into the crowd. He tucks his coin purse into his shirt, since Gabriel won't be the only one in this crowd looking to make back the cost of admission with a little sleight of hand.

"Five shillings," Gabriel says absently. "And you have to show gold, so they know you could afford to bid." He's already looking around the room; studying his odds, most likely.

Drake hesitates. "You know, you don't have to be working. We've coin enough for another week, or two if we're careful."

Gabriel gives him a dubious look. "Carrion back in the den won't keep the fox out of the henhouse, will it?"

"Probably not." Still, at least one or two of the men standing around the edges of the room are wearing the livery of the city guard. "Keep a sharp eye for the hounds, then."

"Always," Gabriel says, but he sounds pleased. "Don't you get yourself in trouble, either."

"Without you?" Drake says. "I wouldn't dream of it."

Gabriel slips off into the crowd, and Drake starts looking around, trying to decide whether he'd rather push his way down to the front and see if he can get a decent view of the platform, or just stay back and keep an eye on the crowd. There's plenty of light from the big windows along both sides of the main hall, each one of them taller than a man and requiring dozens of panes of glass. It's even tolerably warm, thanks to the crowd.

Drake doubts he'd be able to get much of a show down front—right by the rails between standing room and the bidders' seats, people are already pushing and jostling at each other for the space. And if Gabriel is working, Drake doesn't want to get into a fight and get himself thrown out of the place.

He turns away from the platform, looking for someplace out of the way where he can watch—along the wall, maybe. He's picking up Gabriel's habits, feeling better when he knows what's at his back. As he pushes his way through the crowd, the auctioneer bangs a gavel against the podium down front. It doesn't really buy any silence, at least not this far back.

Which is just as well, because then someone grabs at his coat sleeve and says, "Colin?"

The entire world seems to stumble to a halt. Drake turns. He knows that voice, can already see the expression Danny's going to have on—blue eyes wide and surprised, dusty brown hair unruly and straying loose from its tie to fall over his forehead, too pale and too *pretty*, Drake can see now, to ever really look convincing in his huntsman's clothes.

He smiles when Drake meets his eyes, the expression so open and guileless it's painful to see. "It really is you."

"Don't call me by that name," Drake says immediately. It's maybe more cautious than he needs to be, but he's learning as he stays with Gabriel that it's better to be too cautious than not cautious enough. He shakes off Danny's grip, grabs him by the wrist, and pulls him through the crowd, toward the back corner where at least the great pillars supporting the roof will give them something approaching privacy. "Danny, what are you doing here?"

"I could ask you the same," Danny says. He's standing nearer than he needs to. Drake realizes that he's forgotten what it's like to have somebody besides Gabriel talking to him from inside a knife's reach. "When we came back from Nothwn, the stories about you were awful. They're not true, are they?"

Yes, they are. "Depends on what you heard."

Danny leans in closer still. He smells like powder and good tobacco. "I heard you've fallen in with a gang of highwaymen on the Hanaein Road."

Drake laughs a little shortly. "That does sound exciting."

"Then it's not true?" Danny takes Drake's hands in both of his. "I knew it couldn't be. It's just you've been gone so long, and your parents haven't been talking about it, and you know how the gossip gets, and— Oh, Colin, I'm so glad you're all right."

Before Drake has quite figured out how to explain to Danny that "all right" is perhaps overstating the case, Danny is kissing him, every bit as thoughtless as the first time. And Drake, despite knowing better, is kissing back. He's missed the way this feels, he realizes, the soft warmth of Danny's mouth and the solid comfort of having someone else's body pressed close to his own. He lets it go on probably longer than it should, his free hand curled tight in the fine wool of Danny's coat, before he finally remembers himself enough to pull back.

"I'm sorry, I can't do this," he says. "I can't just act like nothing's wrong." His heart is pounding, and Danny's lips are flushed.

"No, I—I know," Danny says. "There must be trouble, or you'd not have left at all, right? But it'll get fixed, you know it will, if you just come home. Your mother's been just heartbroken at every party we've been to this season. Anna's pining for you. Everyone's worried, Colin. Come home."

"I told you, don't call me that here," Drake says, even though he's not pleased with himself for being so short with Danny. "I can't just— I'm in *trouble*, Danny. I'm not robbing coaches on the north road, I'm breaking heads down by the docks. I owe Barron fifty guineas I don't have, I've killed enough men that Captain Westfall would be happy to hang me himself, and I've fallen in with— Oh, Fates." He lets go of Danny and steps back, staring past him. "Hello, Gabriel."

"Who's your friend, Drake?" Gabriel asks, and Danny jumps, turning to face him. "Someone I should know? You've met all of my friends by now."

Drake tries to picture Danny in any of Gabriel's haunts, doing anything but looking for a way home. "He's nobody. It doesn't matter. Did you change your mind about staying?"

Danny makes a little hurt noise, eyes wide, and Drake feels rotten, but it's far better—it has to be—to keep Danny out of this. To keep Gabriel away from him.

"I might have," Gabriel says. He's staring at Danny, who takes a step back, into the wall. "You look awfully upset for Nobody."

"Don't," Drake says. "Really, Gabriel, it's fine. Let's just go."

Gabriel steps closer, so he has Danny pinned. Danny's staring in what looks like terror, but he doesn't back down. "I don't want my dragon to go anywhere," Gabriel says, quietly enough that Drake barely hears him over the roar of the auction. "I've grown used to him. He brings me luck."

Danny looks like he's trying desperately not to panic. Drake lays a hand on Gabriel's shoulder, not quite daring to pull—not when Gabriel's this focused—but knowing he needs to do *something*. "Gabriel. It's nothing to worry about. I'm still here. Come on."

Gabriel doesn't move for another few moments, staring, studying Danny's face. At last he steps back. "Well," he says. "If you're not having fun, Drake, of course we should leave."

"Thank you." Drake lets out his breath in relief. Gabriel turns away as though he's lost interest completely, and Drake mouths *I'm sorry* to Danny as he turns to follow.

"Wait," Danny says, catching at his sleeve, and Drake wants to curse. Gabriel turns back, but Danny goes on, "How do I find you, if I need to get a message to you?"

"You don't," Drake says, even though the crestfallen look on Danny's face makes him feel like a bastard. "I'm a wanted man, remember? Besides, you couldn't pay a reliable messenger to go where I'm staying lately." It's too jarring, trying to confront a part of Colin's life when he's grown used to being Drake. Any answer he could give would be wrong. No matter how much he misses some things about home—not his father's lectures and demands, but his sister's company and all the house's comforts—he can't see how to reconcile that life with this one.

"Then—then promise you'll come to Sebastian's party after the new year," Danny says, fast and low, barely more than a whisper. "You know how little Sebastian cares for the captain. The guard won't be there. You don't even have to come inside, if you don't want to. I'll look for you in the back garden. Please. I want to be able to help you."

"I'll try." In the day-to-day troubles they've had for these last weeks, he's not stopped often to think about his old life, but having Danny here brings all those lost indulgences rushing back.

Danny's smile makes Drake feel like a bastard all over again as he follows Gabriel out of the auction house. It wasn't fair to give him hope like that, especially when there's no way Drake will be able to go, not with how Gabriel sticks to him all the time.

They push their way free of the auction crowd, out onto the street, and Gabriel turns to Drake. "Tell me about this Sebastian," he says. "I don't think I've ever been to a party before."

CHAPTER
FIFTEEN

I t feels like Drake spends the rest of the year trying to explain to Gabriel why they can't go to Lord Sebastian Dunsmuir's party. It's not easy to come up with reasons that Gabriel will accept. The idea of the vast impropriety only makes him stare blankly. And there's no way anyone Lord Dunsmuir could hire for security would intimidate Gabriel, especially when they've already established that the guard won't be there.

Drake suspects that if he could convince Gabriel he didn't *want* to go, that might be the end of it, but that's easier said than done. He's only been to the Dunsmuir townhouse a few times—like most of Colin's old social circle, they usually did their entertaining at their country estate—but he remembers it fondly. In midwinter, he's sure there would be fires lit in all the rooms, and likely there would be musicians, and card playing. And the food—his mouth waters just thinking of it. There would be roast fowl, baked hams, sweetbreads, pastries, winter fruit from the islands, and every last bit of it more tempting than the hard bread and thin stews they've been living on lately.

"They're your people," Gabriel says one chill afternoon as they wait in line to buy coal, casual as if they're already talking about it. "That's the real problem, isn't it?"

Drake shifts awkwardly, changes his grip on their empty coal bucket. "What do you mean?" He hasn't had any cues lately to let him know if they're talking about Casmile's lords and ladies or a menagerie of fantastic beasts.

"Fancy like you," Gabriel says, which doesn't quite clarify things. "You don't want them to see you with me."

"It's not like that," Drake says, which might be true. Ahead of them in the line, a woman is arguing about how much coal she should get for five pence. "It's— It isn't where I belong anymore, is it? You've changed me." *That's* truer than he'd like it to be, really. It's a wonder Danny recognized him at all, when he often doesn't recognize himself.

Gabriel hums, turns to watch a private carriage go by on Falcon Street. "You flatter me, Drake. But if I've changed you, it's made you stronger." His gaze is steady, as serious and reasonable as he gets. In the flat gray light of winter, his eyes have no color at all. "I haven't made you any less than you were. There's no place you can't go now." Drake waits for—hopes for—some cagey statement about dragons to follow that so he can brush it off, but it doesn't come.

"We'll see," he says at last. "I'll tell you if I want to go after all."

"Fair enough." Gabriel drifts toward the coal seller as the line moves along. "I'm looking forward to it."

They reach the front of the line before Drake can argue further, which he'd swear Gabriel did on purpose. He's seen plenty of cases by now where Gabriel managed not to hear things that would make him unhappy.

Really, Drake's surprised that Gabriel hasn't asked about the kiss. He almost wishes Gabriel would, for all that he doesn't know what he would say. The things he and Danny used to do together—well, he's never entirely known what to make of it. Plenty of men in Casmile screw boys; there are nearly as many boy houses on Kite Street as girl houses, and the really fancy ones are every bit as infamous. But there's a difference between having a boy whore and . . . doing what he and Danny used to, and Drake's fairly certain not nearly as many men do that. They definitely don't admit to it, not when they're from good families and there's inheritance to worry about.

Of course, that's probably the sort of concern that wouldn't even cross Gabriel's mind. Maybe it is common for men to lie together down on Cypress Street—though they'd still have to decide eventually which was going to use the other, and there aren't many men in Gabriel's circle who seem like they'd put up with that. But still. Perhaps it's like with him and Danny, touching each other but no more than that, and Gabriel thinks it's not worth mentioning.

Or perhaps Gabriel decided it was another peculiar habit of dragons, and isn't curious any further.

That should be a relief, and yet it isn't. What's wrong with him, that he wants Gabriel to care? That he wants Gabriel to ask him? That he'd like an excuse to tell Gabriel about the times he's gotten a hand in some other boy's breeches to bring him off?

There's an answer to those questions, and he's trying to ignore it. Perhaps the only thing madder than going along with Gabriel's schemes in the first place would be trying to seduce him. But the idea is hovering there, like something Drake can't quite see out of the corner of his eye. He hears Gabriel laughing as they flee the scene of some mischief they've caused, or watches the careful movement of Gabriel's hands as he sharpens his knives, and almost considers it anyway.

CHAPTER
SIXTEEN

O n the day of the Longest Night, it's wet and dreary, and they're
nearly out of coal again, but instead of going to buy more,
Gabriel insists they head nearer to Market.

"You have plans for the holy day?" Drake asks, hands stuffed in
his pockets and his head down against the wind-swept rain.

Gabriel nods as he hurries them up the street. "Doesn't everyone?
What would you be doing if you were still with your own people?"

"Feasting," Drake says. *Dancing*, he almost adds, except that he
doesn't want to explain how dragons dance. "There'd likely be songs.
When I was little, I used to try to stay up until the dawn." He never
managed to last the whole night, not with a warm bed and a warmer
fire, but he always meant to.

"You surprise me so often, Drake. I never expect you to be so
similar."

Similar to what? Drake wonders. Gabriel pushes open the door to
the Red Ox tavern, ducking into the heat and the welcoming scent of
spiced wine. Black Mother, how Drake's missed spices.

But Gabriel doesn't get a table, doesn't even take one of the empty
seats by the bar, just walks up to it and waits for the barkeep to come
over. "Whiskey," he says. "One bottle." He lays three shillings across
the worn oak of the bar.

The barkeep's eyebrows raise a bit—the Ox isn't bad, but it's not
that nice a tavern—but he nods. "One moment, gents, while I fetch
the bottle you're after."

Gabriel nods, waiting patiently, watching the room in general
and still not sitting down. Nobody, Drake notices, is looking at them.
He's not sure if it's because they're so ragged, or if they've become so
notorious that people know their faces.

"Are we not staying, then?" Drake asks.

Gabriel shakes his head distractedly. "You know in the northlands this is New Year's Eve?"

"I didn't." Drake tries to think like Gabriel for a moment. They're not staying at the Ox because in the northlands it's New Year's Eve on the Longest Night. "You want to go call on Deirdre?"

Gabriel beams. "I knew you'd like the idea. She'll be expecting me. I always spend it there."

"That explains why the whiskey's so good." An evening at Deirdre's is no midwinter ball, but it'll be nice to have company for the holy day all the same. He pictures himself explaining to Danny that he spent the Longest Night in the company of a northlands barbarian and an infamous cutthroat, and has to chuckle.

"She'll know the difference," Gabriel says as the barkeep comes back with the bottle. The glass is green, the sealing-wax red: both signs of northlands make. "Thank you." Gabriel takes the bottle, tucks it carefully under his coat. "Shall we?"

"After you," Drake says. He's not really had time to get warm yet, but he doubts that staying in here for longer will make him *more* interested in going back out into the cold. They might as well go now, so they can be sure to arrive before sunset. It's bad luck, he's heard, to stay out after dark on the Longest Night; it's the last night of the year that the Green Lady is free to walk the world of the living. He decides not to mention that to Gabriel, just in case it gives him any ideas about wandering the street all night trying to encounter her face-to-face.

As they head south, away from the river again, they pass a few determined groups of revelers carrying torches that sputter and reek of lamp oil, singing the sunrise-returning songs Drake learned in childhood. *Hail! Fire bright and high*, he hears as they pass one group, and the tune sticks in his head, so that he catches himself humming it as they make their way to Deirdre's little house in the deepening gloom.

When he stops at her door and raps on the window, the last of the light outside is fading. There's a lamp lit inside, though, and he can hear footsteps.

"You're late," Deirdre says when she opens the door. "I was starting to think you'd made other plans."

"Never." Gabriel produces the bottle. "I had to find a gift for you, is all."

Deirdre's eyebrows rise. "Keeping such highborn company's been good for your manners, I see." She takes the bottle and steps back to let them through the door. "Welcome to you both. It's been a while. How've you managed to stay out of trouble for so long?"

"It's all Drake's fault," Gabriel says as they follow Deirdre into the house. She has a fire burning in the front room, and there's a rack in front of it where Gabriel hangs his coat. "He's clever, so we get away more."

"Good to have someone talking a bit of sense into you, at any rate," Deirdre says.

Drake hangs up his coat too, to dry by the fire, and follows Deirdre and Gabriel into the kitchen. The stove's going in there, fire crackling away in its iron belly and a pot on top of it, full of something that smells wonderful.

Deirdre catches the look on his face and laughs. "Don't get your hopes up too much. He was a tough old bird before he went in the pot. He's been stewing since midday to try to coax a little tenderness into him."

"I've no doubt it'll be delicious," Drake says, and means it.

"And besides that, it's tradition," Gabriel adds. He reaches for the handle on the lid of the pot, and then pulls his fingers back, shaking them.

"Tradition?" Drake says. He looks at Deirdre. "Gabriel says you two do this every year."

"Older tradition than that. Something I remember from being a girl in Diere." Deirdre takes three earthenware dishes down from their shelf and sets them on the table. Before she touches the pot lid, she gets a rag to guard her hand. Steam rises from the pot when she opens it. "On the last of the year, you kill the oldest rooster in the flock." She sets the pot in the middle of the table, and fetches some dulled silver and a heel of dark bread. "You pluck him, clean him, and boil him until you've drawn out all the strength left in his old bones."

Gabriel leans over the pot, spearing something on one of his knives and lifting it out onto his plate. "That way," he says, satisfied, like the idea pleases him, "you take his strength with you into the new year."

"I see," Drake says. It's a morbid thought, but no worse than baking death's-head cakes for children on the Lady's holy day. He probably sounded doubtful just now, and he hopes Deirdre won't take offense to that. "Thank you for making it for us." It's easier to believe in Gabriel's dragons and trolls and the like when he's here, and a little extra politeness never harmed anyone in that sort of tale.

"Probably hard to make a dragon stronger," Gabriel says as he fishes more food out of the pot.

"Easy to make him less hungry, though." Drake takes a fork to start claiming some for himself before Gabriel gets all the choicest bits.

The bird's cooked so long that it falls apart almost as soon as they poke at it, coming off the bones into a thick, heavy broth. There are tiny onions and chunks of turnips, and flecks of some savory herb, and Deirdre brings out a big wooden spoon so they can ladle the broth into their dishes along with the meat. It's the best meal Drake's had in months, filling and flavorful and hot. He almost believes that he can feel the strength he's supposed to gain from it seeping into his blood.

When they've emptied the pot and wiped their plates clean with the last of the bread, Deirdre takes up the lantern from the shelf above the stove and turns toward the door. "Now, if you'd care to come with me, I've a fire that needs tending." She picks up the whiskey bottle in her other hand. "And a mind to share what you've brought me, if you'll take a drink or two."

"I wouldn't turn it down," Drake says, and only after that thinks to look over at Gabriel to be sure he hasn't given offense.

Gabriel's smiling back at him, the quiet, dreamy smile that means his head's full of dragons again. "I'd like that. Fire in the hearth and fire in the bottle." He laughs. "And fire in your belly."

"Yours too," Drake says as he gets up from the table. "Let's go."

He can feel Gabriel behind him, too real a warmth to be simply imagined, as they leave the kitchen for the . . . it would be a parlor, Drake supposes, if Deirdre's house were fine enough for that sort of thing. There are two lit lanterns, a moth-eaten sofa, and the drying rack put aside so Deirdre can kneel by the brick fireplace to coax new flames from the logs that have burned down to coal there.

"I wondered about that," Drake says. "The extra fire. It seemed like having two of them—" He stops, realizing he may be about to insult Deirdre's poverty. They're worse off than she is, but he wasn't always, and it seems impolite.

"No, you're right." She feeds another log into the fire. Her skin and hair are the same color in its light. "If it weren't the new year's eve, I'd not bother with this, and let the kitchen stove give me heat for the night."

"Another tradition?" Drake asks. Out of the corner of his eye, he sees Gabriel curling up on one end of the sofa, knees drawn to his chest, boots resting on the edge of the seat.

"The most important one," Deirdre says. "As the days grow shorter, Mathyn Bright-Shining turns away from us. We burn the fires all night tonight in honor of his birth-day tomorrow, and to remind him we want him to return."

"You should tell his story," Gabriel says. "I haven't told Drake that one, because you tell it much better." He sounds quiet, petulant, younger than he has in weeks. Drake frowns at him, worried he might have a fit coming on, but he's still, calm, almost at peace. He watches the fire, and it shines in the black of his eyes.

"For that," Deirdre says, "we'll definitely want the whiskey, to toast him." She sits down on the other side of the sofa and opens the bottle, and Drake, after a moment of hesitation, sits in the middle.

The story Deirdre tells is fantastical, strange, a long poem that she recites in an almost singing rhythm, the story of the golden warrior Mathyn, whose spear is the first ray of dawn or perhaps a bolt of lightning striking the earth, and his twin brother Senan, whose shield is the full moon and whose bow is the crescent. They hunt serpents that might be rivers, and quarrel with a woman made of crows, and pay court to girls as rich as the green hills and as endless as the sea. The whiskey bottle passes among them easily, catching the soft light of the fire. Gabriel shifts against Drake's side when Deirdre's voice rises in the telling of one of the brothers' great battles, and Drake leans into him without really meaning to. It's warm here, the fire and the whiskey and Gabriel wiry and solid against his side. If he could just hold on to this moment, he'd . . . he'd what, exactly? How has he grown so comfortable here?

"And their sons and daughters settled the whole of the free north," Deirdre finishes, "from the hills of Senmae to the seas of Mabvhein, from the snows of Aginau to the plains of Hanaein." Her voice cracks, and she lifts the whiskey bottle in a toast. "May it ever be so."

Drake lowers his gaze. He feels like he should be apologizing, even though he's not the one who caused her troubles.

"You should tell a story now, Drake," Gabriel says. He reaches across Drake for the whiskey bottle. "A dragon story."

"You don't want to tell one?" Drake asks. He suspects he knows the answer, but it might buy him some time.

"Deirdre's heard all my stories before." Gabriel drinks, and pushes the bottle into Drake's hand.

"Go ahead," Deirdre says. She waves as if to grant permission. "I've never heard any dragon stories."

Drake grimaces, takes a pull on the whiskey while he tries to come up with something. He thinks of the tales he remembers from nursery, all those stories about the quick wit of Fox. Gabriel always talks about how clever he thinks dragons are. "Have you heard the story about the dragon who stole a mountain?"

"No," Gabriel breathes, his eyes wide. Of course he hasn't; it's actually the story of why Fox lives in a manor house, but Drake thinks he can change it as he goes.

"Once, far away but not so far as all that," Drake begins, "there lived a dragon. He was young, as dragons go, and small for his age, because he was the last to hatch out of his—out of his brood. But he was quick and clever, and fared decently enough."

"What color was he?" Gabriel asks.

Drake hesitates. "Green."

Gabriel hums. "Not red?" He reaches up and pets Drake's hair.

"It isn't a story about me."

"Tell it anyway." Gabriel takes the whiskey back, and settles down with his head on Drake's shoulder after he's had some.

"When he—when he was old enough to go seek his fortune, he left the cavern where he'd grown up to go find a mountain of his own." He looks over at Deirdre, but she's just watching him, waiting. "He traveled for days and days, searching for a mountain he could claim. Someplace with steep heights for soaring around, and valleys where there might be sheep for him to eat, and a cavern where he could gather precious things to hoard." In the real story, Fox is looking for a fine enough house that Vixen will come to live with him, but Drake decides not to put that part in.

"Eventually, just when he thought he might have to give up and go home in disgrace, he found it—the loveliest mountain he'd ever seen, with a sharp peak reaching to the sky, and bright green meadows circled around the foot, and the inky black opening to a cavern on the sunniest side."

"Was there snow?" Gabriel asks.

"Yes," Drake decides. "Up at the very top of the mountain, there was a crown of snow. And the dragon knew that this was the mountain he wanted. But he was clever enough to know that some other creature probably also thought the mountain fine, and there was a good chance that cavern wasn't empty." In the story with Fox, the monster living in the manor is called Chameleon, but Drake doesn't know what that is, and he's sure Gabriel would ask. "So he asked the creatures he met near the mountainside, and all of them said the same thing: the cavern on the mountain belonged to a giant who could change his shape by magic, and no other creature in all the land was so cruel or so proud or so deceitful. It was— What are you doing?"

"Nothing," Gabriel says. He's holding on to Drake's shirt. "Keep going."

Drake takes another drink of the whiskey, feels the burn of it down his throat, and passes it to Deirdre as he picks up again. "The dragon was almost discouraged, because he was still too young and too small to be sure of himself in a fight against a giant. But it was the loveliest mountain he'd ever seen, and he'd win such renown if he could claim it for his own. So he gathered all his courage, and went up the mountain to the giant's cavern, which was even better than he'd hoped, with glittering, shiny rocks in the walls. But if the cavern was better, the giant was worse, sitting in a nest of bones and picking his nasty yellow teeth."

He's enjoying himself, Drake realizes. It's like boasting in a tavern, only a little easier, because Gabriel wants to believe. "The giant called out to him, demanding to know who dared to enter his cave. And the dragon showed all his teeth, which is a polite way of greeting someone, for dragons, and said that he had come from far away to see the giant that everyone spoke of. 'What do they say about me?' the giant asked, because usually he ate people up before they could say much at all." Drake feels silly when he realizes he's putting on a deeper voice for the giant, but he can't seem to help himself. "'They say you are the cruelest creature anyone has seen,' said the dragon. 'But how could anyone be as cruel as a troll?' The giant cursed and swore at the dragon, who only blinked back at him and showed his teeth, and at last the giant said, 'A troll! I can be every bit a troll,' and he turned himself into one, just like that."

Gabriel's gone so quiet, so still, that Drake thinks he might have fallen asleep, but he's watching intently when Drake glances down. "Keep going," he says.

"The dragon reared back, because the troll was truly frightful. 'They also say,' he said, 'that no creature is as proud. But how could anyone be as proud as a griffin?'"

"A what?" Gabriel asks.

"A griffin. It's an imaginary creature, half eagle and half cat, as big as a horse."

"Ah." Gabriel nods. "I'd seen pictures, but I didn't know what they were called. Thank you."

Drake smiles. "Of course. So the giant turned into a griffin, beating his wings, snapping his beak, and the dragon had to admit he was magnificent. 'Truly amazing,' said the dragon. 'And yet, I have also heard it said that you are deceitful, and where is the deceit in a mighty being like you taking the form of such terrible creatures? It would be true deceit to imitate something harmless.'"

"Oh, clever dragon," Gabriel says, and Drake can't tell whether he means the one in the story or not.

"So the giant, who was as stupid as he was cruel, turned himself into a black-faced valley sheep, and of course the dragon pounced on him, and ate him right up." It's a childish story, perhaps, but Drake's pleased with himself all the same. "And so the young dragon took over the mountain, and for all I know, he lives there still."

"Well told," Deirdre says, and Drake starts. He's nearly forgotten she was listening too.

"Thank you," he says, nodding to her.

"Are you sure you haven't any to add, Gabriel?" Deirdre asks. "Then we'd have gone round the circle."

Gabriel seems to grow smaller, hunching down beside Drake. "No."

"Nothing at all?" Drake says, reckless. His throat feels parched from speaking.

"Once there was a boy whose mother didn't want him, so she set him out for the Lady," Gabriel says quietly. "But She only kissed him and gave him back. The end."

"Gabriel?" The heat of the fire feels too close, uncomfortable all at once.

"The end," Gabriel repeats.

"The end of that story's never been told," Deirdre says. Drake doesn't think she's speaking to him. She gets up from the sofa. "You should sleep, if you can. I'll mind the fire."

"Here?" Drake asks.

Deirdre nods. "It'll be cold upstairs. This old house doesn't hold the heat so well." She kneels by the fireplace, stirring the half-burnt logs to coax up a spray of bright sparks. "Get some rest. You'll feel better in the morning, won't you, Gabriel?"

"I'm fine," Gabriel says, and burrows into Drake's side like they're back in their Cypress Street room and he really does need to be that close to stay warm.

"Sleep well," Deirdre says as Drake stretches out across the sofa's length, and Gabriel shifts to join him.

CHAPTER
SEVENTEEN

Despite the warmth and the relative comfort—still nothing like the goose-feather bed he had a lifetime ago in his parents' house, but so much better than the mat of straw they have now—Drake doesn't manage to sleep through the night. He wakes once to see Deirdre adding more wood to the fire, and again later to hear her humming a tune he thinks he might recognize as she sits by the fireside. She found them a blanket at some point while they slept; now Gabriel is solid and almost too heavy against Drake's side and the blanket holds the warmth in with them both. He can remember tiny scraps of his dreams—books with engraved illustrations of dragons drinking in taverns, northlands barbarians on some sort of sacred quest in the Cypress Street graveyard.

When he wakes for the third or fourth time, the room's gone from near-black to stormy-weather gray, and the fire has died down to a few red embers. Deirdre's gone—possibly in the kitchen, from the sound—and Gabriel is still asleep, wedged between Drake and the back of the sofa. He sighs when Drake shifts to get up, but doesn't wake. Drake eases his way off the sofa and tucks the blanket around Gabriel's shoulders before he heads into the kitchen.

The fire in the kitchen stove is burning brightly, and the kettle's on. Deirdre's sitting in the chair nearest the stove, her hands held out to warm them.

"Good morning," Drake says. "I'm surprised you're up so early. Did you sleep at all?"

"A bit here and there." It shows in her face, heavy shadows under her gray eyes. "It's only once a year. How's he doing this morning?"

Drake shakes his head. "Don't know yet. He's still sleeping." He chews his lip. "Haven't seen him get like that for a while."

Deirdre raises an eyebrow. "You *are* good for him, then, if he's holding it off more of the time."

Drake knows that shouldn't make him so pleased, but he can't help the little burst of warmth at the thought. "You think so?"

"There's another story behind almost any tale you hear," Deirdre says as she rises to measure tea for the pot, "and the one he told last night is no exception."

"And you know the story behind it?" He wants to hear it, possibly more than he can remember wanting to hear anything.

"I know parts, and I can guess others." Deirdre takes the kettle off the stove and pours water over the tea leaves. "The part I know for sure starts about ten years ago, when a boy named Raife and his friends, as nasty a little pack of children as you'll see, brought Gabriel to my door one winter morning—starving and feverish and weak as a runt kitten."

Drake feels something tighten in his chest, and wishes he could deny it. The idea of Gabriel being so lost, so weak— "How old was he?"

Deirdre shakes her head. "Seven or eight, maybe. Perhaps a bit older and just underfed. Hard to know for sure. Raife's gang had been seeing him around the Lady's house for a while, and I think they'd nearly talked him into running with them when the fever took him." Her face softens at the reminiscence, equal parts fond and pained. "They all used to bring their cuts and coughs and bruises for me to fix."

"Was it the fever that . . . made him like he is now?" He doesn't want to call Gabriel mad, he discovers. It might be true, but he doesn't want to say it.

"Nobody knows that," Deirdre says. "It might have been. Maybe he did meet the Lady, like he says. Maybe he was always touched, and that's how he wound up in the boneyard in the first place."

"You could always ask me," Gabriel says.

Drake starts. "Gabriel." The way Gabriel watches him, leaning in the doorway, is alert and predatory—more like a dragon than Drake's ever felt.

"Morning, Drake," Gabriel says. "It got cold, after you left." He sits down at the table. "Morning, Deirdre. Happy New Year."

"I'm sorry," Drake says. He licks his lips. "If I ask you, you'll tell me it was the Lady, won't you?"

"She chose me," Gabriel says. Today he sounds calm about it, casual as if it's no more important than whether there's honey for the tea. "And that was a clear enough sign that the woman who birthed me had done something awful." He picks up the teapot without a care for the heat of it, and pours himself a cup, the water still only pale golden and the leaves swirling to settle at the bottom. "She tried to give me back, but the Lady wasn't ready for me to come back yet. I've trouble to cause here first."

"Of course you do," Drake says. It's close enough to an answer, really. He can imagine the rest—some low-class woman from the docks or the south end, with a child and no husband to help her care for him, and then the boy turns out to be touched and more than a little dangerous. She probably thought she'd do less wrong by abandoning him than by smothering him in his bed. It's a sign of what this life is doing to Drake that he can almost see the sense in a choice like that.

"Now you've heard mine," Gabriel says, picking up his tea. "I'm still waiting to hear yours."

"What, the one that starts, 'Once there was a spoiled rich brat who had no idea what fine things he had'?"

"*Tch*, that again." Gabriel rolls his eyes, but his tone is fond. It's going to be one of the good days, then, the ones where everything's an adventure instead of an ordeal.

Drake stretches, trying to ease out the sore muscles from sleeping twisted up on the sofa. "We should go down to the docks today. See if there's work, or if there's a game to sit in on."

"Mmm." Gabriel holds his cup in both hands, breathing in the steam from his tea. "Feeling lucky today?"

"I am." Drake reads more of his luck than he should in Gabriel's eyes these days, but most often it doesn't steer him wrong. It's a new year today, in the north at least, and Gabriel's alert and clearheaded, and that's luck enough.

CHAPTER
EIGHTEEN

There's nobody looking to hire them in the dockside taverns, it turns out, which is just as well. The cobbles are still slick from the previous night's rain, and the sky's dark with the threat of more. It's a good day to spend inside, instead of tromping across the city on the hunt for someone who's trying not to be found.

So they find a card game, and Drake's luck does hold—it's a bluffing game, and he plays recklessly, not even trying to school his face to calm. He thinks of Gabriel's moods instead, of the way Gabriel's constantly changing, always giving away too much and nearly always misleading with most of it. He's inventing himself, he thinks, making up a Drake who's wild enough to keep company with Gabriel, who laughs at losing hands as much as at winning ones, who knows there's no way for this table to *defeat* him, whatever happens to his coin. It's the best time he's had gaming in ages.

Their luck stays good straight on through Casmile's own New Year, a fortnight later at the new moon—so good that Drake thinks he may change his mind about Lord Dunsmuir's party after all. Gabriel's getting better because of him. Deirdre noticed. They can go for just a little while, and see how Danny, at least, is doing.

The last night of the old year is a quiet one in Casmile—like a deathbed, it's no place to celebrate. The parties all come at week's end, once the new year has started safely. The weather even relents this year, the rain stopping the day before the parties happen so the day itself is cold and bright and clear.

Drake's still debating the idea with himself, unsure if he should bring it up at all, or if Gabriel cares enough to remember when the party's supposed to be, for that matter. There are still so many things about the way Gabriel deals with the world that he only half understands.

"I imagine," Gabriel says in the middle of the afternoon, as they sit on the stone rails of the Willow Street Bridge and make decent people uncomfortable, "you're looking forward to seeing your friends."

"What?" Drake says.

"At this party tonight. Don't tell me you've forgotten."

"Of course not." That settles it—if Gabriel has his wits about him enough to know what day it is, then he's not likely to be dissuaded. Which leaves Drake in the uncomfortable position of figuring out whether he *is* looking forward to it; there are so few people he misses from his old life, and the one he'd most like to see again—Anna— won't be attending the New Year celebration of a known rake and scoundrel. "I just . . . hadn't been thinking about them, really."

Gabriel looks sideways at him. "Not even that boy who asked you to come?"

"No," Drake says, which isn't quite true—he does still think of Danny sometimes, if only to feel guilty about the way Danny turned out to be so much more smitten with him than he realized—but close enough to true, mostly. The other acquaintances he's left behind feel like a blur of bright colors and easy, empty banter, dance steps that Drake—Colin—never liked enough to be good at, and scandals that seem so trivial now he can barely remember them. What does he have in common with any of his former peers, now that he has no finery and little coin? "I suppose it'll be interesting," he says. "I wonder if they'll even recognize me."

"I'd recognize you anywhere." Gabriel lets that statement hang just long enough that Drake starts to try to find an answer, then shrugs and goes on, "But your people might not be so clever. It's a very good disguise, being something they want to not see."

Drake watches the river, a tangle of leaves drifting along with the current. "I suppose it is."

They set out for the party just after sunset, heading up to the far side of town—north of the river, north of Market, too far west for the chaos of Kestrel and Kite. The houses here have wrought-iron fencing in front of their lawns, and there are lanterns burning in the front windows nearly everywhere to complement the lamps on the street.

Drake had almost forgotten what a fully lit street looks like—there aren't even lamps on Cypress, and where Deirdre lives is a bit nicer but the lamps still aren't often lit; thieves drain the oil near as often as anyone should fill them.

There's the guard to fret about, too, though Drake hasn't seen any patrols yet. He used to feel reassured by the knowledge that they were always near, but now the idea raises his hackles. He and Gabriel have no good excuse for being here, none that anyone would believe.

He doesn't remember the number of the Dunsmuirs' townhouse, but he's sure he can find it by sight once they reach Starling Street. And he's not disappointed—he remembers the spreading magnolia in the front, its leaves still glossy in the dead of the year, and the open gate and bright windows make him sure he's right. They stop in the great tree's shadow as a carriage pulls up to the front walk, spilling out a laughing young couple that Drake thinks he should know. He could be there. He could be doing that, coming to this party without a care in the world, ready for it to be the most exciting thing he's done in a season. That could be his life too. He can't quite bring himself to long for it.

Instead he's here in the dark, watching the young couple present their invitation and be escorted into the house. His breath fogs in the chill air, and he can feel Gabriel beside him, the prickling sense of anticipation when Gabriel's almost close enough to touch.

"I'm not so sure about this," Drake says. "Maybe we shouldn't go." He feels unsettled, his nerves jangling, like there's a fight in the making. This isn't his world anymore, but some leftover shred of decorum makes him hideously conscious of how out-of-place they are.

"Don't be afraid," Gabriel says. "I'm not going to let anyone hurt you." There's a glint of light in his hands for a moment. A knife. Sweet Mother Ket, this is going to be a disaster.

"Wait," Drake says, but Gabriel is slipping into the shadows on the side of the house, and what choice does Drake have but to follow? Gabriel stops. "What now? Are there dogs?"

"No. I mean, he has hunting hounds, but there's no reason for them to be in town. It's just—would you at least put the knife away?"

They stand there for a moment staring at each other. Faint music carries through the windows. Drake can imagine the swirl of skirts and lace as people dance.

"For you," Gabriel says at last. "But I will hurt them if they cause you trouble."

"Please don't," Drake says. Gabriel starts moving again and Drake has to hurry to keep up, to make himself heard. "They won't be expecting us at all, and I wouldn't blame them if they were upset."

"You're so kind, Drake."

Kind. Drake follows Gabriel around to the back of the house, not sure where he would begin to argue that description. Anna must miss him at least as badly as Danny does, and he hasn't sent her word even to tell her he's alive. His parents are surely worried. And here he's spent the last few months breaking bones, and worse, at Gabriel's side.

And yet . . . the part Gabriel plays on jobs is usually the nastier one, but he's been nothing but kind to Drake.

Behind the Dunsmuir house is a small brick-laid courtyard, delicately railed like a porch, its posts topped with lamps that have been lit even though it's too cold for the party to spill outside. The garden is orderly, mostly trimmed back for the winter; it doesn't offer any good places to hide.

Gabriel hops up on the railing and perches there, crouching with his head cocked to one side like a crow's, watching people move on the other side of the glass doors. His fingers drum against his knees. Drake wonders if he's nervous, if he's decided that the other partygoers are also dragons by virtue of Drake knowing them. Or having known them, anyway.

"We don't have to go," Drake says softly. "It looks awfully boring, doesn't it?"

And then, of course, Danny comes to the door, a glass of pale golden wine in one hand as he peers out into the dark. His eyes widen, and he unlatches the door to step out onto the bricks.

"Colin," he stage-whispers, nowhere near as stealthy as he probably thinks. "You came after all! I was so worried you wouldn't make it, after—"

Drake vaults over the railing, mostly to get between Gabriel and Danny. "I told you last time, that's not my name anymore. It's Drake."

"Right," Danny says. "I know." There's a flush to his cheeks, either from the cold or from the wine he's already drunk. "I just— Fates, you look like you're wasting away. Can you come in long enough to eat, at least? I'm sure Sebastian wouldn't mind."

"That's very kind of him," Gabriel says.

Drake puts a hand on Gabriel's shoulder. "We shouldn't, and you know it. But I wouldn't turn it down if you could bring some food out here." Really, after dealing with Gabriel's unreasonable demands for months, Danny's seem downright simple.

Danny pulls a pained expression. "I wish you'd come in. It's frightfully cold. But you promise not to leave, if I go get you food?"

"We promise," Gabriel says.

It's clear he was hoping for Drake to answer, but Danny nods all the same. "I'll be right back."

"Nobody certainly likes you, Drake," Gabriel says when the door closes again. The lamplight shines in his eyes. "What did you do to him, anyway?"

Plenty of things, Drake thinks, that he doesn't want to tell Gabriel about right now. "He's just—just friendly. And that's good, isn't it? We'll get a meal out of it."

Gabriel looks away from him, shrugging to get Drake to let go of his shoulder. "You keep so many secrets."

"I'm sorry," Drake says. Gabriel doesn't answer. If he were feeling more clever, Drake supposes he could invent some kind of story about who and what Danny is, but that seems likely to get him involved in Gabriel's private story world, and Drake doesn't want that. So they wait in silence, in the cold, and inside a minuet ends and a waltz begins—trust Sebastian to ask his musicians for the newest and most scandalous dances—and Drake can't decide whether he'd rather be at the party or not.

When Danny gets back with the food, that almost sways him: there are slices of roast duck, and mushroom caps stuffed with herbs and cheese, and rings of grilled sweet pineapple oozing juice across the plate. "Here," he says as he hands over his bounty. "You look like you haven't had a good meal in weeks."

"Haven't had anything like this in longer than that," Drake says. Gabriel takes a slice of duck off the plate; Drake has just enough manners left to ask, "How have you been?" before he does the same.

"It's been awfully boring without you. I haven't gone out anywhere exciting since before we went on holiday, and the things people are saying about you—the things the *captain* says about you!—are dreadful and monotonous both at once, and I'd swear I've nearly gotten in fights over you half a dozen times since we got back from Nothwn, *and* every time there's any sort of social, my parents and Julia's have their heads together, which means they're probably talking about a *wedding*, and who's going to stand witness for me if you aren't around?" He takes a deep breath—talking too much and too fast, like he always does when he's nervous—and adds, "Maiden bless, you must have been starving."

Drake watches Gabriel fumble with and claim the last of the pineapple. "It turns out it's not as profitable as you'd hope, being a cutthroat."

Danny makes an aggrieved noise. "You're not a—" he starts, and then stops. "There's more inside," he says instead. "Plenty more, really. Nobody would miss it."

"Is there, now," Gabriel says. He stares at Danny, hard, while Danny chews his lip and fidgets. "Thank you." He jumps down from the rail and wipes his hand on his trousers. "I won't be long."

"Gabriel," Drake says, reaching after him, but Gabriel doesn't look back and Danny grabs Drake's arm instead.

"Wait," Danny says. "Please."

Drake's stomach does a nervous roll. "He's going to cause trouble in there, Danny."

Danny doesn't let go. "Is he hurting you?"

"What?" Drake blinks at him. "No," he says automatically, and then thinks about it for a moment and realizes it's true. Gabriel's occasionally terrifying and always hard to read, but he hasn't *hurt* Drake once. "No, he— We hurt other people, most of the time."

"You're exaggerating," Danny says, and it sounds like a question.

"I wish I were. I met Gabriel when—" But if he starts to explain who was after Gabriel that night, he'll wind up talking about Morgan, and he doesn't want to do that; mostly he manages to just not think about it, but he knows it would make Danny worry more. "In a tavern brawl, when my father had thrown me out over—" Does Danny know about Barron's thugs coming to the house? "Over my gaming habits, and it's a long story, really, more than I have time for, but we *have* done a lot of awful things together, and Captain Westfall did see us in a fight where I think we killed someone." *I'm something else now*, he doesn't add. *Something that doesn't belong in your world.*

Danny curls his hand in the worn fabric of Drake's jacket. "But it wasn't you, was it?"

Drake looks away. He can't afford to be doing this, not when Gabriel's inside and clearly ready to cause trouble tonight. "What if it was?"

"I mean—" Danny steps in close, wraps his arms around Drake's back, presses his cheek to Drake's. "Lady's shroud, Colin, you're freezing," he murmurs. "I mean, it doesn't have to be, does it?" His breath is warm against Drake's ear, and he's trembling. "If you said it wasn't you—if you said he was the killer, and asked the mercy of the court. Julia's family helped get Judge Colburn appointed, I'm sure we could talk to him and—"

"And *what*?" Drake tries to pull back, but Danny hangs on. "You want me to send Gabriel to hang for something I've done?"

"*Listen* to yourself," Danny pleads. "He's a killer, isn't he? Whether or not you say so. It won't change anything for him. But you could come home again. Even if he didn't get—even if nothing happened to him." He presses his lips to the line of Drake's jaw. "Please, Colin. Come home."

Drake tries to imagine what that would even be like, how he'd feel sleeping in his own bed again and eating like this every night; paying court to a well-bred girl, and taking on more of the plantation's management, and not getting in any more fights or gambling for pennies on the docks or facing down men who've been killers all their lives. It feels like he's two different people, Colin and Drake, the rich boy and—and the dragon. "Danny, I . . ."

As he hesitates, trying to order his thoughts enough to give any answer at all, there's a crash from inside, and someone screams. Danny flinches, and Drake pulls away.

"Don't," Danny says as Drake heads for the door. "Leave him be."

"I can't do that." Drake pushes the door open.

The musicians have stopped playing, the dancers crowding back around the edges of the room. There's a table overturned on the far side, near the fireplace, and food spilled across the floor—the duck carcass, half a ham, sweet honey rolls. In *front* of the overturned table, in a large clear spot on the floor, Gabriel is kneeling over a young man Drake thinks he should know—Brent? Brett? something like that—holding the carving fork like a weapon, its tines pressed to the soft skin under possibly-Brett's jaw. He's not pushing—yet—just watching the boy try not to panic. One of Brett's friends has a bloody nose.

Out of the corner of his eye, Drake sees motion: Sebastian pushing through the crowd, coming closer. Drake curses under his breath. There are too many things going on here.

"Not such fun after all, this party," he says to Gabriel, crossing the room with his tread as heavy and certain as he can make it.

"Bored already?" Gabriel asks without looking up. His voice has the unpleasant flatness it gets when they've cornered someone on a job. "I'd have thought you could keep yourself entertained here for longer."

"You know how it is when you get something you thought you wanted, and it turns out not to be right after all." The escape they want is behind them, and it makes Drake's hackles rise that he can't watch both that and Gabriel at the same time.

"I don't." Gabriel shakes his head. "My Drake is so fickle."

Movement by the table makes them both look up—and Gabriel pushes just slightly, enough to get a fearful noise and some squirming out of the boy under him.

The friend with the bloody nose has drawn a gold-hilted dagger, his eyes wide, his hand unsteady. Drake puts his hands in his pockets, touches brass, and steps between the man and Gabriel's little tableau.

"That's not doing anyone any good," Drake says. "A real fight's much nastier business than sessions in the salon. You ever cut up anything more dangerous than a crown roast?"

"I'm not scared," the man says.

Drake smiles. "Funny." He can't be the rich boy here, now, but if he's the dragon, he thinks he can bluff their way out of here. "Me neither." He watches the way the man's eyes flick from him down to Gabriel and relaxes, just a little. They've won this, as soon as the rest of the room notices. "And if you put that down, nobody has to bleed out on the floor tonight."

"Spoiling all my fun," Gabriel says. Without looking at him, Drake can't tell if it's real petulance or if he's just playing at being bloodthirsty. They're both acting like they're working right now.

"What do you think, Brett?" Drake says. There's a little murmuring from the partygoers, and he tries to tune it out. "Should we be on our way?"

The poor boy makes a strangled noise that sounds a lot like a plea. Drake raises an eyebrow at the friend: *Do you want to make things worse for him?*

"Please," someone says from the crowd, a girl, and Drake would look if he could spare the attention—and the man drops his gaze, mutters a curse Drake can't make out as he tosses the dagger away.

"Good choice," Drake says. They need to hurry. Someone must have gone for the guard. "Gabriel?"

"After you, Drake."

Drake steps backward until he can see Gabriel again—reaching down into Brett's pockets—and then turns to make sure their exit is clear. Danny's standing by the door, looking stricken, and Sebastian is beside him, watching Drake with the cool little half smile he always wore at the gaming table. "Terribly sorry about this," Drake says.

"Think nothing of it. You'll be the scandal of the season." Sebastian winks. "I won't tell our dear friend the captain I saw you, but I can't promise the same for my guests."

"You talk too much," Gabriel says. He pushes past Sebastian and wrenches the door open.

"Happy New Year," Sebastian calls after them as Drake follows. How, Drake wonders, did he ever have the patience for that nonsense?

CHAPTER
NINETEEN

G abriel takes a jagged, purposeful route back to the water, moving at a steady wolf-trot, and it's not until they're crossing the bridge—Drake's not even sure which bridge, in the dark—that Drake catches up with breath enough to ask, "What was that about?"

Gabriel makes an angry spitting noise, and slows to a brisk walk. "I don't care for them much, these friends of yours."

"Right now, honestly, I don't either," Drake says. He hurries to keep up. Was it always that . . . hollow? That obnoxious?

They take a few more turns, and even if Drake isn't sure of the street names, he can tell by the steady downhill slope that they're headed more or less toward home. They turn from one half-lit street down a crooked little alley, and a dozen steps from the next block Gabriel pivots all at once, lunges for him, and shoves him up against the wall, knocking the breath from him.

"I think you've been lying to me, Drake."

Drake holds very still, resisting the urge to deny it immediately. Gabriel's hands are on him, thin and hard, clenched in his jacket and curled around his shoulder. So far he hasn't drawn a knife, and Drake wants to keep it that way. "Lying about what?" he asks. He wishes he could see Gabriel's expression better.

"Your friend Nobody." Gabriel's voice is low and urgent, fierce, the flat coldness from earlier completely gone. "He does matter after all, doesn't he?" His hands knead at Drake's clothes, at his shoulders, hard enough to hurt.

"I'm sorry," Drake says. Of all the bizarre things for Gabriel to find upsetting. "He's—he used to be a good friend of mine." Here he was expecting the problem to be something outlandish and touched—Gabriel deciding not to believe in dragons after all, maybe, after the banality of that scene—and instead it's—

Gabriel presses Drake's back into the wall, like he's trying to hold Drake still with the weight of his body. He feels so lean, bone just under his skin. So *fragile*, despite how dangerous he is. "I won't let him take you away," he whispers. "I won't. You've made things better. I don't want you to go."

Black rot. Instead it's serious.

"I'm not going anywhere." Drake reaches up, slowly, and rests one of his hands on top of Gabriel's. "I'm still here. You don't have to worry."

"I'm not *worried*," Gabriel says, and his voice cracks unhappily. His grip doesn't ease. "I'm just. I don't need you. But you should stay. It's better. Warmer. Less hungry. I don't lose so many days." He lets go of his death grip on Drake's shoulder, as if it's an effort, and pets Drake instead, too hard, still as much of a plea as before. "Your Nobody wants to steal you away."

"Nobody's— I'm not going to let anybody steal me," Drake promises. It's tricky to phrase things right, with Gabriel in a mood like this. "I'm not a thing to be stolen, and I'm here with you on purpose." He rests his other hand on Gabriel's back and strokes, carefully, and thinks about how strange this is, how close to an embrace. "Let's go home, Gabriel. I'm tired. I want to go to bed."

Gabriel slumps a little, leaning his forehead on Drake's shoulder. "You're right," he says after a minute. "This night is no good. We should sleep." He lets go of Drake and steps back. "Lead the way home."

This is probably another test, either to see if Drake does know his way back or if he's willing to call the Cypress Street room home—but that's all right. He can do this. Even with Gabriel at his back and clearly in a reckless mood. He keeps to the smaller streets, avoiding people as much as possible. He doesn't want to deal with anyone right now, and he doubts Gabriel has much patience left, either.

Gabriel doesn't say a word to him all the way back home, and when they get there, he sits on the mattress, silent, staring into the corner while Drake fumbles in the dark to light the stove. When the fire catches and there's light enough to see, Drake thinks perhaps the look on Gabriel's face is melancholy, like whatever fit it was that made him angry earlier has passed, and now he's just worn down. He looks miserable.

Drake shuts the stove door so the light won't keep them awake, and crawls over to the mattress. "Good night, Gabriel," he says as he takes his boots off.

"Oh," Gabriel says, and shakes himself. "Yes." He kicks his boots off and crawls under the blanket, facing away from Drake, pressing close to the wall. "Good night."

Drake hesitates. He should just leave this be, and in the morning things will be normal again, or as normal as they ever get where Gabriel's involved. He's already too close, too tangled up in Gabriel's world.

But thinking like that only makes him ashamed of himself. Gabriel has tried to be good to him. So instead of turning his back, Drake reaches out and rests one hand on Gabriel's shoulder, carefully, gently. Gabriel doesn't move at first—and then he grabs Drake's wrist and pulls, dragging him closer and holding Drake's hand to his chest. His grip is tight, his fingers cold. His breathing shakes.

"It's all right," Drake whispers. "Sleep well."

"Thank you," Gabriel says softly. "I will."

But Drake lies awake in the dark for a long time, and he doesn't hear Gabriel's breathing settle into sleep.

When he wakes in the morning, it's to the smell of damp wood and plaster, and the faint patter of the leak over by the window as rain drips onto the floor. It's light enough outside that he can see fairly well, and he finds he's looking at the curl of dark hair against the dusty skin of Gabriel's neck. Since he came here, he's grown better at keeping still when he sleeps—moving around a lot just risks losing the blanket—and now it seems he's spent the entire night holding Gabriel.

It's a sobering thought. After last night—after last night, he thinks maybe he's been trying too hard not to see the obvious. In anyone else, anyone normal, that episode after the party would have seemed like a fit of jealousy, and Gabriel is touched but he's still human. He might not act on it the same way that other people do, might not know how to show it, but it's strange to think that Gabriel might want to be . . . might want to . . . Drake can't even finish the sentence in his head. It's going to lead him to doing something he can't take back, if he keeps thinking like that.

Gabriel stirs and stretches, making a sleepy, mumbly noise. "Drake?" he asks. "Have you been there all night?"

Drake swallows. "I have."

"You're very warm." Gabriel turns over onto his back, which takes a lot more squirming than it should as he tries not to slip out from under the blanket himself.

"Thank you," Drake guesses. It seems like a safe answer. Gabriel looks over at him, alert but calm now, and it's not so hard to meet his eyes this morning. "How are you feeling?"

"I don't want to go anywhere yet," Gabriel says. "You're not hungry, are you?"

He's always hungry in the mornings, but some days are worse than others. "Not much. I don't mind waiting."

"Good." Gabriel shifts under the blankets, and slowly— tentatively—lays his hand against Drake's side. "This is all right? I thought you didn't want me to. When you first came here, you got up and tried to leave, after."

Drake blinks. Gabriel has been waiting on *him*? "I barely knew you then," he protests.

"Hnn." Gabriel shakes his head. "You barely knew that whore, and you touched a lot more of her."

That was at least a month ago, and Gabriel hadn't seemed to be paying much attention at the time. Drake blushes, and hopes it's still too dark for Gabriel to see. "What about you? I thought you didn't like people touching you."

"Silly Drake," Gabriel says gently. "I don't like *people* touching me." His smile is wistful, sweet. "You're different."

That's reason enough to stop, and Drake knows it. Gabriel's mad, and Drake's not going to be much better if he keeps on like this. And yet—they say no man ever caught the Maiden's eye by playing his cards safely. Drake shifts, and Gabriel just watches him move, and his heart pounds as hard as it ever has when he leans across that last little distance between them and kisses Gabriel's mouth.

Somehow he hadn't thought that Gabriel would feel so *soft* against his lips, but the kiss is delicate and cautious, close mouthed. Gabriel doesn't react, not really, until Drake starts to pull back, and then his hand tightens on Drake's side and a tiny noise escapes his lips. Drake leans back in, and this time Gabriel tilts his head to meet the kiss, so Drake presses harder. When his tongue brushes Gabriel's lips, Gabriel takes a sharp breath like he's startled. His mouth opens uncertainly, and Drake feels dizzy—he's kissing Gabriel, and Gabriel is letting him. It's awkward and slow, as if Gabriel's still not sure about doing this, as if he doesn't know how, oh, Fates, that's a terrifying thought. Drake pulls him a little closer, carefully, and Gabriel clings to him, holding on tight. He leans into the kiss, deepening it—and yet the sounds he makes are tiny animal whimpers, like he's frightened, like he's in pain.

Drake pulls back. "Gabriel?"

Gabriel's eyes are wide and wary. "Why did you do that?"

"Why?" Drake repeats, more to buy himself time than anything. He's pretty sure Gabriel didn't mind, pretty sure he'd know in no uncertain terms if it really weren't all right.

"You see men do it to girls in taverns," Gabriel says, "and Nobody did it to you at the auction. But there isn't anyone here for you to show off to. So why did you do it?"

"Was—" Drake catches himself as he realizes what he nearly asked: *Was the Lady showing off when she kissed you?* But that's madness and no answer, either, and for all he knows Gabriel thinks she was. "It feels good. Isn't that reason enough?"

Gabriel stares at him for a moment as though *he's* the one who's touched, and then laughs. "Sometimes I almost forget how strange you are. How long do you think you would last here, if you just did whatever felt good?"

"All right." Drake tries to laugh, though it feels forced. "That's fair enough." It would lead to trouble in a hurry, that's for sure, with the guard as likely as anything else. Gabriel's hand is kneading at his side, the way a cat would, and it's hard not to squirm when it tickles. "But it was . . . I liked it."

"It means you want something," Gabriel says. "Even the Lady wanted something when she kissed me. What do you want, Drake?"

Drake imagines himself suggesting, for one giddy instant, that he and Gabriel mess around the way he and Danny used to, offering to reach into Gabriel's trousers and take hold of his cock and— He can't do it, can't bring himself to push his luck that far. The Mother only knows what Gabriel would think *that* means. "I want to do it again," he says instead.

Gabriel doesn't relax, not really, but he nods. "Go ahead." He does move this time, leaning into it as Drake presses their mouths together, and he keeps his eyes open, focused and dark.

Drake slides his arms around Gabriel, slowly, trying not to startle him. Then Gabriel's other hand clutches at his shoulder, and Gabriel's tongue slips into his mouth, and he forgets to worry. He leans into the kiss, feeling Gabriel press close against him, lean and bow-taut. He's hard already, aching, strung so tightly—there's been no one since the whore, and he hasn't even had time alone to take care of it himself, with Gabriel always there. If Gabriel—if they—if Gabriel makes any move to take this further, then he'll gladly go along with it. He's not quite foolhardy enough to push for it, but he wants—

Gabriel nips at his lower lip, digs bitten-short nails into his shoulder, growls in a way that sounds almost playful when Drake rocks against him. "You like this," he whispers, still close enough that his lips brush Drake's. "It makes you happy."

"You too?" Drake asks. He's shaking, lightheaded like he gets when they've just escaped from someone who nearly caught them stealing or when he used to bluff high on hands he had no chance of winning honestly.

Gabriel nuzzles him, biting delicately at the line of his jaw, the arch of his cheekbone. It's completely bizarre, but Drake would swear they're friendly bites, and somehow that's charming. "Yes," Gabriel says decisively. "I'm happy."

Drake smiles, letting the warmth swell in his chest, and for once not even fretting about it much. "Good." He rolls onto his back, pulling Gabriel with him, and—oh, sweet Black Ket, he can feel Gabriel hard against his hip. A shiver runs down his spine, and he tilts his head back, holding Gabriel right there.

"You *do* trust me," Gabriel says, his voice breathy and hushed, awed, and he lowers his head to nip at Drake's throat. Drake shudders, can't help it—Gabriel's teeth are sharp, and he doesn't do this with the finesse of a lover, softening the bites with lips and tongue. But it's good, those tiny spikes of pain just enough to make him feel really alive. "So soft." Gabriel's breath is hot on Drake's neck. "I never would have believed it." He bites right over the pulse point, and this time he does linger, his tongue soothing the viciousness of the bite, and Drake moans. He holds on to Gabriel's hips and rocks up, pushing, feeling the way Gabriel grinds against him, so hard, and—

And Gabriel lets go, rolls away from him. The blanket pulls free, and the air outside is cold.

"We can do that again later, if you want," Gabriel says matter-of-factly, like his eyes aren't dilated and his lips aren't flushed, "but first we should go get some food."

"What?" Drake says. "Now?"

"I'm hungry," Gabriel says, pointedly looking away, reaching for his boots.

"All right," Drake says slowly. It isn't really, but he's not sure how to point that out without making it sound like he's demanding that they—that Gabriel let him—no, there's no good way to say it at all. He pushes the blanket off the rest of the way and starts to pull his boots on instead.

CHAPTER TWENTY

B y the time they're halfway up Cypress—Gabriel's quiet, and Drake would rather be distracting himself with just about anything other than thinking about the cold rain dripping down the back of his neck—he's decided that Gabriel must not understand that there's a connection between kissing and screwing, that normal people move from one to the other. He's like one of those boys in the mountains that you hear about sometimes, who get lost when they're small and then raised by wolves. He *looks* normal enough—filthy, but normal—but he doesn't understand why people do ordinary things.

Some things, anyway. He knows how to find food, how to keep the other dangerous bastards on the street from hurting him, how to cut purses in a crowd. How to tell all kinds of fanciful stories. So maybe the comparison doesn't actually work that well. Maybe it's just sex he doesn't understand, and that's not so surprising, with how skittish he is around people.

"Have you ever had a whore?" Drake asks before he has a chance to think better of it.

"Once." Gabriel kicks a loose pebble up the street. "Well. Half a time."

He should know better than to ask these things. "Half a time?"

"Whores lie," Gabriel says. "I don't like being lied to."

Drake considers all the ways that could have ended and decides he'll be happier if he doesn't know. He snags a pebble from a pile of spilled stone that used to be the front column of a house, and tosses it from hand to hand a few times before he throws it at a cluster of pigeons huddled under another house's rotting eave. The pigeons flutter and squawk, but don't leave the relative safety of their perch.

"That's not how you catch pigeons," Gabriel says.

"You can catch pigeons?" Well. Of course you can, he supposes; most likely you can catch just about anything if you figure out how.

Gabriel squints up at the sky. "If the rain stops later, I'll show you."

"I look forward to it," Drake says, even if he's not completely sure. The rain stopping, at least, would be nice. And catching pigeons can't be any more unpleasant than tracking petty criminals through the rotting south city and hoping they're not being led into an ambush.

"You'll get spoiled," Gabriel says, with a little wry smile. "Meat for dinner twice in a row."

Oh. Of course that's why they'd catch pigeons. Gabriel's right; Drake still is the strange one. "Do they taste good?" His stomach twists, and he walks a little faster. The sooner they can get *some* food, the better.

Gabriel shakes his head. "So fancy. How am I supposed to keep up?"

"Don't worry about it," Drake says. "I'm sure they'll be fine." A pigeon is a little like a dove, isn't it? And in any case, it's food.

They get breakfast near the docks, and then spend the better part of the day in taverns, drinking warmed cider as slowly as they can and sitting as close to the fire as there are seats free. It's more expensive than just buying coal for the stove, especially because each place wants to toss them out after an hour or two when they're not in any hurry to spend more coin—but the fires in the tavern hearths burn hotter than their little stove, and sometimes there's a sailor ashore telling stories about Cabiral or Skadthia or some other place so far away that Gabriel probably doesn't believe in it.

And in the afternoon, when they leave the third place they've tried, the rain's tapered off and the clouds are starting to part. Instead of heading further up the row on Front Street, Gabriel turns into an alley. "Catching weather."

"You catch pigeons in alleys?" Drake asks. He's hungry again, and meat—any kind of meat, by now—does sound tempting.

"You can do it just about anywhere. But sometimes it upsets people and they try to make you stop." Gabriel finds a rain barrel with a lid on it, and climbs on top of it, reaching for the low overhang of the roof. "So it's better to do it out of their way."

Drake gives Gabriel a minute to clamber onto the slope of the roof, and then follows. "I wouldn't have thought you'd care about that. Upsetting people, I mean."

Gabriel grins. "Some kinds of upsetting people get you things. This kind just makes it harder to get the pigeons to hold still."

It shouldn't surprise him anymore when Gabriel starts to make sense. It's happening more all the time. "Well, I suppose we wouldn't want that."

"No." Gabriel crouches, staying low against the shingles as he crawls across the roof. "This way, Drake." He waits for Drake to catch up, almost, before he launches himself across the narrow alley nearly from a standstill, landing hard against the gentler slope on the other side.

This is trickier work when it's wet than it was back in the fall. Drake has to take a few deep breaths to steady his nerves before he can make the leap, and he still skids a bit on the landing—and Gabriel's hand whips out, catches him by the shoulder to steady him.

"Careful," Gabriel says.

Drake nods. "You ever fall?" The cobbles can't be easy to land on, and he imagines a broken arm would be terrible to bear, here especially.

"Never. Don't you do it, either."

"It's not something people do on purpose."

Gabriel shrugs. "Not falling *is*, though," he says, and heads for the next roof.

He's moving toward the docks—a little further south, hugging the edges of the row of buildings. Too much further and they'll come to Market, where the streets open wide and even Gabriel can't cross without falling.

They stop just before that, on a broad, nearly flat roof whose far side faces the square. Drake wonders what's below them, whose roof they're borrowing as a pigeon-catching vantage point.

"Now," Gabriel says, "don't move much. And definitely not fast." He takes something from his coat pocket—a scrap of bread, probably left over from breakfast—and starts to tear it into shreds. "I imagine you could do this with rats, too, if you were patient enough."

"Ugh." Drake nearly asks if Gabriel has eaten rats, but thinks better of it in time, for once.

Gabriel nods. "You'd want gloves, because they bite, and I don't think they'd fall for it enough times to make a filling meal."

"I'm just as happy to skip it," Drake says. "I don't think I'd care for eating rats."

"Cats either, I suppose." Gabriel scatters some of the bread crumbs across the roof. "Dogs? Snakes?"

Drake stares at him. "Not if I can help it."

"I thought snakes might be too close kin for dragons," Gabriel says. "They go away in the winter anyway, so it doesn't matter. Now don't frighten the pigeons."

"I won't," Drake promises. Is this what Gabriel would be doing without him? Eating rats and dogs and pigeons when he can catch them, without the money to buy any proper food? Facing the winter with no coat, without the presence of mind to save his pennies for coal?

The first of the pigeons are landing on the roof now, cooing and bobbing their heads as they find the bread crumbs. Gabriel holds one hand out, crumbs cupped in it, watching them with his head cocked sideways like he's a bird himself. He seems almost completely relaxed, still and calm as the pigeons hop closer, as the boldest one comes right up to his outstretched hand. He can't possibly be about to—

He moves so fast Drake doesn't even see it, just the flutter of gray wings and one sharp squawk that cuts off in the middle. By the time the rest of the flock has risen into the air, Gabriel is wringing the neck of his catch.

"Here." He tosses it to Drake. "Hide that one."

"Hide it?"

"They're not clever. They forget about trouble fast if they can't see it. Think it won't come back for them." Gabriel holds out his hand again. "Like Alan, last week."

"Even worse," Drake says, as the flock starts to settle at the edges of the roof and sidle closer again. "It took him, what, two nights before he went back to that whorehouse." The whorehouse was the worst part of that job. None of the girls looked older than twelve. It wasn't a *surprise*, really; Drake's gotten used to the idea that Casmile, Gabriel's Casmile, is full of more kinds of ugliness than he ever imagined before he came here. But remembering those girls made it a lot easier to get the job done when they caught up with Alan the second time, before he could make it in the door.

"Pigeons are much smaller," Gabriel says, quietly, so he doesn't spook the one examining his hand. "So maybe that was like two nights for them."

This time Drake is watching more carefully, and he sees it happen when Gabriel moves: the way his offering hand closes, catching the bird's legs as his other hand snakes out to grab it round the throat. His face is blank and calm when he kills it.

"One for you and one for me," Gabriel says as he tosses the second pigeon to Drake. "And I think we can still get more."

He catches two more pigeons before the rest grow too wary to come close again. "Just as well," he says, "since we're running out of bread to bait them."

That's plenty of this adventure anyway. It's growing dark already, and it's cold on the rooftops. Drake's more than ready to head home.

Once they get there, of course, they have to clean the damn things, plucking the birds awkwardly in the gloom and then gutting them with Gabriel's knife. They roast the pigeons, if that's even the right word for it, on sticks over the coal in their stove, until the skins blacken and the meat smells, if not appetizing, at least edible. It's oily and strong-flavored, but the meat's filling all the same. When he's finished his, Drake wipes his mouth on his sleeve, watching Gabriel strip the last meat from the bones before tossing them on the fire.

"Thank you," he says. He could still eat more—he thinks that's probably true all the time, these days—but he's not hungry anymore, and that goes a long way toward comfortable.

"You're welcome," Gabriel says gravely. "I'm glad it worked today." He seems calm still, stable, like the moon's in the right phase or the tide's at the right height or whatever it is that makes him sensible. And they've had a good day today. Maybe it's safe to ask about this morning.

"Why did you want to stop?" Drake asks. "You weren't just hungry." Gabriel's good at ignoring hunger. Fates know he's seen enough of it.

"Clever." Gabriel turns toward the stove, and looks back at Drake out of the corner of his eye. "It wouldn't have been polite, would it? Rubbing against you like that."

Drake has to laugh. "I didn't mind. I mean, I started it."

Gabriel shifts so he's watching Drake more directly, still crouched by the heat. "You're a riddle. Every time I think I know your answer, you're different."

"*Me*?" Drake says. He might not have dared, some other evening, but tonight the word escapes him with barely a thought.

And it's all right, because Gabriel only smiles. "Am I as bad as you? Truly?" He reaches out like he wants to touch Drake, and then pulls his hand back. "You're like a fire. Always changing. So warm."

"You're like," Drake starts. "No, that's the problem—you're *not* like anything else I know." He licks his lips, watching the way Gabriel's eyes shine in the low light of the stove, the way Gabriel waits for him. "I want— Will you let me kiss you again?"

"You still need to ask?" Gabriel shifts forward, crawls across the bare floor to lean into Drake's mouth.

It's still an awkward kiss, like Gabriel might be trying to bluff his way through but doesn't truly know what he's doing. Drake reaches up and cradles the nape of Gabriel's neck in his hand. Gabriel shivers, clutching at the front of Drake's shirt, catching skin between his fingers. He bites Drake's lip, rubs his face against Drake's like a cat.

"So soft," he whispers. "You feel so soft, Drake." His teeth scrape against Drake's jaw.

"Let's—let's get in bed," Drake breathes. He thinks he might not be able to stand it if Gabriel stops him again, might— No, he knows he *could*, knows he'll manage even if Gabriel wants to pretend this never happened, but Fates, he wants more.

Gabriel nods. "You want to . . . like this morning," he says, and it's so strange to hear him hesitate that Drake is thrown, for a moment, before he realizes what it means: Gabriel doesn't know what to call this, doesn't have a word for what they're doing here.

"Don't pull away this time." Drake can barely make himself let go for long enough to take off his boots, his jacket; he'll want to be able to move, want to be able to feel Gabriel there against him, oh Mother Ket, please. He crawls under the blanket and reaches out as Gabriel slides in beside him. "Don't pull away." His voice is a tight whisper. "It's all right if you want to—if you want . . ." and Gabriel kisses him again, as he falters in search of the courage to offer more.

Drake closes his eyes, presses close against Gabriel along the full length of their bodies, tangling their legs together. He catches himself leaning into the kiss, stops just before he actually pushes Gabriel onto his back. For all the assurances he's gotten tonight, he knows better than that. Instead he wraps his arms around Gabriel's waist, reaches up so he can dig his fingers into Gabriel's back, between the knobs of his spine and the hard wings of his shoulder blades, where the muscle is lean and taut.

"Ah," Gabriel says, holding on to Drake's shoulders. "Drake, what are you doing?"

"Does it feel good?" Gabriel nods. Drake kisses the soft hollow beneath his jaw. "That's what I'm doing. You do things to make me happy. Can't I do that for you too?"

Gabriel laughs, breathlessly, and reaches up to pet Drake's hair. "I want you to be happy so you'll stay," he says, like he's explaining himself, excusing his behavior. "Things are so good with you here."

Drake turns his head, kisses the inside of Gabriel's wrist, nips there experimentally, and feels his cock twitch at the way Gabriel's breathing hitches. It's vulnerability, he realizes at once. His throat, the inside of his wrist, the soft spots where he could be hurt. That he's willing to hold still and lower his defenses that far—it's dizzying.

"Gabriel," Drake whispers, his mouth still against those veins. "When you shiver like that, is it bad or good?"

Gabriel won't look at him, buries his face in the hollow of Drake's shoulder. "Good," he whispers, his breath hot against Drake's neck. "Good because it's you."

Drake moans, rolls onto his back and pulls Gabriel on top of him. He arches up, mouths at Gabriel's throat, bites, and this time sucks on that spot. Gabriel keens and rocks against him, and when Drake lets go, there's a mark there, bruise-red even against Gabriel's dusky skin.

"You want to," Drake whispers. Gabriel's as hard as he is. He can feel it against his belly, and his hands shake as he slides them down Gabriel's sides. "Please—please let me." He gets one hand between them, palm up, cups Gabriel through his trousers.

"Drake," Gabriel says, pushing into Drake's hand. His voice shakes. "Drake, Drake. Ah."

It *hurts*, Drake wants this so much. "Yes," he says. "Please, Gabriel. Can I—can I touch?"

"Do it," Gabriel says, low and fierce, needy. He arches his back, makes enough room between them for Drake to reach his trouser buttons. Drake pushes his own shirt up, out of the way, and fumbles Gabriel's trousers open. He's shaking all the way through. He's going to— He's about to— He's closing his hand around Gabriel's bare flesh, and Gabriel is thrusting into his touch.

"Yes," Drake says to the needy sounds Gabriel makes. "Yes, Gabriel—good, you feel good, I want you to," and Gabriel nods frantically, his grip too tight on Drake's shoulders, his hips rocking hard. For a heartbeat, Drake lets himself wonder what it would be like to take this further—to be pinned under Gabriel's lean weight like this, Gabriel thrusting above him, inside him—and then he's moaning too, terrified at how tempting that sounds, at how willing he would be to let Gabriel— Not now, though, not tonight, when Gabriel's already tensing over him, breath harsh and gasping, taut and desperate. He bites down hard on Drake's shoulder as he shudders, as he splatters Drake's belly with his climax. It hurts, but Drake swallows the protest as best he can.

"Drake," Gabriel says, "Drake," with the same fervent tone most men use to curse. He leans to the side, just enough so that when he collapses he's only tangled with Drake's legs instead of on top of him. "So good, my dragon. So clever."

"Thank you." Drake reaches down to unbutton his own trousers, to take himself in hand. He needs it so much. "I liked it. Fates, I liked it." He's already stroking himself when Gabriel's hand covers his. "Y-you will?"

Gabriel pushes his hand out of the way, takes hold of him. "Of course I will." His grip is firm, his hand callused, nothing like anyone else who's ever done this for Drake. It takes a few careful strokes before he finds a rhythm, but only a few, and then he's fast, confident, hard. It's almost too much, the rough treatment, but Fates, Drake's needed this for so long—he holds Gabriel close against him and pushes and pushes and feels the pleasure hum through him in a rush of golden heat as he spills.

He has to reach down to stop Gabriel, afterward, when he grows too sensitive and Gabriel doesn't seem ready to stop touching him yet. He can't find words, so he just lies still like that, his fingers laced with Gabriel's and his heart pounding.

"You make so many things better," Gabriel says softly. Admiringly, it sounds like.

Drake laughs. He's still giddy, though the tension's gone now. "I'm glad," he says. "That was so good."

Gabriel smiles, and lets go of his hand to pet him instead. Drake wipes as much of their mess off his belly as he can, and then has nothing to do with it but smear it on the floor. He should have brought up some water for washing, he supposes. Would have, if he'd known they would be doing this. He'll try to be better prepared next time.

Not now, though. Now there's no way he's getting up to go fetch water outside in the cold, when he could stay here instead and pull Gabriel into his arms again.

"My dragon is happy?" Gabriel asks. He tugs the blanket up to their shoulders, curls into Drake's side.

"Yes." He kisses Gabriel again, because it's still so amazing that he can. "Good night, Gabriel."

Gabriel tucks his head against Drake's shoulder. "Good night, Drake."

CHAPTER
TWENTY-ONE

They do it again in the morning, before they get out of bed, and Drake's pretty sure that the second time, Gabriel starts it. His neck feels sore, tender from too many bites, by the time they're done, but he can't complain. He catches Gabriel preening as they pull their boots and coats back on, like he's proud of himself.

Outside, where it's lighter, Gabriel squints at Drake, brow furrowed. "You never seemed so delicate," he says, reaching up to touch Drake's neck. His fingertips are chilled, and Drake flinches. "I've hurt you."

"I'm fine." Drake laughs weakly. "Left marks, did you?"

"Little red ones." Gabriel frowns. "If I bite too hard, you should say so."

"You didn't. I promise, it's fine."

Something wary and feral flits across Gabriel's face, and he straightens. "Come on. We should go."

He's moving before Drake can answer, heading down Cypress at a deliberate pace like he's going somewhere important. "Wait," Drake says. "Where are we going?" There's nothing *there* at the bottom end of Cypress, definitely no place where they can find food. Just more rotting houses, sinking into the swamp, and the Lady's house.

"Someone's after us," Gabriel says quietly. Drake's heart sinks. They'd been doing so well lately, with everything making sense and now last night. He should have known it couldn't last.

"Who?" he asks, hands in his pockets, trying to stay calm.

Gabriel shakes his head. "Men who know what they're hunting. Nasty ones. Turn here."

That makes it worse. Drake follows Gabriel's lead, turning off Cypress down some crooked alley too small to have a name. If the answer had been something fantastical, ogres or trolls or even the Lady's hound, it would have been easier to shrug off. They move faster now that they're off the main street, Gabriel's breath steaming silently in the cold morning air, his eyes alert and seeking. Drake finds himself listening, trying to catch some sign that their pursuers are real without seeming to be looking for them. There's a noise from behind that could be footsteps sliding on moss-wet cobbles, and a rustling from one of the empty houses that could be a rat or a man trying to be stealthy—and his heart is pounding despite himself, like he believes Gabriel's pronouncements whether or not he has evidence.

Then they make a turn and come to a pile of rubble where the street ought to be, where a house just slumped forward and collapsed across the road. Gabriel stops.

Drake watches him. There are questions at the tip of his tongue: *Now what?* and *Where are they?* But he doesn't say them, just waits. The hair stands up on the back of his neck. Something scrapes behind them.

When Gabriel moves, Drake's ready; he can see the tiny changes in stance that mean Gabriel's about to lunge. And that means he's moving, too, bolting with Gabriel toward the rubble, up onto the crumbling brick, and a knife strikes the stone where he would have been.

Someone curses behind them, but Drake can't spare a second to look back. "Circle round," the man behind them orders, which means there must be at least two more. "Don't let them get to clear ground."

Gabriel lands hard on the cobbles on the other side, and Drake with him only a heartbeat later. The shock thrums up his ankles, but he doesn't dare stop to fret about that now. He sprints for the mouth of the alley, his stride matched to Gabriel's, and at the next street, Gabriel says, "Split up," before he veers left.

Drake turns right, his heart pounding, and takes off. He doesn't like this, doesn't want to get separated when they don't know how many people are following, doesn't want to fight without Gabriel to watch his back—doesn't want to leave Gabriel unprotected, because these bastards have to be after him. Up one block, and there's movement at the next, some bruiser with a club, so Drake ducks into the house to his left, pelting through its rotten inside and praying the floor won't give out under his feet. Only a little ways to go—there's a window with its glass long gone, gaping open to the gray light of day. The floor sags, cracks under his next step with a wet creak, and he runs faster, reaching for the windowsill. There, he's there, and as he closes his hand around the window frame to boost himself out, there's pain, a nail or a shard of remaining glass scraping his palm, but he holds on anyway, one boot up on the windowsill to launch himself out to the street.

Still not far enough. Someone shouts as he lands on the cobbles, and he turns left—toward Gabriel, he hopes. He *can't* lose Gabriel now, not when things between them are finally so good.

At the next corner someone tackles him, knocking him to the ground and landing hard on his chest. "Got him!" the man yells as Drake tries to strike out. "He's down here!"

Drake gets one hand free, scrabbling for a weapon. He grabs a loose rock from the paving cobbles and lashes out with it. He hits his attacker in the temple, once, but there's no force to the blow and the man grabs his wrist, slams it down on the cobbles hard enough that his fingers go numb and tingling and the rock falls from his grip.

"Hurry it up!" the man calls, and Drake tries to lunge for his arm, teeth bared to bite. "The little shit's not—"

Gabriel lands on the man's back, knocking him halfway off Drake, and his breath hisses through his teeth as he brings his hand down on the back of the man's head. He's holding a brick, and he smashes it into the man's skull until bone cracks and blood splatters.

The man's allies are coming, though—someone's turning a corner off to the right. "Gabriel," he says, struggling free of the man's deadweight. "Gabriel, hurry."

The panic in Gabriel's face fades as he meets Drake's eyes. "Come on," he says, dropping the brick and offering his other hand to haul Drake to his feet. "This way."

He doesn't let go, holding tight to Drake's wrist as they flee down the next alley. The rest of the thugs will be worse now, with their man down. Drake wonders what they want, why the first one didn't try to kill him when he had the chance.

They're headed south again, bearing left as they go, until Drake thinks he knows where they're headed. They come out on Cypress again at the far end of the street, alley cats scattering as they pelt toward the Lady's house. They slip past the gates, the twisted iron and mess of brambles, and Gabriel slows.

"You think we're safe here?" Drake asks softly. He keeps moving, and Gabriel comes with him, beyond the first rows of graves, toward the mossy granite tombs in the back.

"No one's ever safe anywhere," Gabriel says, but his shoulders relax and the hunted look leaves his eyes.

Drake lets himself breathe a little easier, too. And then back by the entrance someone says, "You three hold the gate. There's only the one way out of here. Me and Hawk'll take the rest in to flush him out."

"What about the little one?" another man asks.

"If he don't have the sense to run, kill him. He ain't what we're here for."

Drake feels sick. He looks over at Gabriel, hoping for some cue, but Gabriel has frozen, eyes wide, hands clenched at his sides. "Come on," Drake whispers, reaching up to touch Gabriel's shoulder. His hand is bloody. He blinks at it, and shakes himself. Gabriel's gotten him out of plenty of trouble already. "Let's get moving. Never safe anywhere, remember?"

He puts his other hand, the not-bleeding one, on Gabriel's shoulder, and Gabriel starts like he's just been woken. *Not now*, Drake prays. They can't afford for it to get really bad now. He takes Gabriel's hand and pulls.

By the time they've reached the back fence, Gabriel at least seems alert, but still panicky. Drake holds still for a moment, listening for their pursuers. The iron fence is too tall to climb, rain-slick rails that stretch up higher than Drake can reach. Gabriel leans into him, fingers curling thin and needy into his sleeve. There has to be another way out.

Drake leads the way along the back fence, looking for a weak spot they can use to escape. They've made it about ten paces when he sees movement between the graves, three men coming up the path. He pulls Gabriel down with him into the hollow beneath a tangle of briars. They could face three and probably do all right if Gabriel were feeling better, but like this . . . He ducks down, watching the tramp of the men's boots through the tall grass.

"Gives me the fucking creeps," one of the thugs complains as they get closer. "You think it's true? Think the other one really is Gabriel?"

"Don't care if he is," the second one says. "Gabriel's a man, same as you. Gets in my way, I'll fucking kill him."

"Lady's cowl, did you see Matty's head?" the first man answers. "He beat it to fucking porridge."

"Shut up, the pair of you," the third one says. "You want him to know where you are?"

Drake looks around. He needs an escape, needs it soon, before the thugs realize they must have gone to ground somewhere and start searching less obvious places than the standing tombs. He needs—

There's a spot in the fence a little ways down, just beyond their briar patch, where the years of winter rain have worn the dirt away and formed a ditch running out underneath the iron and toward the edge of the swamp. Drake glances back at Gabriel, finds Gabriel watching him with an awful sort of pleading expression. He points toward the ditch, nods once. Gabriel blinks, and nods back. Good. Now they just need a chance. If the Lady favors them the way she's supposed to, then—

No. He can't depend on fairy tales. Look what it's doing to Gabriel, to have that not work. He watches the path for movement, waits for the thugs to turn. He shifts forward on his elbows, carefully, edging toward the ditch as best he can without leaving their cover yet.

And then the screaming starts.

"Get it off!" someone is yelling. "Fuck! Fuck, get it off! Kill it!"

The thugs near them take off running toward the noise, calling to their man as they go. "What is it?" one of them is asking. "You find the little shit?"

"Come on," Drake whispers, taking Gabriel's hand to lead him toward the gap under the fence. But he still hears the answer as they start to crawl toward their escape:

"There's fucking snakes in here!" one of the thugs yells over the sound of the one still screaming. "Davy got bit by a black fucking cottonmouth!"

Drake's blood goes cold. It's midwinter. The snakes should all be gone, dead or hidden underground where they can wait for spring. And yet those men found one alert enough to bite, and it's one of the

Lady's own: the ones whose bite makes a man's skin split and rot while he still lives.

"Thank you," Drake whispers, just in case the Lady's listening. "Please keep us safe." He lets Gabriel go first, keeps watch as Gabriel squirms through the muddy ditch and out of the graveyard, but the thugs haven't recovered enough to keep hunting. They're arguing now, yelling about whether they should keep looking, whether Gabriel set the cottonmouth on them and what else he might be capable of. Drake gets down on the ground, sliding through the ditch belly-up so he can keep an eye out for pursuit.

And Fates but it's cold, wet as it is, and the ground beyond the graveyard fence is just more sucking mud, with twisted trees for cover as the dark swamp spreads out beyond. Still, they don't dare stick too close to the fence, not if they want to lose their pursuers. Drake reaches for Gabriel's hand again, and holds on as he leads the way into the swamp.

CHAPTER
TWENTY-TWO

"You're all right?" he asks quietly, when they've gone far enough that he dares to make some noise. The trees around them are bare but for the silvery hanging tendrils of Lady's moss, and the wet black branches seem to reach for them, skeletal as Her hands.

Gabriel nods slowly. "Where are we going?" His breath is a tiny puff of fog in the air.

Drake shakes his head. "I'm not really sure. Away from those guys. There were too many of them." This is all wrong. Gabriel shouldn't be asking *him* to lead the way.

But Gabriel doesn't seem to have really recovered yet, because he stays quiet as they pick their way through the swamp. In some spots the ground is dry enough to support them, and in others the water has seeped up to the surface, black and still, and sometimes the cover of fallen leaves makes it look like they have stable footing until they take the next step and find themselves sinking into sticky mud. Drake's stomach growls occasionally, and he tries to ignore that along with the stinging chill in his hands and feet. If they can get far enough west, he's pretty sure they can come back up into the city without anyone knowing to expect them. It's easier said than done, though, trying to keep his bearings in the gloom under the cover of the trees.

Getting back into the city is only the start of things, anyway. After that they'll have to deal with the men who came hunting them, which Drake's not looking forward to at all. He's going to need Gabriel if they're going to have a chance, and right now it seems like Gabriel still can't deal with the idea of people coming after them in the Lady's house.

"We're going to be all right," Drake says, not because he's sure of it but because he feels like it needs to be said. "You'll see."

"You sound so sure," Gabriel says quietly. At least he's willing to argue, Drake thinks. It's a start.

"We get help when we need it." He tries to sound certain. "And we make our own luck when we have to."

Gabriel hums, and goes quiet again. The silence is eerie, after the city—there's no place in Casmile, not as far as Drake can tell, where it gets this quiet. There are always people out doing *something*. Here the sound of their feet breaking twigs or kicking up leaves seems loud. If there are birds in the trees, they aren't singing, and if there are animals in the underbrush, rats or frogs or snakes— Fates, Drake wishes he hadn't thought of that. If there was one black cottonmouth out and about in Casmile today, there could be another in the swamp, under a fall of leaves or in the knot of a tree's roots. For all that he said they make their own luck, Drake's not sure if he trusts it to hold when they're out here. It's a lot harder to bluff the swamp than a gang of dockside toughs.

When he sees the movement through the trees for the first time, he thinks he's going mad. He's cold and wet and miserable; what if he just *wants* to find some reason to hope? What if he's finally caught whatever it is that Gabriel has, seeing the Lady in shadows and hearing things that aren't there? But the apparition is the first thing he's had to guide him since they got through the fence, and right now he'll take it. He picks up his pace, heading toward the movement he thinks he saw.

A few steps later he sees it again, and Gabriel hisses like he sees it too. That has to be a good sign, doesn't it? If they're both seeing it, then neither of them is mad. They walk faster, toward the flicker of dull color through the trees. Drake wants to ask Gabriel what he's seen, wants to call after whatever—whoever—they're following, but the silence has grown too thick, too potent, and he doesn't dare disturb it.

The part where his heart leaps, where he starts to really hope, is when they can smell fire, a little further into the swamp. He breaks into a jog, and Gabriel lopes along beside him, head up and eyes alert at last. It's the wrong season for wildfires. Everything out here is soaking wet. The only way for there to be a fire out here is for someone to have tried hard to build one.

Puddles splash under their feet, and for a moment Drake is caught, the heavy mud sucking at his boots, but he pulls free; he can't afford to get lost now. Maybe they've made it back to the city's edge, and once they reach the streets they can find a tavern where—

But this isn't the city at all. They come through a dense thicket of trees, brushing the hanging moss away from their faces, and there are people here, facing off with them in the muck of the swamp.

The man's dark, probably Jua'zan, his hair long and his face thin and hungry. He's holding a pitchfork, a rusted old gnarled thing that's likely spent more time down here in the swamp than doing honest farm work. The woman has a sickle, and she's wearing trousers, like a pirate or a field slave. She says something in a language Drake doesn't know, harsh and clicking.

A third voice answers, a girl's voice, and Drake looks past the adults to see the girl herself half-hidden behind the trunk of a tree. The color they've been following through the trees, he realizes, is the dull blue of her dress.

"When we need it," Gabriel says softly, and he's not tensed for a fight at all. He has his arms wrapped around himself and his hands hidden in his armpits.

Drake nods. "Please," he says to the woman, "will you let us sit by your fire for a little while? We won't ask for anything else, but it's so cold, and we're wet through."

"Who's after you?" the man asks. He hasn't lowered the pitchfork, but the set of his shoulders says he's not looking for an excuse to use it, at least.

"Nobody, I hope." When that makes the man's expression darken, Drake explains, "We fled the city this morning, and I don't think the men after us are still following." He looks at Gabriel. "We'd have heard them by now."

"Yelling," Gabriel says. "They did a lot of that." He's shivering, little shudders wracking him as he stands there. They need that fire.

"We'll be on our way as soon as we're warm. Please." Drake doesn't think they have anything they can barter with, or he'd offer—anything for a little aid right now.

The man and the woman trade a few words—and the strangest thing is that it sounds like a few of the words are Casmilan, every fourth or fifth one; Drake thinks he hears "hounds" at one point, and possibly "rest" in the answer to that, but most of the words are nothing he knows.

"If you bring the bounty hunters with you," the woman says eventually, "we kill you both."

Gabriel's lip curls back from his teeth, and he hisses like a snake himself. Drake puts a hand on his arm. "We bring no one."

The woman nods, and beckons. "This way." She sends the little girl first, furthest from trouble, and Drake follows, still holding on to Gabriel. He's not sure which of them he's trying to reassure. The man walks behind them, and he hates the feeling of turning their backs on someone with a weapon, but he can't blame these people for not trusting them.

They're dressed like Casmilans, despite the strange language and the man's dark skin. The clothes are simple and a bit threadbare—there's a patch on the right sleeve of the woman's jacket with ragged, uneven stitches, and the hem of the girl's dress is muddy and torn. But they're ordinary enough; they don't wear the bright colors of the travelers, and Drake's not quite far gone enough to think they're the fair folk.

He follows the woman and the little girl—her daughter, probably, for all that she's more light-skinned than either of the adults—along a narrow trail that he'd never have noticed without them going first. When they turn one last bend, and what he'd taken for another dense thicket turns out to be hiding a little ramshackle house, Drake almost stumbles as he realizes where these people must have come from.

They're escaped slaves. Hiding in the swamp where their old masters' hounds couldn't sniff them out, and then just staying there. It's a fanciful enough story for Gabriel, and yet he'd bet it's true.

"In with you," the woman says, pulling back the flap over the door. A deer skin, it looks like. "We'll build the fire back up, see if you thaw."

"Thank you," Drake says. It's dark in the little house, and it smells of something odd and sharp that he can't place, but even with the fire banked and low, it's warmer than they've been all day. He sits down on the floor—more skins, there, between them and the cold wet ground—and scoots as close to the fire pit as he can comfortably get.

Gabriel crawls halfway into his lap, not so much sitting beside him as leaning across him.

"So clever," Gabriel mumbles into Drake's shirt.

"Just lucky," Drake says softly. He drapes his arm over Gabriel's back, and watches the woman feed the fire. Her hands are broad, the knuckles twisted with years of hard work.

When the first red tongues of flame curl up from the fire pit, the woman sits back on her heels and meets Drake's eyes. "What are you running from?"

There are a lot of true answers to that question, Drake realizes. He thinks of Captain Westfall, of Sebastian's party and Danny's expectations, of the scraps they've had with dockside toughs. "This morning," he says slowly, "there were men after us that we'd never seen before." That isn't quite right, though. "After me, I think. They didn't—they didn't seem to care whether they got both of us."

"Mmm." The woman nods, holding her hands out to warm them by the fire. "Lawmen?"

"No. Not this time." Drake wants to move—Gabriel's weight on his leg is giving him pins and needles all down it—but he thinks he shouldn't just yet. Not until Gabriel feels a little less tense under his hands. "I think they wanted to take me away." Gabriel clutches tighter, and growls in his throat. Drake runs his fingers through Gabriel's hair.

It's because of the party, he's suddenly sure. Someone there said something about it to his friends, and the rumors would have spread, and now the people who know who he used to be also know who he's become. Those men this morning were looking for Colin.

"We can't go back to Cypress Street," he says, as much to himself as to Gabriel. "We're going to have to start over." If he counts up all his copper, he might have a shilling to his name, and he can't imagine Gabriel's much better off. They're in for a rough night or two unless their luck changes in a hurry. They might be able to go see Deirdre, but staying with her would just get her involved in it, too.

"You can't stay here," the woman says firmly. "We've trouble enough already, and no room to take on strangers."

Drake nods. "I know. Really, I meant it. We'll be on our way soon."

"Just so you know," the woman says. She gets up from the fire. "We can spare you a bit of broth, at least, as long as that's clear."

"Thank you." Drake's fingertips ache with the warmth coming back to them. He watches the woman bring in a pot of water and hang it over the fire. She adds some flakes of something from a leather bag. Fish, it smells like when it starts to heat up. They must live off what they can find or catch in the swamp.

"Either of you carry brands?" the woman asks, stirring the broth slowly. She says it casually, like it's no big deal, like it would be no surprise.

"No." Drake tries not to bristle. Probably better if she does think they could be slaves too, if she thinks his pale skin means he's part barbarian. He remembers Barron's thugs threatening to sell him off back when he'd first met Gabriel. What if they could do that? Would anyone believe him if he declared himself now? Would it even matter to the sort of men who'd buy him in the first place?

"You might be able to take the road, then," the woman says. "If you want, Hajari will take you out to the mountain road when the sun goes down."

Drake hesitates. It would mean starting over, that's for sure. He's not sure what they'd do in Deradan or Port Clair, save that he'd need to leave being Colin behind for good. But it would get them away from their troubles here. "I'm not sure. Thank you for the offer. I'm just, I don't know if . . ." He brushes a lock of hair off Gabriel's forehead. "If we're ready to leave Casmile just yet."

"Your choice." The woman produces two wooden cups, and dips the first one in the broth to ladle some out. "Waiting on your friend?"

"Yes." His friend. Gabriel is that, he supposes, odd as it is to think of him as anything but simply Gabriel. "Gabe?" he says gently. "You want to sit up and have some broth?"

There's no response for a minute. Drake would almost think Gabriel had drifted off to sleep if he weren't still holding on so tightly.

"Please, Gabriel," he says. "Come back. We're going to be all right. Come back to me." He cups Gabriel's face in one hand, strokes Gabriel's cheekbone with his thumb. Gabriel's throat works as he swallows, but he doesn't move otherwise. "I didn't go away when you asked me not to. Don't you go away from me, either." Drake leans down and brushes gentle kisses across Gabriel's brow.

Gabriel stirs and peers up at him. In the dim light of the hut, his eyes look pure black. "Drake?" he says hopefully.

"I'm here." A knot of tension eases behind Drake's ribs. "You hungry?"

"Always," Gabriel says with a little wry twist to his mouth. He sits up and reaches out to take the cup of broth. "Thank you," he says to the woman as he raises it to his lips.

Drake accepts the second cup gratefully. The broth is thin, and the flavor of the fish is strong, but it's hot and it's the nearest thing they've had to a meal yet today. He drains his cup as fast as Gabriel does.

"Welcome back," he says to Gabriel when he's done. He'd like to ask for more, but he's already gotten more generosity here than he had any reason to expect.

"I didn't really go away, you know," Gabriel says. "I don't think I've really gone away since you came." He smiles. "You keep me here. I'm glad I did that for you, too." He holds out his cup to the woman. "Is there more?"

The woman laughs. "You're not shy at all, are you, Gabriel?" She takes his cup. "There's more. You hear what I said to your friend earlier?"

Gabriel nods. "About leaving. Yes. We'll go soon. Back to Casmile."

"You sure?" Drake asks. If it's what Gabriel wants, he'll go, of course. But he can't help worrying about their odds. "You want to go back?"

"Those men wanted to take you." Gabriel sits up straighter, and his eyes narrow. "I'm not going to let them."

They leave almost as soon as they've finished their second cups of broth. Outside, the two adults talk things over for a minute in their odd half-familiar language, and then the man nods to them.

"This way," he says. His Casmilan is accented, like he wasn't born on the plantation he must have run from. "Take you up to the south gate."

"There's a south gate?" Drake asks. The only ones he's ever heard of—the only ones anyone ever uses—are the north gate, toward Hanaein and the barbarian territories, or the west gate, toward Deradan and the mountains.

"Not anymore," Gabriel says. "But you can still see where it used to be."

The fact that Gabriel knows about it makes Drake feel better. They'll be back on familiar ground. This doesn't seem like a trolls-and-dragons afternoon, either, so they should be able to get their feet back under them in the city.

Their guide doesn't talk to them, just leads the way through the tangle of the swamp, past the standing pools, under the trailing moss. Beneath the trees it seems like it's barely raining anymore. Drake's hand is sore where he cut it this morning, but the bleeding stopped by itself, so it can't be too bad.

When they can smell wood smoke through the trees, Hajari stops. "Keep on that way," he says, pointing ahead of them. "You'll come to the city again. I don't go further."

"Thank you for all your help," Drake says.

"Just get gone. Don't send any trouble our way."

"We won't," Drake promises. There'll be trouble enough—Gabriel's shifted into that too-alert stance that means he's waiting for a reason to cut someone—but not here. Not for the people who helped them.

Hajari nods and turns away, heading back into the deeper cover of the swamp. Drake looks to Gabriel.

"Shall we?" Gabriel bows, gesturing to the faint trail ahead of them.

"You know," Drake says as they start moving again, "someone might be waiting for us here. If they figured out where we went."

"That would be nice. It would save a lot of trouble hunting them down." Gabriel sounds cold, almost but not quite like he gets on a job; he sounds angry, Drake realizes. When was the last time Drake actually saw Gabriel angry?

He thinks it's possible there was only the once, that very first night.

"Somebody must have sent them," Drake says, holding a stray branch out of the way until Gabriel passes. "They acted like they wanted me for something in particular."

Gabriel nods. "We'll find out who it was. And I don't care if it's the captain himself. He'll be sorry."

"Planning to take his eyes?" Drake tries to keep his tone light, but he doesn't think it works.

"Done that before," Gabriel says. "I might have to find something really unpleasant for this one."

CHAPTER
TWENTY-THREE

T he trees thin out at last, and Drake spots the first houses ahead of them—little ramshackle things, barely more than the swamp runaways' hut, scattered through the trees. The trail underfoot becomes clearer, more defined.

One or two people come out of houses to watch them as they go past, but they don't speak, don't try anything. It's probably for the best. Gabriel wouldn't have the patience for anyone getting in his way right now.

The houses grow more densely clustered, but not much more well made, as they walk onward. There is almost a road now, not like the broad ways out by the main gates, but near enough to the single-cart lanes that wind from one estate to the next. And ahead of them, in the weak winter light, Drake can see stone walls.

The little ramshackle houses go right up to the edge of the city wall, some of them even leaning against it. Everything feels cramped, too close together and just this side of falling down. Drake wonders if this little outlaw town has ever caught fire, how fast the whole thing would go up.

"Over here," Gabriel says, bearing left, leading Drake along until they come to the real gap in the wall—not just a spot where stones have come loose and fallen, but the remains of the south gate. Parts of the wall have come down here too, a pile of rubble littering the ground. Fragments of the old gate still hang from rusted hinges, but the wood is soft with age and water, crumbling away in pieces. The shape of the gate that must have stood here, high and arched, is barely suggested by the remains of the western-side wall.

"How old is this?" Drake asks. "When did the gate come down?"

"Years and years ago," Gabriel says, climbing onto the rubble of the wall. "Deirdre said it was already like this when she first came here."

Drake follows Gabriel over, trying to balance himself with only his uninjured hand. "It looks like there used to be something down here, apart from just the swamp."

"Everything used to be something else, didn't it?"

"I guess so," Drake says, as he climbs down on the city side. The cobblestones are about half missing, and there's grass growing up through the spaces between them, but it's a Casmile street, and that makes Drake feel better than he ever thought it would. Ragged and dangerous as it is, the city—*Gabriel's* city—has still become *home*. "Let's go get some proper food."

"Feed my dragon to make him strong," Gabriel says, "and then we'll go see what we can learn about your new friends from this morning."

Even that can't put Drake off his food. It's about time, as far as the stories in taverns and gaming dens go, for Gabriel to do something terrible again. What good is a legend that's not still growing?

By the time they get clear of the no-man's-land around the south gate and all the way to the river—fairly far into the heart of the city, as near as Drake can tell, closer to the gallows square than he'd really like to be—it feels as though they've been walking for ages, and Drake half thinks his stomach is trying to devour itself in despair. "Here," he says when they come to a tavern, never mind that it's likely more expensive than something down nearer the port. Tonight he's sure he'll be sorry, but right now he doesn't care.

The heat and the scent of something savory make him sag with relief the second he pushes the door open. He stops a barmaid before they've even taken a table—Gabriel's headed for the one in the corner—and says, "You have some kind of stew on?"

"We do," she says, and looks him over. He must be a mess, he realizes at once, muddied and waterlogged and smelling of swamp. "It'd be eight pence for you and your friend, and the ale extra."

Drake digs in his pocket and comes up with the copper. He has precious little to spare. "Two bowls, then, and some bread to go with it." They can always get more money, can't they? Especially if they're well fed and strong enough to fight.

The stew, when it comes, has some strong-flavored meat in it that Drake doesn't recognize. Gabriel says it's goat and sounds amused that Drake doesn't know that, which seems like a good sign all around. If Gabriel's feeling that much better, they can start making plans.

"We need to figure out who sent them," Drake says when Gabriel is pushing the heel of his black bread around the bowl to sop up the last of the gravy. "The ones after us this morning were just doing what they were told."

Gabriel nods, licking gravy off his fingers. "We should go back home."

Drake blinks. "Are you sure?"

"Remember the pigeons. They'll expect us to be pigeons, too. Coming home to roost. Someone will be waiting for us."

"I'm not sure that's what we want." Drake wishes he had more coins, enough to buy a pint of ale. "There must be easier ways to learn who they were."

"If we knew names," Gabriel says. "If we'd seen more of them close up. Maybe then we could ask someone. But we don't, so this will be faster." He smiles his working-an-ugly-job smile. "Besides, this way we can make them sorry they thought they could have you."

That's going to be nasty, no matter how it goes. "All right," Drake says. "If you think it'll work better." The barkeeper is watching them, now that their food is done and they don't seem to be ordering anything else. "Should we get going, then? We don't have all that long until dark."

Gabriel shakes his head. "Today they'll still be nervous. We wait out tonight. Let them get bored. Sloppy."

"You have a plan for tonight, then?" Drake can't summon any enthusiasm for the prospect of sleeping on the street somewhere. "I don't have the coin for a room, even a cheap one."

"Plenty of empty rooms in the city." Gabriel's eyes flick sideways—he must know they're being watched—but he doesn't move to get up. "We'll find something. Don't worry."

They wind up sitting in the tavern long past the first hints that they've outstayed their welcome, until the barkeeper sends the girl out somewhere and she comes back with a hulking brute of a man in her shadow. It's almost funny, after this morning—they could handle *one*, no question—but Gabriel gets up and stretches anyway. His shirt rides up, and Drake tries not to let himself stare at that sliver of bared skin.

"You want to go now?" he asks instead.

"Nothing to gain by staying," Gabriel says. "All we get if we win is more of them coming in to help out."

"Fair enough." They do have better fights to get into. He pushes back his chair, nods to the barmaid as they get up to leave. He'd like to think the bruiser looks glad—not a fighting man, maybe, just a local who has the muscle to make people listen.

The sun's going down outside, as nearly as Drake can tell; the thin light coming through the clouds is getting weaker. This doesn't promise to be a good night. Gabriel wanders away from the tavern without looking back, wearing his distracted hunting-for-things face. Drake follows, trying to have faith. Just a few hours ago he was sure that this would be enough, wasn't he? He should try harder to trust Gabriel now.

At one corner they hang back, watching the proprietor of a smoking den place torches in the sconces by the door. Gabriel investigates those when the woman has gone back inside, tugs one free of its wrought-iron clasp, and hands it off to Drake. He nods once in silent satisfaction and heads into the worst of the south-city blight.

It's full dark by the time they find anything Gabriel deems promising, and by then the cold is settling in seriously and their torch, smoky and sputtering, feels absurdly conspicuous. Drake realizes to his own dismay that he misses their room on Cypress, which may have been squalid and awful but was at least always *there*. Lady's foresight, it's called, realizing things could get worse only when they actually do.

"Let's try this one," Gabriel says. The house he walks up to is barely worthy of the name; it seems to have taken damage in a fire and then never gotten fixed. About half the roof is just gone, a black hole with ragged edges. The door's been boarded over, but there are windows on the ground floor that haven't been treated as carefully, and Gabriel pries the shutters off one with only a minute of tugging. The wood makes a thin screeching noise as it comes free of the old nails. Gabriel tosses the shutters inside, and boosts himself up on the sill.

Drake brings over the torch and holds it up. "Look all right?"

"Think so," Gabriel answers. "I'll hold the light for you once I've gotten inside." He jumps down into the dark, and there's a squelching noise.

"Are you all right?" Drake asks.

"Fine. It's just muddy."

"Muddy? Inside?" That can't be good. Drake peers in the window. There aren't any floorboards. Instead there's just bare ground, most of it a thick layer of wet ash that Gabriel's boots have disturbed. The house probably wouldn't be standing at all if the outside wasn't brick.

"Hand me the torch," Gabriel says.

"Here." Drake passes it in to him, and the light throws flickering shadows through the room. Something skitters away into the dark in a far corner, and Drake tries not to think too hard on it. The tenement in Cypress probably had rats too, and they got by.

He climbs through the window—was it just this morning that he was fleeing another house like this? Trouble only ever seems to catch them in plenty. The mud underfoot is thick and sucking, the ground soaked right through from all the winter's rain.

"I'll get you a fancy house," Gabriel says softly, watching him. "A fine house and a hoard of treasure to fill it up."

"You don't have to do that," Drake says. He stops studying the room and looks at Gabriel instead. *I'll settle for someplace dry*, he could say, or *If we could build a fire that would be enough*, but neither of those things is really what he means. "You don't need anything like that to make me stay."

He almost can't face Gabriel's smile after that. It's too much. He's in so far over his head. "Thank you, Drake," Gabriel says. He turns away a minute later—he doesn't know what to say either, thank the Fates—and starts to look around the house.

There are some jagged remnants of interior walls still standing, and bits of stone on the ground that probably supported the floor that used to be here. They make their way to the back of the house, where the old kitchen hearth still stands: a brick fireplace, and a spreading half-moon of brick paving in front of it, slightly cracked and blackened but still there and mostly dry.

"This'll do, won't it?" Drake asks. "If we look around, maybe we can find something to use to build up a fire there."

Gabriel actually seems to think about it before he answers, like he doesn't already have a plan in mind. It's both unsettling and comforting, somehow, to know that he doesn't just know all the answers, that he's bluffing his way through as much as Drake is.

"Yes," he says at last, and he probably means it to sound certain, but it's been a long day and Drake's had enough time to get used to him, and the worry shows through just a bit. "Good idea."

They wind up having to pry up some splintered floorboards from the less damaged side of the house, and then sort through for the least damp ones to get a guttering, reddish fire going—but it feels like a victory to have even that much hissing and popping in the hearth, enough to warm their hands by. Drake stacks the rest of the scavenged wood next to the fire so it might dry out enough to burn, and stretches in front of the hearth.

"It will get better," Gabriel promises as he lies down too. They really have lost ground, if even Gabriel thinks this is too poor a life.

"It will," Drake agrees. "Tomorrow." He drapes an arm across Gabriel's shoulders.

He's already closed his eyes, trying to convince himself to sleep, when Gabriel says, "Drake."

"Mmm?" It sounds like Gabriel just wants his attention, not like anything is actually wrong. Like the tone Anna would use to ask for a story when they were little.

"Do you believe in things?"

Drake blinks the sleep away. "Things?" If he's understood the question correctly, this is important. "What sort of things?"

Gabriel shrugs against him. "Luck. The Lady." There's a pause. "Dragons."

The fire hisses, crackles as the wood shifts and settles. Drake licks his lips, thinks carefully about his answer. "It isn't enough for you to believe in them yourself anymore?" he asks. "You need someone else to agree?"

Gabriel's fingers curl in the fabric of his jacket, holding on loosely. "It's horrible if they're not real. But sometimes—this morning..." He trails off, shakes his head.

"Because those bastards followed us to the Lady's house?" Drake asks. Gabriel nods. "You saw what happened when they didn't believe, though, didn't you?" This is easier when it's about the Fates. They're *supposed* to be a mystery. "They didn't think the Lady could hurt them, and she did. And we got away. Remember? It's all right." He thinks of the stories Gabriel has told him, Troll Bridge and the Lady's kiss, and how much uglier they'd have been without something to believe in. "The Lady was watching over us this morning, Gabriel. You're her favorite. Everyone knows that."

"You always know what to say," Gabriel says softly. It doesn't really sound like a complaint.

"Dragons are supposed to be clever at word games, aren't they?" Drake asks. "Stories. Riddles."

"Is that why you stay with me?"

"Because you're a riddle? I suppose it is, in part." Drake wonders if Gabriel has forgotten calling *him* the riddle, or if he's just all right with trading places now and then.

"You should tell me the dragon story."

"The one about the mountain?" Drake tries to remember how it went the first time.

Gabriel shakes his head. "The one about you."

"Someday," Drake says. "When I'm sure I can tell it right. Will you wait for that? For me to be sure I have all the important parts of it by heart?"

"Promise," Gabriel says. "Promise you'll tell it then."

"I promise." It's not so bad, being Gabriel's dragon. And he still doesn't have to tell the story any time soon.

Gabriel relaxes against him. "I'll wait, then."

CHAPTER
TWENTY-FOUR

By the morning, their store of firewood is almost completely gone, and there's a dead rat on the hearth next to the smoldering embers. "It came up to see if we were dead," Gabriel explains. "It's bad luck, though. We weren't."

"I imagine that'll be plenty of people's bad luck today," Drake says. Gabriel laughs. "It will."

They have just enough left of their fire to cook the rat. It tastes terrible. Drake wishes there were more than one of them.

By the light of day, he can get his bearings a little better, and it turns out they're not so far from Cypress after all—a little further inland, but near enough. They keep to the side streets as they circle back toward their room, watching for anyone who might be watching for them. How are they going to spot their quarry? They don't have much to go on.

It turns out it's easy. There's a little cluster of them lounging on the stoop outside the building, and they're obvious as a canker. Plenty of people spend their time on the streets around here, with no honest work to do, but none of them look like that—broad shouldered, heavyset, like they've never gone hungry for lack of skulls to bash in. Drake glances at Gabriel. How are they going to do this?

Down, Gabriel motions. He crouches there, in the alley across the street from their opponents, and studies their surroundings. After a moment he touches Drake's sleeve, points to the door of the building on their side, then up at the second story. Drake nods.

The door is locked, but the wood's old and soft, and when Drake leans on it a little, they get inside with no trouble. The hallway is a lot like their own, filthy and dark, and the stairs stretch upward beside them. "What's our plan?" Drake asks.

"We're going to keep watch. They must switch off sometimes. Going for food, things like that. Then we can take one alone." Gabriel starts up the stairs. "And talk this over with him."

"Sounds good to me. I don't much care for running and hiding."

Gabriel laughs. "You sound angry. That's good." He opens the first street-side door upstairs without knocking.

There's yelling almost immediately. Drake reaches the door just in time to catch a boy, maybe eight or nine years old, trying to bolt. He drags the boy back into the room, where Gabriel is facing off against a woman with a kitchen knife and another child hiding behind her.

"Get out," she says to both of them. "You've no business here."

"We need to borrow your window," Gabriel says. He steps over the rags on the floor—blankets, maybe, or spare clothes. "We don't have to do anything worse than that." He has one of his knives out all the same, held at his side as he turns just far enough to glance out without really turning his back on the woman.

Drake hauls the boy further into the room. "Can you see from there?"

"Well enough."

"You're the ones those men are looking for," the woman says. She glances from Gabriel to Drake, and then to the door.

"Don't run," Drake says. "I'll break your boy's neck, Lady's truth."

The woman glares, but the boy whimpers, pulling weakly at Drake's arm, and that makes her relent. Drake's glad. He doesn't know if he could have actually brought himself to do it if she'd called his bluff.

"What are they offering?" Gabriel asks.

"Five guineas," the woman says.

Drake stares. That's an outrageous sum down here.

"Like to choke them to death with their five guineas," Gabriel mutters.

"Oh, come on," Drake says. "*I'd* turn me in for that kind of money." The boy squirms, trying to pull away again, and Drake shakes him. It makes him feel like a brute, but he's already set himself up for the role and now he needs to be convincing. "Stop that."

"When we take care of them, we'll take the money and buy you all the fancy things you want."

"All of them?" Drake asks. They're going to pull this off, no question. He can tell just looking at Gabriel's stance. "We'd better hope they're carrying plenty of coin."

The woman makes a little disbelieving noise. "What do you think you're going to do? There's at least six of them."

"Only six?" Drake says. "See, they lost more after we left them in the Lady's house."

Gabriel looks grimly pleased. "I suppose it's our turn, then. We can't expect her to take care of all our problems."

"You're both mad," the woman says.

"As moon dogs," Drake agrees. "Sit tight. With luck, we'll be on our way soon."

He loses track of how long they wait. They've had jobs like this, where they spend most of their time just watching for a good opportunity to get their man alone. It's not his favorite kind of work, especially hungry. But this isn't a job they can turn down.

They're there long enough for the woman to lower her knife, to settle in to waiting with her little girl beside her. The boy squirms a bit, but Drake doesn't have to pay too much attention to him.

"There," Gabriel says eventually, coming alert, his posture growing tense and ready all at once. "They're changing up. Some of them stay on guard to wait for the pigeons to come home, and the others go out searching."

"How many?"

Gabriel shakes his head. "Haven't learned. There are only two going each way."

The boy tenses against him, so Drake leans down to look him in the eyes. "Don't do anything stupid," he says. "We're going to leave, and you're not hurt. If you—if any of you—try to go warn those bastards, you'll earn no coin, only some very dangerous enemies."

The boy flinches back from him, bristling like he'd desperately love to fight but doesn't dare.

"Time to go, Drake," Gabriel says.

They leave the room at a stroll, like they're going nowhere in particular, and then take the stairs in leaps and bounds, back out to the alley. Gabriel doesn't even slow down, turning and heading northward through the twisted side streets that cling to Cypress like the Lady's moss. The men they're following are walking up Cypress itself, casual enough that Drake thinks they might be taking a break, not actually hunting right now. They carry themselves like they're hoping trouble will try them, and people get out of their way. Stupid bastards.

When they turn off Cypress it's toward Dock Street, about as far south as that comes. There's nothing respectable this far down it, that's for sure—nothing but half-empty warehouses, crooked gaming houses, and smoking dens. Gabriel jogs across Cypress in pursuit, and Drake follows his lead. Between Cypress and Dock is their best bet, in the cramped old streets that used to serve the harbor when ships moored on the south shore.

They're about halfway to the first bend in this little alley when their targets stop. Drake's reaching into his pocket for his brass knuckles, and Gabriel already has a knife drawn.

The first one turns—not entirely blind to his circumstances after all, more's the pity. "Come out of hiding at last?" He draws a knife of his own.

"Can't let the Lady have all the fun with you," Gabriel says with a smile.

The men both have knives, and they lunge for Gabriel first. But Gabriel's fast, jumping back and slashing in return—knife in each hand now—and the bastards are in each other's way when they attack the same target in such close quarters. Drake steps into his first punch, catches one of them right in the ribs with a solid crack of bone. The thug swipes at him as he falls back, cursing, and Drake's not as fast as he should be; a blade bites across his arm. Son of a whore.

Gabriel catches the other thug in the face, and both Drake and the first thug jump at the screaming. There's blood everywhere—always so much blood from head wounds—and the guy's retaliating strikes are wild enough that Gabriel has no trouble dodging.

Drake sees his chance and takes it: while his thug is reacting to the spectacle, he swings, slams his bare fist into the back of the guy's neck. The thug drops, and Drake kneels beside him to make sure he's out but still alive; they're going to want some answers after this. Gabriel takes another nasty swipe at the other one—he's as bad as a hunting cat—and the prick tries to run.

Nobody outruns Gabriel when he's this angry. It takes two steps before Gabriel catches the collar of the man's shirt with his right hand and stabs with his left, driving the knife home below the ribcage. There's more screaming for a few seconds as the man collapses, and then the screams turn to gurgling when Gabriel cuts clean across his throat.

"Such trouble." Gabriel crouches beside the body, wipes his knife on the dead man's pant leg, and starts going through his pockets. "Won't tell us anything now. Yours?"

"Still breathing," Drake says. "Might not wake for a bit, though."

"All the better." Gabriel pockets the dead man's knife and coin purse. "Let's get him off the street before the guard comes by."

They manage to get their new companion more or less upright between them, one arm over each of their shoulders. He's damn heavy, but they make do, staggering away from the mess they've left behind and turning at the first opportunity. With any luck, they'll look like they're helping out a friend who's spent too long in the smoking dens—nothing makes people look away faster, Drake's found, than someone who might ask for help.

Just a little way off Dock Street, someone has left a warehouse door ajar—or maybe, from the look of the splintered wood around the lock, someone didn't bother to hire anyone to guard their wares at harbor. Inside, the building smells of mildew and earth and rotting fruit. Some old barrels sit shattered, half strung together by old shipping cargo nets.

Drake and Gabriel dump their captive in the middle of the room, next to one of the beams that support the rafters overhead. Stripped off the barrels, the netting makes decent enough rope for Gabriel to tie the man's hands behind his back around the beam, while Drake uses the man's torn sleeve to bind up his arm.

Gabriel crouches in front of their captive and pries up one eyelid experimentally. "No," he says, "don't think he'll come around for a while." He lets go, then helps himself to the man's coin purse before he stands. "Stay and watch him?"

"Of course," Drake says. "Where are you going?"

"Further up." Gabriel picks at the knot on the stolen coin purse, tugs it open, and shakes the contents into his hand. "I'm going to go get food."

There's silver in that handful of coin, a good deal of it, enough to make Drake feel weak with relief. They can live on that for days, even if they have to keep finding other places to stay. "Sounds good. Hurry back."

"I wouldn't dream of missing the fun." Gabriel turns for the door, then stops as if he's just remembered something and turns back.

"What—" Drake starts to ask, and doesn't get any further before Gabriel kisses him. It's not a lingering kiss, just enough to be solid and certain. Drake catches Gabriel around the waist and kisses back—for all the times Gabriel has changed moods since, he still wants to do this again, and that's luck if Drake ever heard of it. "I'll be waiting for you."

"I won't be long," Gabriel says, and this time he actually does make it out the door.

It's chilly in the warehouse, and the light from the ventilation windows high under the eaves isn't terribly bright, but Drake can think of worse places to be. Though possibly not for their guest, whose day is likely to go sharply downhill from here. Drake tucks his hands into his armpits to keep them warm and paces, five steps from one end of the clear space to the other, turn and another five steps back. He wonders if Gabriel will want to ask the questions. He wonders if people are likely to hear them if the man starts to scream. He wonders what's become of Colin, who would have shied away from business like this; he feels all dragon right now, ready to extract vengeance from everyone who's dared to cross him.

He's not sure how long it's been when the man stirs, tries to sit up straighter, starts to pull on the ropes that bind him.

"Hold still," Drake says, coming closer.

"Fuck you," the thug says. "Where's your pimp?"

Drake kicks him a few times. "If your boss told you Gabriel was the only one who could hurt you, I think you're going to be disappointed."

It takes a second and some wheezing before the thug can answer, and when he does, it's not that impressive. "Whatever you're looking for, fancy boy, you're not going to get it out of me."

"Sure I am." This is theater, as much as anything that happens in a playhouse, only with more riding on a convincing performance. Drake gets down on his knees in front of the guy and punches him in the mouth, does it a second time when it looks like he's recovering enough to answer. Blood trickles down from a split in the man's lip. "I'm getting it right now."

"You said you'd wait for me," Gabriel says, and Drake catches the moment of terror that crosses the thug's face. Good. That'll help.

"Sorry," Drake says as he stands up. "He's got a smart mouth." He dusts off his hands. "What'd you get? It smells great."

Gabriel holds out two half-moon–shaped pastries. "Meat buns. Ate mine already. These are for you."

"You're a prince." He takes the meat buns—still warm, even, and the pastry flaking in his fingers—and steps back. "If you want to kick him around a little while I eat, or anything, feel free."

"Wouldn't dream of it." Gabriel's watching their captive avidly. "This is personal. Your business. Like Morgan was for me."

Their man flinches just slightly at the mention of Morgan. "I was new then," Drake says around a mouthful of his meat bun. "I wouldn't have known what to do with Morgan if you'd asked me." He takes another bite. "This is delicious." The crust is stuffed with tangy, shredded meat, slow cooked and laced with sweet simmered onions. Drake's pretty sure he would have appreciated it anytime, but no time more than now, when he's so badly starved.

Gabriel crouches on the floor in front of their man. "Should I cut him up a little, then?"

Drake wonders if he could keep eating while he watched something like that. He thinks maybe he could, and wonders when he got so cold. "If you start cutting now, he won't last long, will he?" He smiles when their captive glares at him. Right now this is a bluffing game, Gabriel's favorite one: how badly are we going to hurt you? "I mean, it's not like we have anything to stop the bleeding with, if you nick a big vein too soon."

"I'm more careful than that," Gabriel says, pouting. "I don't hit the big veins until I mean to."

"Told you once already," the man says. "I got nothing to give you. Don't bother with the show."

"Too bad for you," Gabriel says sympathetically. "All we can hope for is that you last for a while." He throws a punch, a quick jab that snaps the man's head back and makes his eye start to blacken almost immediately.

"Son of a whore," the man says.

Gabriel cocks his head to one side. "What's that have to do with anything?"

"His ribs are cracked on the right side," Drake offers as he stuffs the last of his food into his mouth. He's not looking too closely, but whatever Gabriel does with that information makes the man hiss and kick weakly to try to push Gabriel away. Bad move.

Gabriel pulls his heavy knife, flips it around in his hand, and brings the pommel down hard on the man's leg right below the knee. There's another cracking sound and what's definitely meant to be a curse, for all that it barely has any breath behind it.

"All right," Drake says. "I'm done. I could take over again for a bit." There's sweat standing out on the man's brow, despite the chill in here, and if Gabriel makes him go into pain shock too soon, it's not likely he'll even be able to barter his way out by volunteering information.

"Of course." Gabriel gets up. "He's all yours, Drake."

For a while after that, Drake tries not to pay too much attention to what he's doing. He aims his kicks so they'll hurt, but not do too much lasting damage. It's a means to an end, not something he does for its own sake, and personal or no, he would probably still leave most of it to Gabriel if it weren't for what a good threat Gabriel makes.

When they reach the point where Drake can throw a punch and pull it, and have the man still flinch, he figures they're about ready. "You want to take a turn? I'm getting bored with him."

"Now can I take some pieces off?" Gabriel asks. He's rolling one of his knives over the back of his hand, catching it, and setting it in motion again.

"Don't see why not."

"What do you bastards *want*?" the man slurs. He sounds hopeless. Just about right.

"Nothing too unusual," Drake says. "Bloody rotten vengeance on the men who wrong me, that's all."

The man huffs a little angry sound that's probably supposed to be defiant laughter. "You're as bad as they say, aren't you?"

"Flattery won't get you out of this," Gabriel says. "Come on, Drake. He's not good for anything else. Get out of the way so I can cut him."

"Wait," the man says. He's trying to focus on Drake, but his eyes are going glassy and the left one's swelling shut. "There's got to be something you want to know." Drake looks at Gabriel like he's considering the idea, and the guy adds, "Please."

"Were you really going to pay up the five guineas if someone handed me over to you?" Drake asks. Easy questions first, just making conversation.

"Course not," the man says thickly. "Way too much of the take to give away."

"Makes sense," Drake says. "How much is the take? What am I worth?"

The man's mouth curves in a bitter smirk, but he stops when that makes his split lip start oozing blood again. "Twenty-five."

Drake whistles. "Make all of you rich, wouldn't it? Even more now that there's fewer ways to split it. What was your man going to do with me, if he would pay that much? That's no hangman's bounty."

The man hesitates, and Gabriel says, "This is boring. He doesn't have any good stories." He shifts, knife raised, takes the man by the hair.

"I don't know," the man protests. "Sell you, probably. That's what Tom figured." He keeps looking from Drake to Gabriel's knife and back again. "To your family if they'd pay up, or else on a ship going south."

"Not bad." Drake gets down on the floor so he can look their captive in the eyes. "You know you need to get out of town yourself now, right? If you go back to your friends after this, there's no way they'll believe you didn't talk to us." He makes his tone as gentle and reasonable as he can. "So you've got nothing to lose but your life here."

Gabriel's knife traces a slow, careful line up the right side of the man's face, stops beside his right eye. He presses just hard enough to make an indent in the flesh. "I wouldn't say *nothing*, exactly."

"I'm talking already," the man says. His voice breaks. "What do I got to say?"

"Who's the man with the money?" Drake asks softly. "Who gave you bastards the job?"

The man swallows hard. "He's called Barron."

So Barron's still that angry, months later—trying to pick up where he left off, as if he hasn't already turned Colin's life upside down.

"Thank you." Drake steps back so the mess won't get on him, and Gabriel slits the man's throat, quick and easy, from one ear to the other. Blood pours from the wound, drenching the front of the man's clothes, steaming in the chill air.

"We've tangled with Barron before," Gabriel says.

Drake nods. "He might not know that. I don't think any of that first group got away. Westfall's men picked them up." He watches Gabriel step back, take off his jacket, roll up his sleeves. "What are you doing?"

"Letting Barron and his boys know that we're unhappy. Could you see if there's anything in here I can wipe my hands on afterward?" He picks up the knife again.

"Of course." Drake wonders as he turns away if Gabriel's trying to spare him from watching whatever he's going to do to the corpse. It's hard to tell whether it would be more like him to worry about Drake's sensibilities or to simply not realize the sight could be upsetting.

The stores left in the warehouse look like exports, mostly—the empty barrels held peaches or peach brandy, from the smell, and there's a broken crate whose timbers still smell faintly of tobacco under the top layer of mold and rot. How long has it been since he last had a good smoke? He almost can't remember what it tasted like. The dizziness of a good pipeful belongs to a different life, a different story from the one he's in now.

There is at least one bolt of spun cotton in the back, mildewing around the edges and its dye faded unevenly, but serviceable enough for this. Despite himself, Drake looks for the weaver's mark on the end of the bolt, but it's not one he recognizes. Nobody who dealt with his family's plantation, then. He pulls, and the cloth tears off the bolt raggedly, too damaged by the damp to hold together.

When he brings it back to the body, Gabriel is just standing up. His hands are streaked red, and the body is—

"Arhon's shroud," Drake says, looking away from the blank hollows where the eyes were. "His own mother wouldn't know him."

Gabriel nods. "Everyone will know who did it, though." He takes the cloth and wipes his hands. It stinks of blood in here, sharp like wet copper, and the smell makes Drake uncomfortable despite his best efforts to stay calm. "Help me with him?" Gabriel bends down to cut the ropes binding the dead man to the pillar.

"Not enough chance he'll be found if we leave him here?" Drake guesses. At least the position means there isn't too much blood on the arms, so they should be able to carry him out all right.

"Not nearly enough. The rats would get him first for sure, and they don't tell stories." He stops. "Not in taverns, anyway. Maybe they tell each other things."

"About old Graywhiskers, who went to see if the humans were dead or only sleeping?" Drake steps over a small pile of wet red things and doesn't look too closely at what they are. "The next day all anyone could find of him was his tail and a few burned pieces of bone."

Gabriel reaches under the body on the other side to help lift it. "If you go back there on a moonless night, though, you can hear the skitter of his claws on the stone."

CHAPTER
TWENTY-FIVE

They prop the body up outside, against a wall, as close to Dock Street as they dare. Gabriel digs out one bright, polished shilling. He leaves it in the corpse's open mouth, and his hand comes away bloody again. Drake wonders if it's a gesture with a history in Casmile's underworld, or if the language is Gabriel's own. The message is clear enough either way—here's payment for their informant, for the last job he did.

Gabriel wipes his hand on the wall, leaving a trail of bloody smears across the brick. "Ready to go?"

Drake nods. He's more than ready, really. They don't want to be here when the first unlucky bastard comes stumbling out of a tavern up the street and sees this.

They've made it a good four or five blocks away when Gabriel says, "Do you want to go after Barron tonight?"

"Is it up to me?" Drake asks. That seems odd; usually Gabriel is the one who makes the plans, unless there's something they absolutely need, like more coal or the rent. Of course, as far as Gabriel's concerned, it's entirely possible that vengeance is the same kind of emergency.

"He's your trouble," Gabriel says. That feels like a challenge as much as an offer—*he's your trouble, so what are you going to do about him?* "If you want to take him down right away . . ."

"I can let it wait for a night." It's been a long day already, and the idea of starting another hunt now, when he's fairly sure the afternoon is more than half gone, doesn't sound too tempting. "We're rich now, aren't we? Let's get a room for the night and have a few drinks, celebrate a bit."

"Anything for you, Drake. I did promise." Gabriel strokes Drake's cheek, and Drake kisses his palm.

"Come on, then," Drake says. "Let's find ourselves some luxuries."

The inns by the harbor come in two basic varieties: the ones for the sailors, and the ones for the merchants. Extravagant as it is, Drake leads them into the Leaping Dolphin, a merchants' inn, and even though it'll cost them more for a night than their old room cost for two weeks, he can't bring himself to regret it. When the proprietor suggests, almost without wrinkling her nose, that they could have a bath and their clothes washed for an extra shilling, he doesn't even try to barter that down. How long has it been since he really felt clean?

Gabriel seems rather suspicious of the whole endeavor. "The water's hot," he says, watching steam rise from the wooden tubs.

"I should hope so, for what it's costing us." Drake strips, piling his clothes on the floor beside the tub—the serving boy doesn't seem to want to come close enough to fetch them while they could still get at him easily, and Drake supposes that's reasonable—and climbs into the water. "Ah, Fates, it's been too long." He has to keep his left arm clear of the bath so the bandages won't get wet, but he lowers himself down until most of the rest of him is soaking, and that feels wonderful.

When he cracks one eye open, Gabriel is following his example, warily, setting knives and coin purses beside the second tub where they'll still be in reach and dropping his clothes in the pile. The suspicion slides off his face as soon as he gets into the water. "Oh," he says, and lowers himself carefully, holding on to the sides of the tub. The serving boy gathers up their clothes and flees, no doubt glad to be gone.

"Good, isn't it?" Drake reaches for the coarse washcloth and the cake of soap between the tubs.

"You'll get me spoiled, Drake," Gabriel says, but he sounds pleased. "Did you do this often?"

"Fairly, I suppose. Less in the summer when the heat's everywhere anyway."

"Wouldn't have thought the heat would bother you." Gabriel watches Drake wash, and it isn't even a particularly lascivious expression, just interested, but Drake finds himself starting to get hard anyway. He's warm and comfortable and he knows where his next meal's coming from, and Gabriel's admiring him, and that feels like more than enough.

"Here," he says, passing the soap and cloth across the space between them. "Your turn."

Gabriel laughs when the soap slides from his fingers, like he wasn't expecting it to do that, and reaches down into the water to retrieve it. He doesn't remark on it when he starts to wash himself clean, but it looks as though he's mimicking motions he hasn't really practiced. Drake thinks he's probably being rude by staring, but he can't help himself.

They trade the soap and washcloth back and forth, and neither of them does a terribly good job of not watching the other, so Drake supposes it must be all right. The serving boy comes back just before the water's really grown cold, when Drake is rinsing the second round of soap out of his hair. "Robes for you, sirs," he says, still fidgeting a bit. "Your clothes are by the fire in your room, number six, and here's the key." He shifts from one foot to the other.

Drake's about to thank him, tell him that's all they need, but Gabriel gets up first, rising out of the water with an easy, almost predatory motion. The boy flinches, tensed and ready to bolt when Gabriel reaches down for his pile of things, but it's only the purse he's going for. He walks across the room dripping, not even trying to cover himself, to take the key from the boy and give him a handful of copper in trade. "Thank you," he says.

The boy bows. "Enjoy your stay, sirs," he says in one rushed breath before he turns and runs for the door.

Gabriel watches him go. "Was that wrong?"

"No." Drake's smiling as he gets out of the tub himself. "Totally polite. He's just scared to death of you, that's all. You look much fiercer than the fat merchants he probably waits on most days."

"You're such a flatterer, Drake."

"It's only the truth." Gabriel might not be big, but he's wiry and scarred and carries himself like a hunter—like he knows he's the most dangerous thing in any room he walks into, even naked and unarmed. "Here." Drake picks up one of the robes and hands it to Gabriel, the material heavy and thick in his hands for all its plainness. "Let's go upstairs and see if our clothes are dry yet."

Gabriel shrugs into the robe, and then pulls it tight around himself as if he's noticed how warm it is. "Let's. After you."

Drake leads the way up the inn's back stairs, finds their room at the end of the second story hall. They're on the side facing the alley, not the water, but that's all right. They've both seen the harbor plenty of times. Their clothes are hung on a drying rack in front of the fireplace, and the fire leaps and crackles like it's been fed recently. There's a little stack of split wood beside it, even, so they'll be set all night.

"So fancy," Gabriel says, shaking his head.

"Not complaining, are you?" Drake feels the fabric of his jacket. Still pretty damp.

"Not complaining," Gabriel says. "Does my dragon want to go in search of dinner?"

"In a little while." The curl in Gabriel's hair is more obvious when it's wet, and the robe is just a little too big for him. He looks feral, out of place here, like something from one of his stories. Something wild disguised as a boy. "Come to bed with me?"

Gabriel stops in surprise for a moment, and then smiles. "Not for sleeping, you mean."

Drake shakes his head, reaches to turn the lock on the door. "No."

Gabriel nods. "I'd like that." He looks surprised again when Drake slips off his robe before crawling between the sheets, but he follows suit, and makes a low, pleased humming sound when he slides into Drake's arms and they're both bare.

"Yes," Drake says quietly, sliding his hands down Gabriel's back, feeling bone under the skin, the flex of muscle, the tight lines of scars. This is a luxury worth craving, the sweet smell of clean skin, the smoothness where the grime has been washed away. "Yes, Gabriel. Here. Like this." He shifts, and Gabriel meets his mouth for the kiss, pressing close against him.

It doesn't take much this time to get Gabriel to move with him, hips rocking, bare skin sliding against each other. Fates, that's Gabriel hardening—that's what it feels like when he's half-hard and pushing against Drake's thigh for more friction, and his hands hold so tight. He bites at Drake's tongue, keens in his throat, kneading at Drake's back hungrily.

"Let me," Drake says against his mouth. "Can I, Gabriel, Fates, can I look at you?"

"You're ridiculous," Gabriel says. "You look at me all the time." But he shifts back, lets Drake push the quilt down all the same. His ribs are too plain, and even in the firelight the shadow of his hipbones is deeper than it should be. Clean, his skin is a warmer color than Drake is used to, except where the worst scars have streaked it white. His cock lies against his lower belly, flushed, mostly hard.

Drake reaches out, runs his fingers along the smooth line of Gabriel's collarbone, trails them down over the plane of Gabriel's chest. He lays his palm flat in the hollow of Gabriel's belly, where the arch of rib cage drops away to softness.

"You've never looked more like a dragon," Gabriel says softly. He rests his hand over Drake's.

"No?" Drake meets Gabriel's eyes. "What am I doing?"

Gabriel shakes his head. "I think you must be confused. You look like you've found a treasure."

Drake ducks his head. "Nobody else has this," he says. "It's just for me." He shifts his weight, leans down, presses his lips to Gabriel's shoulder.

"Most people would call you mad for wanting it," Gabriel says. One of his hands slides into Drake's hair, holds on. "Drake. My Drake. Please, more."

His skin tastes like soap, the salt and dirt washed away. Drake licks at his throat, bites carefully at the soft hollow there, shivers at the low noise Gabriel makes when he does it. He reaches down a little further, takes Gabriel loosely in his hand. Gabriel pushes, thrusting against him, and Drake's body responds in kind. Fates, so good, so much— He lifts his head to watch what he's doing. His hand looks so white against Gabriel's skin—even now, after months of living here, he's so much paler than Gabriel is. No wonder he seems otherworldly.

"Move, Drake," Gabriel whispers, and Drake realizes that he's almost stopped, that he's let himself get distracted.

"Sorry." He takes a firmer grip, and Gabriel rocks against him.

Drake leans down again and presses his lips to Gabriel's throat. The way Gabriel responds to him, Fates, to his mouth, to his touch—he could go further than this, he thinks, and knows the idea won't leave him alone as soon as he has it. The rules are different with Gabriel. It wouldn't have to make either of them the other's boy, not if they're the only ones who know. And Gabriel is holding tight to him, breath shaky, making sweet needy sounds.

"Gabriel," Drake murmurs. "Do you—" He doesn't have to ask that. He knows Gabriel trusts him, strange as it is. "Will you let me try something new?"

"Of course. You've had so many good ideas." There's laughter in his voice, Drake thinks, like this is all still strange for him, too; like they're having another adventure.

Thinking about actually doing it makes Drake's heart pound, makes his nerves jittery. "Hold still, then," he says, and lets go, pushes himself up on his hands and knees so he can slide down the bed to kneel between Gabriel's thighs.

Gabriel watches him, eyes wide and alert, lips parting when Drake curls his hand around the base of Gabriel's cock.

"Tell me," Drake says, and licks his lips. His mouth feels dry. "Tell me how this feels." He leans down and parts his lips, and Fates, he wouldn't have thought he'd have to stretch so much to do this—to take Gabriel in his mouth.

"Drake," Gabriel gasps, his voice shaky, almost panicked. "Drake, Drake—" He reaches down, groping blindly, and Drake takes his hand. Gabriel holds on so tight it's almost painful, and Drake is just starting to worry that maybe this is actually upsetting Gabriel when he takes another shaky breath and says, "Please, yes."

Drake moans a little, as close as he can get to saying yes, to telling Gabriel he wants to. It feels a lot more awkward than he would have expected—the angle is completely unnatural, and he thinks his neck will start to really ache soon, and he has no idea how the Kite Street girls managed to get him all the way in their mouths, because he's taking barely half of Gabriel and he feels like he's going to choke. But he doesn't want to stop, either. Gabriel moans and shivers, and he feels so smooth against Drake's tongue—and nobody has ever done this for Gabriel before; that's plain from the way he reacts, and Drake wants to make his first time good, wants to spoil him and maybe show off a little, too.

After a few careful strokes, he starts to get the hang of it, how to guard his teeth with lips and tongue, how to move so that he keeps a rhythm going, so that he doesn't take more down his throat than he can stand. Gabriel's thighs tremble, and he croons little encouraging noises that never quite turn into real words. Drake can taste salt against the back of his tongue, wonders if—

Gabriel comes, silent and tense under him, and Drake's mouth is full of bitter heat. He coughs a little, not prepared for it, and then swallows, twice, three times.

"Oh, Drake," Gabriel says, barely more than a whisper, hushed and reverent. "So clever. So very good."

Drake sits back on his heels, meets Gabriel's eyes, and lets himself smile a little in relief. His jaw feels odd, and he can still taste it, tingling at the back of his throat. The bitterness is somewhat less than thrilling, but that scarcely matters when it's Gabriel. "Good. I'm glad." He feels giddy, unable to believe he actually did that—and hard, too, for the needy way Gabriel looks at him, for the fact that he just made Gabriel come. With his *mouth*. Fates.

"Come here," Gabriel says, reaching for him, and Drake lets himself be pulled up to stretch out next to Gabriel for a kiss. "So very clever," Gabriel tells him, stroking his back, his sides, pushing him onto his back and reaching down to take hold of him. "Is it hard to do? I never have."

Oh, Maiden's mercy. "I hadn't either. Didn't really think I wanted to, until—until you." Even with Danny, he'd only wondered about it occasionally, and then mostly about whether Danny would be willing to do it for him.

"I want to try, then. If you'll let me."

"Fates, Gabriel, of course I'd— Yes. Please." Drake's so hard just thinking of it that he aches. He knots his fingers in the sheets and watches Gabriel kneel between his thighs. His breath comes short, and he feels dizzy.

Gabriel leans down, nuzzles his way into Drake's groin like a pushy cat, rubs his face against Drake. His breath is hot. He licks, like he's tasting it, like he's curious, and Drake moans without being able to help himself. Gabriel laughs.

"Something else you've been wanting and not asking for?" he says. "Silly dragon. I can't guess at everything."

Drake doesn't even know how to start arguing the point—Gabriel makes it sound like he was trying to be difficult, like he didn't have a good reason to hesitate—but then Gabriel leans back down, and he loses interest in trying to argue anyway. Gabriel's mouth closes hot and wet around him, careful lips and tongue, and it's all Drake can do to just hold still. He wants to push, wants to rock deeper into *Gabriel's mouth*, oh, Mother's blessing—and when he looks down, Gabriel has closed his eyes, his cheeks hollowed, his lips stretched around Drake's shaft. He hums as he slides down further, little noises like he's . . . like he's fascinated, like he's trying this out to see how it goes. The idea makes Drake want to laugh at how incredible all this is.

"Don't stop," he says instead, and he sounds just as unsteady as Gabriel did a few minutes ago, just as overwhelmed. "You're so good to me, Gabriel, I, ah—" And he falters, gasping, when Gabriel's teeth scrape his skin for just a second. Gabriel makes a soft, sorrowful noise, and strokes Drake's hip in apology. "It's all right," Drake says. "You didn't hurt me." The pain didn't even slow him down, didn't do anything to ease the aching tension that's drawing every last scrap of him toward Gabriel's mouth. "If you . . ." he manages, and he's so close, it should take longer than this, but he *wants*. "If you wanted t-to do that again—"

And when Gabriel does, teeth raking delicately over his flesh, Drake loses what's left of his control and spills in Gabriel's mouth. He's shaking with exhaustion and so relieved to be here, like this, things finally going their way. When Gabriel looks up, wiping his mouth on the back of his hand and wrinkling his nose at the taste, Drake can't help laughing, wrung out and content, more relaxed than he's been in ages.

"Thank you," he says, reaching out to pull Gabriel close, to hold on to him. "Oh, Gabriel." They fit so well together by now, used to the puzzle their limbs make. "This is— I feel so good right now."

Gabriel settles his head on Drake's shoulder, curled close against him, and bites Drake's collarbone affectionately. "Good. You make things better, Drake. So much better."

Drake closes his eyes and nuzzles Gabriel's hair, so soft now that it's clean. He's warm and comfortable and they have a real bed to sleep in tonight and another meal coming to them yet today, and Barron's not going to walk away from this one. The Fates do play favorites after all.

CHAPTER
TWENTY-SIX

T hey doze for a while without really meaning to, wake up near sunset and get dressed—their clothes not only dry but warm from hanging by the fire—so they can go downstairs to have dinner. The Leaping Dolphin has a roast on for the evening meal, and casks of smooth northlands lager for their taps. Gabriel tries both with enthusiasm, and from the look on his face at the first bite of roast beef, Drake guesses he's never had its like. There are so many things that he'd like to show Gabriel, if he only has the chance. Maybe after Barron's dead, that should be their next plan.

After dinner and a few pints apiece, they go back up to their room and suck each other off a second time. It's sloppier, messier when the lager has gone to both of their heads, more potent and more plentiful than they're used to. The sex still feels just as good, though, dizzying and clumsy and wet. Afterward, Drake sleeps more heavily than he has in months, naked with Gabriel under the blankets. It's warm enough that when he wakes in the morning, he discovers one of them pushed the blankets down in the night, and neither of them woke at the exposure of bare skin to air.

Gabriel is still asleep beside him, his mouth soft and relaxed, his hair curling gently over his forehead. He looks young, and still so hungry, his cheeks hollow—but better, Drake wants to believe. Less desperate. Less of a shadow.

He touches Gabriel's face, gently, stroking the line of Gabriel's jaw—

And manages not to flinch, barely, when Gabriel's hand snakes out and grabs his wrist.

"Sorry," Drake says as Gabriel's eyes open. "I should let you sleep?" No wonder Gabriel could catch the rat that came to investigate them; he strikes before he wakes.

"It's all right. My dragon's woken up hungry again?"

Drake's about to deny it—he doesn't especially need anything just yet, and if Gabriel wants to rest a little longer while they have the chance, that's fine—but then Gabriel rolls over, pushing Drake onto his back and settling on top of him. He's already getting hard.

Drake reaches down between them, shows Gabriel how, if they lace their fingers together, they can rock against each other at the same time and both reach for it at once. Drake finishes first, and decides he likes that, because then he can be watching, can see the moment of off-balance breathless need on Gabriel's face as he gives up control and shudders into Drake's hand.

"Now," Drake says afterward, when they've wiped themselves clean on the sheets and are pulling their clothes back on, "I think I'm hungry." It's not bad today, though, the way it is when they're barely getting by. Anything seems possible, at this point. "We'll get some breakfast on the way to Barron's house. How's that?"

Gabriel touches the spots where his knives are hidden, like he's taking stock of them. "Sounds good to me. I'm looking forward to meeting Barron, after hearing so much about him."

Breakfast is a batch of warm sweet rolls, bought from the front door of a bakery and smothered in peach butter. The air's still cold, but the clouds hang high and distant, no real threat, not likely to carry any real rain. Drake and Gabriel walk up the broad expanse of Market Street, taking their time, passing the shops and tradesmen along both sides of the way. The merchants' district lasts until the second bridge, more or less, and then gives way to some finer taverns, private clubs, and the high-stakes gaming houses that were the center of Colin's version of Casmile. A few houses here are worth checking for rumors, if they need to track Barron to ground, but Drake figures they might as well start with the most likely option, so the Peacock it is.

The Golden Peacock is as flashy as its name suggests, brightly painted, edged in gold leaf around all its ornate moldings. The lamps are always lit, no matter the time of day or night; Drake's never seen the house closed up. Inside the walls are hung with imported silks, and the chairs around the gaming tables are heavy, dark polished wood and overstuffed velvet, the kind of things a man can just sink right into and relax comfortably until he's gambled away every shilling to his name. There's reserve brandy for sale, by the bottle or the glass, and some of the most finely cured tobacco that a man can find anywhere in the city. The whores who make their living off the winners aren't terribly discreet about it, entertaining in rooms in the back of the house, and Drake's never been sure if that was because they were legal or because the guard can be bribed.

He tries imagining what this must look like now from Gabriel's perspective as they show silver and walk through the front door. Dragons everywhere they look, he thinks, cunning old serpents guarding their hoards and brash young ones hoping to steal from them. The air smells of smoke, curls of it wreathing the one table that's active right now. There's no dice game this early in the day, not enough traffic to keep the table going, just the guarded faces of the men around the card table, and the flash of coin being tossed in to ante.

There's no sign of Barron, not yet. Drake watches the cards flutter as the dealer shuffles them, counts them off as he deals the new hand. Three card brag, it looks like.

Gabriel elbows him in the ribs. "Your man here?"

"Don't see him. He might be in the back, though. Or he might be coming in later." Barron owns a stake in the Peacock, though Drake can't remember if it's a quarter or an eighth. At any rate, it's his gaming house, the one he's most likely to show up to. "We probably don't have that long to wait." There's a boy at the table about Drake's age, someone he'd swear he met at one party or another, who's just won the last hand and looks like he thinks he can't lose. "Maybe we should get comfortable, sit in on the game for a bit."

"Mmn," Gabriel says. "Costs a lot to play here, doesn't it?"

"We're still flush, though," Drake says. Robert? Is that the boy's name? Roland? Something like that. "Wouldn't it be something if we could use Barron's money to win more off him?"

"Drake," Gabriel says sharply. He steps in between Drake and the active table, and the crease to his brow keeps Drake from trying to see past him. "I know it's very shiny, all that coin piled up there. Of course you want it for your own. But greedy dragons never see the knights coming for them, do they?"

Drake opens his mouth and realizes he's about to argue, about to try to claim that he could play just one hand, and stops. "Sorry," he says instead. Robert or Roland, whichever, makes an aggrieved, disbelieving noise from the table, and Drake doesn't let himself turn back no matter how much he'd like to. "You're my luck, Gabriel. If you say no, I guess we don't play today."

"Not today," Gabriel agrees, and pets Drake's arm as if he's done something clever. Drake hopes nobody's watching them too closely. "How do we find out if he's in the back?"

"We ask, I suppose." There aren't many whores in the house when it's slow, but there's always someone willing to work the winners. Drake studies the side of the room, where a few girls are lounging, watching the table, watching them. One of them—the younger one, with her hair in braids and rouge on her mouth, in a clinging wine-gold dress that makes her skin look dark and warm—smiles just a little when he looks at her, and beckons.

Drake takes the invitation, threading his way between the dead tables to get to the couch where the whores wait. He can feel Gabriel just behind him and to his right, close enough to touch. Close enough to lay a claim, and the whores can tell, from the raised eyebrows.

"Good choice," says the girl who beckoned to him, and winks. "That table's got no luck at all today, but you'll always get a good time over here." She leans forward, so Drake can see down the front of her dress. "You up for it, handsome?"

"Looking for someone," Drake says. "Have you seen Barron today?"

"Haven't seen him," the girl with the braids says. She glances at the other whore, who might be a little older, or maybe just more tired, her eyes heavy despite the paint she's wearing to hide it. "Kate?"

"Haven't seen him, don't miss him. He was in a damn foul mood last night. Don't think anybody's in a hurry for him to come back."

There's something entirely too satisfying about that, about the idea that Barron's nervous knowing they're still out there in Casmile somewhere. "You know what he was upset about?" Drake asks.

Kate shakes her head. "I know plenty about him, handsome, but I'm working right now, and you don't sound like you're buying."

"Of course." Drake glances at Gabriel for confirmation, and Gabriel shrugs one shoulder. It's still odd to be making all their decisions, even if it's clear he does know more about this particular tangle than Gabriel does. "How much?"

"Just you?" she says. "Six shillings."

"Both of us," Drake says. He doesn't want to get separated, doesn't want to leave Gabriel here with nothing to keep him entertained and plenty to make him uncomfortable. He needs Gabriel steady today. Clearheaded enough to help.

"What kind of girl do you think I am?" Kate asks.

One who only costs six shillings, Drake thinks, which he knows isn't fair, because there are plenty of awful things he'd probably have done for that much money a week ago, and he probably will again.

"I won't touch you," Gabriel says. He's smiling, close mouthed, one of those unnerving expressions that Drake often thinks he does on purpose—the ones that look like he doesn't quite know what they're for, and he's just doing them because other people do.

Kate glances from him back to Drake, shifts like she's not sure where the threat is coming from. "You're going to make trouble if I don't, aren't you?"

"It'll be the easiest money you make all day. Come on. If I wanted to hurt you, I'd be trying to get you to leave the house with me."

"I still want extra," she says. Her expression is guarded, like she expects one of them to get nasty, like she's used to men who get violent easily. "Ten."

"All right," Drake says. They can always change their minds later, but best to start friendly. "Lead the way."

Kate gets up. "They give you trouble, you just yell," the other girl says, watching Drake. He gives her one of Gabriel's just-showing-my-teeth smiles, and she looks away.

Drake and Gabriel follow Kate to the back of the house, past a silk hanging with a spread-wings design painted on it, to a row of small rooms. There's a lamp already burning in the room Kate chooses, and under the tobacco smoke it smells like every whorehouse Drake's ever been to: stale sweat and sex.

She turns back to them as Gabriel closes the door, and her posture is stiff, worry lines tight around her eyes. "You want a show, then?"

"No," Gabriel says. "I want a story."

"You sleep with Barron?" Drake helps himself to one of the chairs, and gestures for Kate to take the couch.

"Girl can't get a job here if she doesn't," Kate says.

"You don't like him, though."

Kate laughs harshly. "You want me to say I'm waiting to be rescued? Looking for a nice boy to take me away from all this?"

"No," Drake says.

"More like we're waiting for you to say you wish somebody would take care of the greedy pig," Gabriel says. This time he smiles like he means it.

Kate's eyes widen a little, and she glances between them. "You mean it?"

"I owe him," Drake says. "He's sent plenty of trouble my way, and I owe him for it." He waits for her to meet his eyes. "I hope you meant it, when you said you knew him."

"What do you want me to tell you?"

"Where to find him when he's not here. Where he lives, if you know. Whether he's hired himself any bodyguards."

"He'll kill me for helping you."

"That's if he gets to kill anyone after we're through with him," Gabriel says. "And there isn't much chance of that."

Kate takes a deep breath. "You promise you won't hurt me if I tell you?"

Drake nods. "Lady take the liar," he says, and Kate shudders a little, because she has enough sense to be afraid, but she nods too.

And she does know plenty, from the sound of it. How nervous Barron got last night after the bad news, the bravos he hired a few days earlier, the fact that last night instead of taking a whore home with him like usual, he took two of the Peacock's guard instead. There's a joke to be made about that, an ugly one, but none of them bother with it. Kate's voice rises and falls steadily, reciting information. How to get to Barron's house from here—the son of a bitch has one of the old row houses on top of the Bank Street ridge, fronting right on the drop to the water. How many ways there are into the house, how much the street is lit most nights. Which room is his, up the stairs. Where he keeps his coin.

That part Drake hadn't even really thought about yet—but Fates, what luck that would be. Barron's rich enough to have lent him alone probably twenty guineas over the last year or so, not even counting all the other debts he bought up. If he keeps even a fraction of that on hand instead of in a bank, it'll be enough for them to live like dragons for a good long time. They can stop worrying, stop counting coins to make sure they'll have enough food to eat and coal to burn.

Kate's running out of answers to give them, her voice dry now, when someone knocks at the door. Gabriel gets up from his perch on the arm of the couch, drawing one of his knives. Kate takes a sharp breath, and Gabriel motions for her to stay quiet.

"What do you want?" Drake calls. He tries to sound impatient, irritated at the interruption. It doesn't take much acting.

"Kate," whispers a voice from the other side. The other whore, it sounds like. "Open the door."

Drake gets up, opens the door, and pulls the girl inside. It didn't look like she had anyone with her, but he shuts the door again anyway. "What is it?"

The girl flinches like he's holding on to her too tightly, but Drake doesn't let go. "Barron's here." She glares up at him. "He's asking about you. And I don't give a fuck about you, but I don't want Kate caught up in your mess."

"Fair enough," Gabriel says lightly. He turns to Drake. He looks ready for anything. "Shall we go pay our respects?"

"Let's," Drake says, letting go of the girl. He hands Kate a generous pile of silver. "You stay here. No reason for you to get hurt."

Kate shakes her head, reaching for her friend. "Who are you bastards, anyway?"

Drake slides his brass knuckles on and flexes his fingers to settle them. "Drake and Gabriel." He can't help himself. He bows like they're at a midwinter ball, or in the theater. "Pleased to meet you."

"Now, Drake," Gabriel murmurs, hand on the doorknob. Drake nods, and they go.

CHAPTER
TWENTY-SEVEN

B arron's in the middle of talking to someone at the gaming table when they come back out to the main room. He looks almost exactly as Drake remembers him: well fed, gaudy, his clothes a little too extravagant for the house and definitely for the time of day. He's gesturing like he has everything under control, like whatever story he's telling is amusement and nothing more, but his posture's too tense to hold that up.

Then he glances around the room—casually, like he's looking for an illustration of his point—and meets Drake's eyes. He falters in his story, and Drake would swear he turns gray, the blood drains from his face so fast. There's a big nasty type over by the wall, who starts toward them as soon as it's clear Barron's upset.

"Gabe," Drake says.

"Get him," Gabriel answers, and turns toward the tough.

Someone screams when Gabriel raises his knife, and the players get up from the table. Drake launches himself toward it, up *onto* it, coins and card scattering and the wood creaking in protest as he lands—and Barron's not stupid, he's turning for the door, trying to put some distance between them—so Drake dives for him, the table crashing down behind him as he throws himself at Barron's shoulders. The bastard goes down heavily, and there's more yelling, everyone panicked now.

"You corpse-fucking—" Barron snarls, trying to push Drake off, and Drake punches him, the hand with all the brass, and there's a dull, sloppy crack under his hand. Barron stops struggling, but it can't be that easy, so Drake tangles a hand in his hair and slams his head down on the floor for good measure, once, twice, and there's blood everywhere and more cracking noises, and he doesn't want to *stop*, angry now at the way they've had to run, and at Barron's stupid thugs wanting to kill Gabriel, and that they weren't safe anywhere, and there's less crunching now and more just wet noises and—

"Drake!" Gabriel is yelling, like it's not the first time he's tried. He's pulling on Drake's sleeve. "Come on. We have to go." He glances toward the door. "They're crying for the guard."

Fuck. "Right." Drake lets Gabriel pull him up. "You're all right?" he asks, because there's a lot of blood on Gabriel's front and some of it might be his own.

"Fine," Gabriel says, and doesn't let go of Drake as they start for the door. "Just fine."

Nobody's stupid enough to get in their way—plenty of men might want to see criminals brought to justice, but not many want to take the risk of doing it themselves. Outside it's starting to rain, the sky dull, the city gray, the cobbles slick under their feet.

Gabriel turns right, away from the harbor, and Drake goes with him. No good came of separating the last time. He can hear more shouting now, the guards' whistles, the clatter of hooves. They need to get off the main street, out of sight, now.

Drake pulls on Gabriel's hand and tugs him down a side street. It's too quiet up here, too many houses and not enough shops, not enough places for them to get lost. A whistle blows again in the distance, and they turn a second time, then a third. If the mounted guard find them, they'll get run down in no time. There aren't nearly enough escape routes here, not even an easy way up onto the roofs, with how widely spaced the houses are.

"Across the river," Drake says at the next corner. They need someplace where they can hide.

Gabriel nods, and they take off again. He's moving easily, keeping up, so he can't have gotten hurt back there, not really. Fates, it all went to rot so fast, the plan unraveling as quickly as they'd made it, and now—they turn south toward the river again. If they can get into the burned quarter, below the river, they'll have no end of places they can hide, and streets so cramped and narrow the horses won't be a help to the guard anymore.

When they come out on Market Street, they're about fifty paces from the nearest bridge, and downriver someone shouts before they've taken more than three of them. They run faster, trying to reach the bridge— Are those footsteps behind them? They can outrun a man, surely. The way is clear up to the bridge, and they duck around an ox cart that comes creaking up to its foot. Someone curses behind them— Good, let the guard get tripped up there.

There are only a few people on the bridge, one of the narrower ones, and Drake's already thinking about which way to go on the other side when he sees the horseman riding up the bank, from the right—on a gray, even, and he prays it's not the captain.

"Left," he says, as they weave through the scattering of people on the bridge.

"Just go," Gabriel says, maybe agreement—he has to hope so— and then they're across and turning left, and a whistle sounds behind them again. Damn the guard for being so well organized today.

Drake doesn't even see the second horse until it's too late, until it turns the corner in front of them and rears, and they flinch back but not fast enough—and there's a sickening cracking noise as one of those flailing hooves glances off Gabriel's temple.

He drops instantly, crumpling to the street, and Drake dives for him, pulling him back to keep the guardsman's horse from trampling him outright. "Gabe," Drake says urgently, cold with panic. There's blood, fresh and bright, streaking Gabriel's face, and he's limp in Drake's arms. "Gabriel, please. Wake up. Wake up."

He hears the snort of a horse behind him but doesn't look up. Gabriel's still breathing, that's the important part. "Touching, Harwood," Captain Westfall says. "But your luck's run out."

He should be looking for a way to bolt—between the legs of the bay in front of him, maybe—or preparing for the attack he's sure comes next, but Drake can't make himself do either. He holds on to Gabriel instead, watching for the flutter of eyelids that means—yes, thank the Maiden, there—he's fighting his way back to wakefulness.

"You'll come quietly now, won't you," the captain says as the other guardsman dismounts, "or I'll kill your friend right here."

Drake glances up long enough to nod—hates the satisfaction on Westfall's face, the rotting bastard—and presses the heel of his hand to Gabriel's temple, as if he could stop the bleeding by wanting alone. Gabriel's eyes almost focus on him, clearing slowly.

"Up you go," the other guard says, grabbing Drake by the back of his coat. Drake pulls against the grip instinctively, and gets a blade at his throat for his trouble. "Up, I said." He doesn't even sound angry, just bored. Doing his job, like he and Gabriel when they're working someone over themselves.

"Let me help him up?" Drake asks, and when the pressure of the blade eases a little, he takes that for the most encouragement he's likely to get. He pulls Gabriel closer, gets his hands under Gabriel's arms, tries to stand up slowly. At first Drake staggers, but then Gabriel gets his balance, and they both manage to climb to their feet.

"Drake," Gabriel says weakly, his fingers catching in Drake's coat. "You should have run. They'll hang you."

"Save your strength," Drake says. He can feel the little shivers running through Gabriel's frame, wonders how bad the injury really is. When he turns, Westfall is holding his crossbow at the ready, aimed at Gabriel.

"Take their weapons," he says.

The guardsman strips off Drake's brass knuckles, searches him roughly for anything else dangerous, then starts to confiscate Gabriel's knives. It's a sign of how bad things have gotten that Gabriel doesn't really fight the effort. The guard finds three knives, all told. Is that all of them? They've been through so much lately that Drake's not sure whether he still has a fourth.

By the time the search is done, a few more guardsmen have shown up to help. Worst luck they've had in days, and that's saying something. Their hands are pinned behind their backs, and Gabriel's lip curls in the beginning of a snarl when the rope's pulled tight around his wrists, but he's still too unsteady on his feet to manage any kind of real threat. People are gathering on the street to stare. Drake hates all of them.

"All right, boys," Westfall says, his tone flat and satisfied. "You know where we're headed now."

The guards on foot patrol march them up the street, and Westfall follows on his horse. It's not terribly far, up Bank Street and then south along Raven to the prison, barely a stone's throw from the hanging square. Real fear starts to crawl along Drake's limbs. They can't bluff their way out of this, can't leave it to chance, can't come back another day when their luck's better. The prison is squat and ugly, its foundation rain-blackened stone, the door heavy oak. Inside it smells like damp straw, old piss, and fear.

"Revell," Westfall says, "take our fancy boy upstairs."

"What?" Drake asks. "No, wait, I— Don't, I want to stay with him."

"Don't make it worse for yourself," Revell says, taking a grip on Drake's collar and tugging him toward the stairs. Other guards are dragging Gabriel through a door downstairs, and he stumbles once before he disappears down the hall. "You might have a chance up here, at least."

"But— I—" Drake lets Revell drag him up the stairs, too numb and hopeless to struggle hard. Revell's a big man, broad across the shoulders, and he pulls Drake along like it isn't difficult. "What'll happen to—to my friend?" he asks as Revell pushes him into a cell.

Revell at least meets his eyes, wearing the unhappy face of a man who doesn't want to be as hard as he has to be. "He'll hang, once the magistrate's had a chance to hear the case against him. Tomorrow or the next day, most likely."

The bottom drops out of Drake's stomach, and he feels like his legs won't hold him. "No. You can't— There must be some way—Wait, please," he says as Revell closes the cell door. "Can you send word to my family, at least? To the Harwood plantation, out on Mockingbird Lane. I'll pay for it. Whatever I have left, you can have it."

"Save your coin. We'll send someone out to tell your family. They'll likely want to hire someone to plead your case when it's your turn." Revell shakes his head. "Don't get your hopes up too high, though. You've already got the Lady's eye by the time you walk in the prison door."

He turns away, and Drake can't even summon the energy to call him back. Fates. He slides down into a little heap on the floor and wishes for a miracle, for lightning to strike and break open the walls, for the ground to open and swallow him up here, *anything* but having to sit here and wait and think of Gabriel somewhere in a cell below, hurt and alone and due to hang.

It's hard to know how long he sits there, not moving; it seems like ages, but the light from the thin barred window hasn't really turned, so it can't actually be that long. There aren't any other prisoners up here with him, and the quiet is oppressive. The rope around his wrists is rough, scratching at his skin, and his fingers tingle like the feeling's going out of them. There's no sign of Revell in the hall, or any of the other guards, either, when Drake struggles to his feet to look. Nobody to come and untie him.

If he were the clever dragon Gabriel tells him he is, he'd have an escape plan by now. He'd have some elegant way of tricking the guards, or he'd know how to pick the lock on the door, or he'd pull the walls of this rotten place down around him to go free. He'd be—

Drake stops, makes himself take slow, deep breaths. He needs to keep his wits about him, now more than ever. First thing, he needs his hands free, and after that he can start to work out the rest of the plan.

The cell doesn't offer much in the way of assistance. The bed is a straw mat on the floor, like Gabriel's on Cypress Street, and the only other furniture in the room is the chamber pot, which looks to be painted iron, not porcelain, so he can't break that for an edge. The bars are sturdy, and Drake searches for a raw join, a seam where the iron's rough enough to work as a file, but no luck there. Lady take the captain and all his men, and the builders who made the jail so solid. Drake hangs his head, tries to stay calm and figure out what to do next—and realizes he's staring at the little round heads of the nails holding the floorboards down.

He kneels, awkward without his hands to catch him, and turns around to try to find the edges of the nails with his fingertips. They lie almost flush against the wood, too close to do him any good, but surely there must be others, mustn't there?

"He's one of yours," Drake mutters as he searches for other nails, "and I'm one of his. If you make exceptions at all—" which is ridiculous, and he knows it perfectly well; even if the Lady is real and even if she's listening, why should she make exceptions for anyone? The gallows would just bring them to her. "Please," Drake says anyway, because he has nothing to lose at this point. His fingers find another nail under the edge of the straw mattress, the head bent out of true just enough to leave it sticking up. "Please help us."

The rope is heavy stuff, tough fibers that don't fray easily, and Drake drags his wrists across the nail until his shoulders ache before he dares to stop and feel for progress. He thinks it's working, thinks the twisted strands are splitting where he's been worrying at them. The light is starting to change, warming as though the sky has finally cleared now that they're not outside to see it. And he has nothing else to do in here—nothing save worry about Gabriel, and wonder what horrible things Westfall might have done to him when he was too badly off to fight back—so when his shoulders recover enough that he can make himself keep moving, Drake goes back to sawing at the ropes.

By the second time he has to stop, the light from the window is turning orange. There's not enough time, not enough chances. Drake wonders if someone will come by to feed him tonight, and if so, how long it'll take. He feels too nervous to eat, his stomach in knots, but it'll be the best chance he gets. He can't just keep sitting here. The rope is frayed now, still holding, but more than half-cut. He pulls, flexing the muscles of his arms and shoulders, straining against the unforgiving tension of the rope. It burns, digging into his wrists, and he bites his lip, pulling harder. The cut on his arm from the fight with Barron's goons starts to ache in time with his heartbeat. *No*, he thinks, gritting his teeth against the pain. He's not going to let it end like this.

The rope gives all at once, so suddenly that Drake almost loses his balance, falling backward. He catches himself on his hands and sits up again, brings his hands in front of himself to see how bad the damage is. Both of his wrists have red, angry welts across them, and when he curls his fingers inward, the tendons ache. But his hands are free.

Drake gets up, takes two steps across the cell to examine the window. Even without the bars, he thinks he'd have trouble getting through it; the opening's narrow enough that he'd have to turn sideways to fit, and high enough off the floor that he'd need some way to boost himself up. It's not the way he wants to go anyway—when he leaves, he wants Gabriel to be with him.

He looks past the bars, out into the city. The sun's setting in the distance, and the roofs nearby glow gold. The streets open out only a few blocks away, where— His cell faces the hanging square, Drake realizes. He steps away from the window, feeling sick. Tomorrow, Gabriel—

No. No, it won't happen. Can't. He won't let it.

The lock on the door is sturdy, and he doesn't have anything to pick it with in any case. If he's going to get out of here, it'll depend on someone else opening the door. Surely someone will come to feed him soon, won't they? It sounded like he was being given special treatment because Westfall knows who he is.

The sun sets before he hears movement on the stairs, though—there've been a few sounds from below, muffled through the floor, but nobody coming up to this wing until now. Drake pulls back, gauging his odds. The lid for the chamber pot is the nearest thing he has to a weapon right now. When the cell door opens—

And then the light of a lantern warms the hall outside, and he sees who's come to visit him, and he stops. "Anna?" He remembers just in time to put his hands behind his back so it won't be clear he's freed them. He should have thought to hide the rope, but by lamplight perhaps the guard—not Revell this time, someone else—won't notice the curl of it beside the straw mat.

"Colin," Anna says, rushing up to the edge of the cell, wrapping her hands around the bars. "Oh, Colin, what have you done?"

He has to hang his head. "I'm sorry. Of all the ways I could have seen you again, I promise this isn't the one I'd have chosen."

"Of course not," Anna says, reaching through the bars for a moment before she pulls back and turns to the jailer. "Please, let me in to see him."

The guard frowns. "Against the rules. And forgive me for saying so, but you'd have to be mad to want to get close to a killer like him."

Anna draws herself up proudly, and Drake thinks, *How can she have grown up so fast? It's only been a few months, hasn't it?* "My brother," Anna says sharply—Fates, she learned that tone from their father— "will not hurt me, and I will see him."

That shouldn't work, should just lead to an argument or outright dismissal—or maybe Drake's forgotten what it was like to be important, because it's the jailer who looks away first. "There'll be no rescue if he turns on you," the guy says—gutless little bastard—but his hand hovers over the ring of keys at his belt.

"I'm not in any danger," Anna says. Drake could kiss her for her faith in him. She stands waiting, proud and determined, until the jailer shakes his head and lifts the ring of keys.

The temptation to lunge for freedom now, to push his way through the open door, is so strong Drake can taste it, but he makes himself hold still. He doesn't want Anna to get hurt, and he thinks his chances will be better when she leaves anyway. The jailer unlocks the door, and the iron bars swing back, and Anna slips inside with him.

"It's good to see you," he says. "You're looking well." The cell door closes again behind her, and he tries not to flinch.

"And you look awful," Anna says, crossing the floor toward him anyway.

The jailer *harrumph*s, and picks up his lantern again. "I'll be back for you when I've seen to the bastards downstairs. You have that long and no more."

For a moment Anna frowns like she's going to call after him when he turns away with the lantern, but she doesn't, and when the light fades down the hallway, Drake lets his hands fall to his sides.

"You were the only one who'd come, were you?" He can't even imagine how much of a scandal his arrest will be, but he'd have expected his parents to at least show up.

"Father wasn't at home when the messenger came, and mother said it wouldn't be proper to come to a place like this without him. She said he'd escort us tomorrow."

"And you didn't care about the impropriety? You should be careful of that sort of thing. Look where it's landed me."

The noise Anna makes is too pained to be a real laugh, and then she's flinging herself into his arms, holding on tight, and all Drake can think of is the filth on his clothes and how she must be ruining her dress. "You idiot," she says into his shoulder. "You idiot, Colin. Why didn't you come home?"

Drake shakes his head, wraps his arms around her carefully. "I meant to, at first. But there were Barron's thugs after me, and then Westfall making it worse, and . . . I met someone, and he—" Fates, there aren't words for it. "It would have been hard to leave him."

"But . . ." Anna says, and Drake doesn't want to hear the good reasons he should have done things differently, doesn't think he can bear it.

"He's the reason I need to get out of here now," he says before Anna can marshal reason against him.

"We'll get you out, I'm sure of it. Even if father doesn't approve, he wouldn't abandon you here. He'll get someone to advocate for you, and it'll be fine."

"No, that's not what I meant." Anna tries to pull back, and he holds on tighter. He's not sure he can meet her eyes. "I need to get out tonight. I don't have any time to wait."

Anna squeezes him tight. "I know it must be awful to be stuck here, but—"

"It's not that. I don't even *want* to go back to the house, not really," and he can barely believe the words himself, so he's sure she won't. "And if I could— It's not me I'm worried about. It's Gabriel."

"Gabriel?" Anna says, very softly. "The same Gabriel from the stories you used to tell me?"

"He's not . . . he's not much like the stories," Drake says. "And he's looked after me since the night I left home, and now he's downstairs in one of the other cells and they're going to hang him in the morning unless I get him out of here tonight." His voice is shaking by the time he finishes the sentence, and he's holding her too tightly.

"Colin," Anna says, and he nearly tells her that's not his name anymore. "You can't— You would throw away this chance for him? He means that much to you?"

"Yes." Admitting it out loud feels like letting go a breath he's been holding for months. "He does."

Anna takes deep, slow breaths, and her shoulders are shaking. "I've missed you so much," she whispers. "So much, Colin."

"Don't cry," Drake pleads. "Don't cry, Anna, please. I'm sorry."

"I'm not crying," Anna insists, even though her voice is choked. "Where would you go, then? If you c-could escape with him."

Drake hesitates. They will have to flee the city, won't they? Too many of the guard know them now. He takes a breath to make a guess, Nothwn perhaps, or Deradan, and there are footsteps on the stairs.

"Promise you'll write," Anna says.

"What?" Drake asks. When the jailer and his lantern come back into view, he hastily hides his hands again. Anna has tears on her cheeks but her mouth is set in a determined line. "I promise."

Anna nods. "Good," she says, and steps back.

CHAPTER
TWENTY-EIGHT

"Time's up," the jailer says, his keys rattling as he steps up to the door. "Said your good-byes?"

"I have." Anna sounds sorrowful enough that Drake wishes there were anything he could do to have made this go some other way.

The jailer pauses with the key in the lock. "Back, you," he says to Drake.

Drake steps back half a pace, trying to estimate the time he'll have, the way he'll need to move. The key turns in the lock and the door swings open, just enough for Anna to slip through—only Anna stumbles as she takes that last step, crumples in the doorway with her arms flung out in front of her. The jailer curses when her grasping hands wrench his grip free of the cell door, and Drake lunges for it, pulling the door open wider.

"You whore!" the jailer shouts, trying to tear his hand free of Anna's grasp, dropping his lantern when she won't let go. He draws his hand back as if to hit her, but Drake reaches him before he can land the blow. Fear and hunger have made him weak, and he nearly trips on Anna himself, but he manages to crash into the jailer hard enough that they all topple into a heap in the hallway. Drake lands on top, snarls a hand in the jailer's hair, and cracks his head against the floor before he can pull the cudgel from his belt.

"That noise will bring others," he says, rolling free and offering a hand to help Anna up. The lantern's broken, oil spilled across the floor and blazing bright, throwing wild shadows down the hall. "Are you all right?"

"I'll have some nasty bruises on my knees, but I'll live." Anna smiles bravely. "And I don't think there are any other guards in the jail right now. You have your chance, brother."

Drake stares at her. "You tripped on purpose, didn't you?"

Anna raises her chin defiantly. "You're not the only troublemaker in the family."

"Thank you," Drake says, reaching for the keys that still hang from his cell door. "Now don't let it get the better of you. You don't want to end up like me." He pockets the keys and turns for the stairs.

"Colin!" Anna says. "You can't— You're not going to just leave him there, are you?"

Drake looks back. The fire from the lantern isn't going out. Some of the oil splashed far enough that the flames are reaching for the edge of the straw mat in the cell now, and if that catches—the flame licks at the cloth, turning blue, coiling up in smoky tendrils—then the building itself may light. The guard lies where they left him, out of the fire's reach for now but likely not for long.

The flames will wake him, Drake nearly says, but the way Anna stares makes him waver. "You'll have to help me," he says instead.

Anna nods, and when Drake reaches for the man's ankles, she takes his wrists. It's awkward, and the man's heavy, but they get him more than halfway down the stairs before Anna stumbles.

"Let him down," Drake says. "That'll do, won't it?" He can smell smoke from upstairs, and if the jail's going to burn he can think of someone he'd far rather be carrying out of it.

"I rode here," Anna says as they make their way down the last of the stairs. She takes his hand. "I'm going to get a carriage home. Take my horse."

Drake stops, stunned for a moment at the lavishness of the gesture. "Thank you." He can remember when that would have seemed an easy offer to make, but barely. "You're better than I deserve."

"Write me from Deradan," she says. "Or I'll come looking for you."

"I'll write," Drake promises. "Dragon's honor."

Anna laughs just a little, a surprised sound, and then leans in to kiss him quickly, her lips brushing the corner of his mouth. "Good luck. Lady spare you."

She has, Drake thinks. "Thank you," he says again. Upstairs there's a crackling, popping noise, like the fire has found itself some fuel worth the effort. They're out of time.

Anna turns, pushing the front door open, and flees into the dark. Drake watches until she's gone, then turns for the lower wing of cells.

The door to the wing is locked. Drake pulls out his ring of pilfered keys, trying one, then another. The third one turns, the tumblers of the lock sliding back, and he pulls the door open.

Inside the air reeks of mold and human filth, bad enough that Drake flinches away at first. It's dark, the only light from the cells' tiny windows. He takes a cautious step inside. "Gabriel?" he says.

There's movement from one of the first cells. "Who's there?" someone asks. Not Gabriel, the voice too rough, too low.

"I'm looking for a friend of mine," Drake says. "Came in this afternoon. He's young, slight. He was bleeding when he got brought in."

The man in the cell grunts. "In the back. Hasn't said a word since the captain left earlier." Drake starts down the row, and the prisoner raises his voice a little more. "You going to help the rest of us out, then?"

"Once he's free," Drake says without looking back. His stomach's in knots. He tries not to think too hard on what Westfall might have done to Gabriel, alone in the dark down here. His eyes are adjusting now, slowly, and he can see a shape slumped against the wall in the last cell. "Gabriel," he says softly. There's no answer.

His hands are shaking when he tries to fit a key into the lock. He can't be too late. It can't end like this.

The lock gives reluctantly, sticky with rust, and Drake shoves the door open with a creak. He drops to his knees, reaching out. "Gabriel," he repeats. His voice cracks.

Gabriel shifts in his arms, limp, half falling against Drake's side. His breathing stutters, and he twitches weakly. The blood on his face is still there, dried dark.

"Wake up, Gabriel," Drake says gently, holding him close. "Please, wake up. We need to get out of here."

"Drake?" Gabriel's voice sounds thin, small and vulnerable, but thank the Maiden he's awake.

"It's going to be all right." Saying it will make it true. "We're leaving now." He pulls Gabriel's arm over his shoulders and lifts, staggering under the awkwardness of Gabriel's limp weight. Gabriel's head falls forward, and he sags. "Stay with me," Drake pleads. "Don't go anywhere."

"Trying." Gabriel sways, still unbalanced. "Cold. Talk to me, Drake."

Drake winds his other arm around Gabriel's waist. "If I tell you a story, will you stay awake for that?"

Gabriel's fingers curl in Drake's sleeve. "You tell good stories. Yes."

Drake swallows hard. "Once upon a time," he says, and guides Gabriel through the cell door. "Once upon a time there was a dragon." He thinks he hears Gabriel's breath catch, and prays it's surprise, not pain. "Once upon a time there was a young dragon who thought he knew all there was to know about the ways of the world. He wasn't terribly wise, but he was clever, and he thought that was enough, so one day he left the glittering cavern where he'd grown up— Gabriel, can you hear me?"

"Mmm." Gabriel lifts his head for a moment, and stumbles. "Clever. Go on."

"That's right." It's slow going with Gabriel mostly deadweight across his shoulders. "So he came to the city of men looking for—for treasure." There's muttering from the other cells they pass now, as the prisoners start to wake and realize what's happening.

"Here," one of them says. "You've got the keys, don't you? What about the rest of us?"

"Getting there." Drake stops at the first cell on the row, shifting Gabriel's weight against his side, and holds out the keys to the man who'd first talked to him when he arrived. "Take them and pass them down when you're out. And make it quick. There's a fire upstairs."

That makes noise break out in all the cells at once, men yelling in alarm and demanding to be next, to be let out. Gabriel's grip tightens faintly on Drake's sleeve.

"You all have the time," Drake says as they reach the door, as the first prisoner unlocks his cell. "Don't panic, just go." He pushes open the door, leads Gabriel out of the cell wing. The smell of smoke out here is too strong for just the banked fire in the jailer's little fireplace. Drake wonders if anyone outside has noticed it yet. He can't hear any shouts, any alarm bells, but it can't take much longer, he wouldn't think.

"Roused the dragon to fire," Gabriel says softly, and Drake squeezes him close. He's going to make it. He has to.

"I couldn't leave you there, could I?" Drake says. Anna left the door open when she fled, and Drake helps Gabriel out into the dark now. "I don't suppose you know how to ride."

Gabriel laughs for a moment, though the sound dies in a hiss of pain. "No."

"Well, let's see how fast you pick it up." Anna's horse is waiting, a handsome chestnut gelding that stamps and snorts when they draw close but doesn't actually shy away. Drake wishes he could remember this one's name. "Here, reach up and take hold of the saddle. Are your hands all right?"

"Yes," Gabriel says, and curls his fingers gingerly around the pommel. "No. Hurts."

Drake winces in sympathy. "I'm sorry. You don't have to hold on for long."

Gabriel nods, but barely. Behind them there are shouts as someone notices the fire in the jail's upstairs windows, and low curses from the prisoners just now escaping. Drake glances back, wary of an attack—someone trying to take the horse, or to recapture them—but the other prisoners are fleeing on foot, scattering down the streets.

"We should hurry." Drake laces his fingers together and leans down, the way his riding instructor used to do for him when he was little. "Put your foot here, and I'll boost you up. And then we're getting out of here."

"So clever," Gabriel says, and steps into Drake's braced hands. He's shaky, almost doesn't manage to get his leg over, and the horse sidesteps a little. But Drake holds him steady until he manages to more or less get settled, slumped forward in the saddle.

Drake unties the reins from the hitch and throws them over the horse's neck. There's a low swelling *whoosh*, and then a sharp outburst of crackling noises, heat washing the back of Drake's neck. The fire's reached the roof, then, caught the pitch there. Now the alarm bells do start to ring, and the horse tosses his head nervously, shying as Drake reaches for the saddle.

"Come on," Drake coaxes, nervous, his heart racing. "I don't like it, either. Let's get going, then." He gets a foot in the stirrup and pulls himself up, sliding an arm around Gabriel's waist to reach for the reins as he settles his other foot in its stirrup. He tugs at the reins and the horse wheels under them—Mother, but it's strange to be riding again after all these months—toward the river, toward their escape.

The clatter of hoofbeats on the cobbles comes almost in the same moment as the first sharp sound of a guard whistle. *Not now*, Drake thinks, when they're so near—but the captain comes around the corner before he's even had time to finish the prayer.

"You rotting bastard, Harwood," he calls. "You could have lived."

There are shouts from behind them too, so Drake knows the way back isn't clear either. He needs to move, soon, before one of the guards comes up with a crossbow—there, Lady Arhon take him, someone jogging up to the captain's side—and something bursts in the roof of the jail, sends flaming debris scattering down between them. Drake leans over the horse's neck, shielding Gabriel as best he can, and digs his heels into its sides. His horse bolts forward, and Westfall's horse rears, screaming like the fire must have caught it. They drive straight into the space between Westfall and his lieutenant, close enough to clip the horse's flank, and Westfall loses his seat as they gallop past.

Let the fall kill him, Drake prays. *Let him crack his skull on the cobbles.*

The horse runs with pure terror to drive him, and Drake doesn't try to rein him in just yet, holding on to Gabriel and doing his best to keep them both in the saddle as they tear down the darkened streets away from the fire. When they're far enough that the scent of burning pitch isn't quite so strong on the air, he pulls back a little, reins in the full gallop to a rolling pace that he doubts either he or Gabriel will want to keep up for long. He turns toward the harbor before they've reached the river itself. The west gate will be closed at this hour, but they need to get out of the city.

"Gabriel?" His voice feels raw in his throat. In the distance, he can still hear the shouts and alarms as people try to tame the fire.

"What is it, Drake?" Gabriel sounds tired, and he's shaking a little in Drake's arms.

"Help me find the way to south gate?" He might be able to find the way himself, but he wants Gabriel awake for his own peace of mind.

Gabriel takes a deep breath. "Find Cypress. I'll show you from there."

"All right." They're probably entirely too conspicuous like this, riding double and clearly in a terrible hurry, but Drake thinks he'd rather run that risk than try to go on foot. They need the extra speed right now. And with any luck, the fire will keep the guard from sparing a thought for them until it's doused.

He finds Cypress easily, and nudges the horse into a canter as they start south. As long as it's still safe, they may as well. The cobbles become too broken and uneven for that before long, and they slow to a walk. Drake spares one hand from the reins to just hold Gabriel close against him. Soon, now, it must be.

"There," Gabriel says, lifting one hand—not really pointing, like his fingers don't want to curl that way, but at least gesturing. "Turn right there."

Drake pulls lightly on the reins. It's strange to see this part of town from horseback, to look down on the collapsing buildings and crooked alleys from a vantage point like this. He'll miss it, he realizes. Gabriel's Casmile. Broken and ruined as it is, they've shared so much here, and now they'll be starting over in a place that's strange to both of them.

"Left," Gabriel says. He rocks in the saddle with the horse's gait. "Then straight on to the gate."

It's a wide street, the one that leads down to the south gate's remains. Drake wonders what it's called, farther north where it matters. He peers into the dark ahead of them, looking for the gate, or what's left of it.

Crossing the pile of rubble on horseback is tricky work; Drake winds up having to get down and lead the horse, nervous the entire time that Gabriel will lose his precarious balance, fall, and hurt himself further. As the excitement wears off, Gabriel's starting to fade again.

It worries Drake that he can't tell whether that's thanks to injuries, or just the way he retreats when he's troubled enough.

Gabriel *does* slip, and start sliding off the horse's neck, when Drake boosts himself back up in the woods beyond the gate. "Are you all right?" Drake asks, catching him, trying to keep him balanced.

"Tired," Gabriel says, leaning back against him. "That's all."

"I know," Drake says. "Me too." The horse shifts impatiently, and Drake nudges him to start moving again. If they keep the city wall on their right, they should find their way out of the wood and make it to the Deradan road. "We'll stop to rest as soon as it's safe."

CHAPTER
TWENTY-NINE

A nna's horse picks its way through the swampy wood, careful of its footing in the dark. Casmile's fire bells ring in alarm, quiet enough at this distance not to drown out the breeze through the pines or the squelch of mud under hooves.

"You should tell me the rest of the story," Gabriel says softly. He takes a deep breath. "About the dragon."

"All right." It'll help to pass the time, and give him something to do besides worry. "Where were we?"

"You came to Casmile looking for treasure," Gabriel says. One of his hands rests carefully on Drake's wrist.

"That's right." This isn't just a story about him, though, even if it could have been at first. "The dragon had seen a—seen a star fall," he says, thinking of Deirdre's northlands stories. "It was one of the jewels of the Green Lady of the Grave, fallen down to earth. Surely, he thought, if he could find such a rare and precious jewel, it would bring him luck. So he set out for the city to search for it." He's not sure how far the woods extend, but they seem thinner up ahead. They'll have more light when they can get clear of the trees, and then they can cross the open fields to the road.

Gabriel pets his arm. "I knew you had to be after something. Go on."

Drake takes a slow breath, thinking back to that first night, the chaos, Morgan's toughs showing up at the Dragon's Head. "The city was nothing like he expected, and he found himself lost almost at once despite his cleverness. Men were so loud and impatient, so quick to anger."

"But that's all right," Gabriel interrupts. "Dragons are fierce when they're angry."

"I'm getting to that," Drake says. Gabriel's head rests against his shoulder, so he kisses Gabriel's cheek before he goes on. "But not everything about the city was bad. The dragon happened upon a boy who wasn't like any of the others, a boy who knew the Lady himself and knew the city just as well. He was as fierce as any creature the dragon had ever heard of, but he was also kind, and he took the dragon home with him, offered him food, and showed him the secrets of the city of men. The boy could see through the dragon's disguise, but he loved secrets, so he told no one."

"The dragon paid him well for his kindness," Gabriel says. "By keeping him warm and fighting beside him, and making everything make more sense." They *are* coming to the edge of the wood now, and the torches at the west gate are visible off in the distance. Drake turns the horse left a bit, away from the wall. They should try to put some distance between them and the city before they stop. He hopes the guard won't know where to start looking for them, but it never hurts to be careful.

"They had all sorts of adventures together," Drake says, and he finds he's smiling despite how awful this day has been. "Everything they did was new and strange, and the dragon nearly forgot what he'd been seeking at first."

Gabriel hums. "Flatterer." He sounds pleased. Drake kisses him again.

"No, it's true. So they lived together in the city, and people told tales about them, and perhaps they could have gone on that way for years, except . . ." This is the tricky part, he thinks, the bit he really needs to get right, only he's not sure how to say it.

"Except," Gabriel says after a minute, when Drake still hesitates, "except that they were caught in a trap, and the huntsmen of the city came to take the dragon away."

A chill runs down Drake's spine, and part of it is the cold night air but part of it is the memory of the view of the hanging square. "And when the huntsmen locked him up and took the boy away . . . all the colors went out of the city at once, like a spell breaking, and it was the ugliest place the dragon had ever seen." His voice is getting hoarse, his throat tight. "And that's when he knew. He'd found the Lady's lost star after all. It had been right there with him the entire time. The—the boy must have swallowed it, because it was in his heart now, and its, its magic touched everything around him." He has to stop, to swallow hard, to hold on to his composure.

"Drake," Gabriel whispers. "Tell me the end."

"So—so what else could he do? He smashed his way out of his cage and went to find the boy, who was the very treasure he'd always wanted. And the boy had grown sick—"

"Heartsick."

"Heartsick," Drake corrects himself, feeling his own heart pound, "without him. But the dragon lifted him up, and held on to him, and wished with all his might—" It's become a true story, so he'd better give it the ending he wants. "And the boy recovered, and the light of his star grew bright again. The boy and the dragon fled the city to terrorize people on the wild roads beyond. And if nothing more wicked has come along—" his voice cracks, but this is how tales should finish "—they must be living there still."

There's silence for a long minute, broken only by the steady beat of their horse's hooves as they make their way onto the packed road. Gabriel shifts, turning in the saddle enough to look back over his shoulder. "You love me," he says very softly, "don't you?" He sounds awed, and hopeful.

Drake nods. He can see starlight reflected in Gabriel's eyes. "I do," he says, stretching forward for a kiss. The angle is terribly awkward, but he doesn't care. He's shaking with relief and with nerves and it feels so strange to have said it, but he wouldn't dream of taking it back.

"Everything's going to be all right," Gabriel says when he pulls back, relaxing into Drake's arms. He sounds more certain of that than he has of anything in days.

"Yes," Drake agrees. It won't be easy, getting to Deradan from here, and the Fates only know what they'll do when they get there. But they have enough determination between them that they'll get by. "I suppose we'd best hope we're bringing all our luck along."

"Don't worry," Gabriel says. "We have each other. We can always bluff the rest."

PART III
SPRING

CHAPTER THIRTY

The caravan rumbles into Deradan late in the afternoon, shaggy draft ponies plodding up the street with their heads down. Drake barely looks up from the card game he's playing outside a travelers' inn. He doesn't want anyone to remember him being particularly interested, and besides, he's winning.

He plays three more hands after the last wagon rolls by, down the cobbled main street toward the heart of the city. Then he collects his winnings—"Better take the blessings the gods give me and be grateful, aye?"—and sets off down a side street, whistling.

Deradan still feels small to him after Casmile, nestled as it is in the shadow of the mountains, bounded by sturdy cliffs at one end and the walled pass at the other. By the northmen's standards, it's a bustling metropolis; small wonder they always looked ill at ease back home.

Except Casmile isn't home anymore. Drake circles through Deradan's backstreets, the crooked and narrow lanes that wind behind artisans' shops and miners' bunkhouses. Along the north sides of buildings, where the shadows are never broken, dirty snow is still heaped against the walls. This doesn't feel like home either, but it's what he has for now.

When he judges he's gone far enough, he cuts back inward to pick up the main road, following it down again to meet the caravan at its destination. The merchant in charge, a stout Casmilan with fashion sense that Drake would have scorned to tears a lifetime ago, is directing the unloading of the wagons.

Drake saunters up to the man. "Extra pair of hands might finish the job quicker," he says. His accent is still terrible, he's fairly sure, but only real northlanders seem to notice.

The merchant glares at him with the suspicion reserved for beggars and swindlers. "Not looking to hire day labor. Move on."

Drake pulls a pendant from under his shirt so it hangs where the merchant can see it. "There's always room for one more."

The combination of the pendant and the passphrase makes the merchant's spine stiffen. "Yes, well. I suppose I could spare a shilling."

"The very soul of generosity," Drake says with a little bow.

"You're new," the merchant says.

"Connall an Hanaein," Drake introduces himself, offering his hand.

The merchant takes it in a firmer grip than Drake might have expected. "James Sheffield."

They're both lying, and that's fine. Drake smiles. "Good to meet you at last, after all I've heard. A mutual friend would like to offer you an invitation to supper, once your work here is done."

Sheffield smiles back. "So good to be welcomed back by friends. You'd better hurry with the unloading, hmm?"

"Sir." Drake goes to join Sheffield's crew in unloading the wagons. Most of them look like they were hired for their ability to discourage highwaymen more than anything else, and they're ready now to take their pay and go. Nobody does more than grunt acknowledgement when Drake joins them. Suits him fine; the less attention they pay to him, the better. He doesn't particularly want to be remembered, after all.

He hefts a keg of peach brandy and carries it into the warehouse to stack beside the others. He can't decide whether or not he's disappointed that Sheffield was so quick to believe him. On the one hand, it makes his work easier; on the other, tokens can be stolen and passphrases learned through any number of unscrupulous methods. Small wonder Sheffield's stuck running some piddling overland slave route, if he thinks that's precaution enough.

Darkness falls fast in the mountains; the sun slips behind the peaks to the west and the light vanishes almost immediately. The hired swords grumble as they finish unloading in the gloom, eager to be off. They've had a good two weeks on the road, at a wagon's pace, and probably not a pint of lager to be seen. Drake hangs back while Sheffield pays them.

"Rotten scavengers," Sheffield mutters as the last of them leaves.

"Ah, don't be so harsh," Drake says. He's enjoying the persona he's falling into—a bit of Sebastian's casual generosity, a bit of Deirdre's lilting tease. "Mayhap they've loved ones to hurry home to." A beat, just long enough for Sheffield to frown. "Or it could be they're afraid to linger and meet the huntsman."

"Another of you people's ridiculous legends? Come on, I have an appointment to keep."

"Course, your lordship." That part is entirely Deirdre, the ability to sneer the word *lord*. "Wouldn't do to keep a friend waiting."

Drake leads the way down a darkening side street; here and there a lighted window spills illumination over a patch of ground, but they're few enough in this part of town. At the next crossroads, he turns toward the darker street without a pause.

"Can you still call the blind huntsman a legend, though, when there's evidence?"

Sheffield scoffs. "A blind huntsman, hmm? Can't be much good at it."

"Well, he wasn't always blind, was he? They say once he could see clear enough to know the perfect shot, every single time. He could drop a boar with a single arrow, he was so good."

Sheffield makes another *harrumph*ing noise. "And then he did something foolish, of course."

"You know the way of tales," Drake agrees. "He wronged a woman—and here no man is sure, you understand, whether she was a fearsome mortal maid or the Red Rider herself, but either way, the huntsman mistook one of her hounds for a wolf and shot the beast dead." He glances over to see Sheffield watching him warily, and shrugs as he goes on. "She changed into a wildcat's shape and set upon him. Tore his eyes out, savaged him, left him for dead."

They turn another corner, down a narrower street. Sheffield stumbles once. "Still nothing to be afraid of. Pathetic, if he ever really existed."

"The frightful part comes after." Drake lowers his voice to a hush. There's a prickle up the back of his own neck now, a sense of being followed. "It's his ghost that stalks the streets . . . and takes the eyes of lonely wanderers, trying to replace the ones he's lost."

Sheffield makes such a sour face that Drake has to bite back a laugh. Do they still tell stories of Gabriel in Casmile, or has he disappeared from the streets' legends already?

"But perhaps you're right after all. This way." There are no lamps down this alley at all, as he knew there wouldn't be. "Silly to be scared of ghost stories, isn't it?"

"It is," says a sweet tenor from behind them. "There are much worse things than ghosts abroad at night."

Drake stuffs his hands in his pockets, watching out of the corner of his eye as Sheffield startles and turns around. "Worse things, hmm? Like what?"

Soft, delighted laughter. "Oh, any number of monsters. Dragons."

There's screaming after that. But not for long.

Gabriel's the first back to their lodgings, but only by a second. Drake catches him around the waist before he can get the door open, and they both stagger, laughing, breathing hard in the thin mountain air.

"All right, you've won your damned race," Drake says, letting his head fall forward to rest on Gabriel's shoulder. "Now name your forfeit."

Gabriel squirms in his arms, turning to face him. "I'm sure I'll think of something." He nips Drake's lower lip, his fingers curling possessively in Drake's coat.

Drake kisses him lightly. "Come on. Inside." That's different here, too; Deradan's people are considerably more suspicious of men whose love for each other is physical. A year ago, Drake might have imagined that someone like him wouldn't care about that, would dare anyone to take offense at it. But when they arrived in the middle of the winter, chilled and starving and slowly losing the battle against fever, more trouble was the last thing they wanted.

The room they found to recover in was one of a row lined up against the cliffside above a tavern. They've kept it in the months since; though the stone back wall always seems to bleed chill into the room, it's sturdy and they've no complaints about the wind finding a way in. Gabriel stirs the fire back to life when they slip inside, and firelight makes the room look warmer immediately, even if it won't feel that way for a good deal longer.

Gabriel looks up from the fireplace and frowns. "What's wrong?"

Drake shakes himself. The cold, the local taboos, the thin air that never carries the heavy brine smell of the harbor... "It's still not home, I suppose."

"Mmm." Gabriel sits down on the little pallet they share and starts tugging his wet boots off. "We could leave," he offers. "That was the last of them, wasn't it?"

"One more payment to pick up, and then we're through," Drake agrees. Sheffield was the last act of a revenge cycle they'd been hired for after a slave ring stole the wrong boys for merchandise. The whole city's been talking about the killings. "Probably won't get work like that again anytime soon."

"Not enough people, and definitely not enough travelers." Gabriel sets his boots by the fire to dry, then raises an eyebrow, gesturing for Drake to do the same. Wading through slush got the blood off their boots, but it doesn't have much else to recommend it. "We'd have to be quiet for a while if we stay here. Not make any trouble."

"We could afford that, though," Drake says, lining up his boots beside Gabriel's. The man who hired them to ruin the slave ring owns a substantial stake in the silver mine, and he's been generous. "We could probably make it to summer on this job if we tried."

"I bet you'd get bored." Gabriel tugs on the hem of Drake's coat, pulling him down. "You're not the sort of dragon to just sit on his spoils and guard them."

Drake stretches out next to Gabriel, easing an arm under his narrow shoulders. "Don't think you'd be pleased, either, with all the best stories happening to someone else."

Gabriel hums, nuzzling Drake's throat. "Maybe not. Where are we going, then? Won't be safe to go back to Casmile yet, not with the size of that fire."

"I swear the fire gets bigger every time a new traveler comes in to talk about it," Drake says. "To listen to some of them now, it sounds like Deradan should have seen the smoke." Gabriel bites him. "Ow. Right. Where to next?" He rolls the question over in his mind for a moment; there were so many places that only seemed like distant tales when he heard about them in Casmile, and they must have been all the more unreachable from where Gabriel was standing. "Ever seen a mermaid?"

"Don't think they like places as busy as the docks," Gabriel says, shaking his head. "Why, have you?"

"I might have, once, when I was very small." If he closes his eyes, he can picture the beaches from that trip to Jua'za, the golden sand and the distant lumped shapes of rocks half-submerged beneath the waves. "Only at a distance, though, and not for long."

He tries to dredge up more details from his memory so he can tell a decent story, but Gabriel only says, "They like warm places, don't they."

Drake laughs. "Had enough of snow?" Gabriel nips his collarbone again, and Drake shoves at Gabriel's ribs, and their planning is abandoned for a minute in favor of a wrestling match, squirming and grappling and laughing. This time Drake wins, pinning Gabriel, lean and bright-eyed, beneath him, and he claims a kiss for his prize.

"All right," he says, breathless. "I'm sick of the cold too. We'll go south as soon as it's warm enough to travel, how's that? Find someplace along the coast that we can terrorize."

Gabriel smiles up at him, twining both arms around Drake's neck. "Leave the Blind Huntsman here, become something else on the road. They'll tell different stories of us every place we go."

Drake traces the line of Gabriel's cheekbone with his thumb, his heart at once so light and so full he can barely stand it. "And being with you will be better than all the stories together."

Dear Reader,

Thank you for reading Laylah Hunter's *Gabriel's City*!

We know your time is precious and you have many, many entertainment options, so it means a lot that you've chosen to spend your time reading. We really hope you enjoyed it.

We'd be honored if you'd consider posting a review—good or bad—on sites like **Amazon, Barnes & Noble, Kobo, Goodreads, Twitter, Facebook, Tumblr,** and your blog or website. We'd also be honored if you told your friends and family about this book. Word of mouth is a book's lifeblood!

For more information on upcoming releases, author interviews, blog tours, contests, giveaways, and more, please sign up for our weekly, spam-free newsletter and visit us around the web:

Newsletter: tinyurl.com/RiptideSignup
Twitter: twitter.com/RiptideBooks
Facebook: facebook.com/RiptidePublishing
Goodreads: tinyurl.com/RiptideOnGoodreads
Tumblr: riptidepublishing.tumblr.com

Thank you so much for Reading the Rainbow!

RiptidePublishing.com

ACKNOWLEDGMENTS

No author is an island, and no book is written without a tremendous amount of support and influence. This one owes a great deal to Rachel, my editor, who took my manuscript and honed it to a knife-edge; to Kiwi, who breathed life into Gabriel in the first place; to Ariel, who kept pushing me forward when I doubted myself; to my parents, who still thought it was wonderful that I was writing even when I turned out to be writing street thug romance with lots of stabbing; to the small crew of alpha readers who cheered on the very rough first draft; and to the fans of the Bijou, who convinced me that I could move people with stories of my own. Thank you for everything you've given me.

ALSO BY
LAYLAH
HUNTER

Resurrection Man
(in the *Bump in the Night* anthology)

Ground Mission

Cultural Hospitality

Safe Harbor
(part of the *Evergreen* collection)

Ivory Black, Flecked with White
(in the *Snow on the Roof* anthology)

Direct Connection
(in the *Wired Hard 5* anthology)

ABOUT THE AUTHOR

Laylah Hunter is a third-gendered butch queer who writes true stories about imaginary people in worlds that never were. Most of hir work deals with queer characters, erotic themes, and the search for happy endings in unfavorable circumstances.

Hir mild-mannered alter ego lives in Seattle, at the mercy of the requisite cats and cultivating the requisite caffeine habit, and dreams of a day when telling stories will pay all the bills.

Connect with Laylah:
Website: laylahhunter.com
Twitter: @LaylahHunter
Goodreads: goodreads.com/Laylah_Hunter

Enjoy more stories like
Gabriel's City
at RiptidePublishing.com!

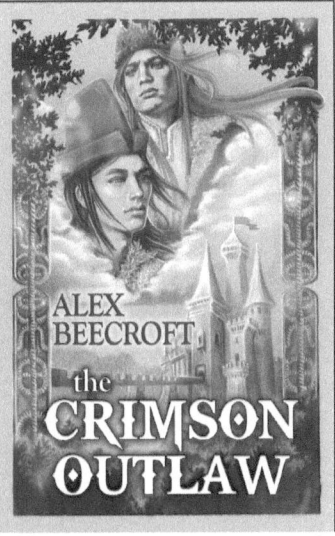

Earn Bonus Bucks!

Earn 1 Bonus Buck for each dollar you spend. Find out how at RiptidePublishing.com/news/bonus-bucks.

Win Free Ebooks for a Year!

Pre-order coming soon titles directly through our site and you'll receive one entry into a drawing to win free books for a year! Get the details at RiptidePublishing.com/contests.